Forbidden Road

Reut Barak

Copyright © Reut Barak

Reut Barak has asserted her right to be identified as the author of this work in accordance with the Copyright, Designs and Patents Act 1988.

This novel is a work of fiction. Any references to historical events, real people, or real places are used fictitiously. Names and characters are the product of the author's imagination and any resemblance to actual persons, living or dead, is entirely coincidental.

Cover Design by Domanza
Development Editing by Dr. Liron Gibbs Bar
Line Editing by Graeme Smith
Copyediting by Faith Williams

ISBN 9798649996754

All rights reserved. No part of this publication may be reproduced, stored in a retrieval system, transmitted in any form or by any means, electronic, mechanical, photocopying, recording or otherwise, without the prior written permission of the publisher once it is officially being published, and made available for purchase.

"If there is a book that you want to read, but it hasn't been written yet, you must be the one to write it."
- Toni Morrison

To Graeme, Liron and Ben who made it all worthwhile

About the Author

Reut Barak is an author based in Edinburgh, Scotland. She started her career as a singer and learned about European history and myths. Inspired by Arthurian legends, she started creating a magical world of wizards and witches, which links to the rich folklore of Scotland and to modern love stories. She is also an online chef and founder of RawMunchies, a creative venture for healthy vegan recipes. She's a freelance journalist, previously published in *National Geographic* online, and has worked and traveled internationally. She has an MBA from the University of Oxford and...

Well, no, not really... The true story is:

Reut was born in Camelot in the year 1201, following the famous explosion of the northern dragon tower.

She has a degree in fantasy and science fiction from the University of Atlantis and this record can be found in the central library, now twenty thousand leagues under the sea.

She likes phoenix riding, dragon fighting, and painting the roses red. And Grimm's Fairy Tales, too.

Preface - How it all got started

The Evans Witches

www.evanswitches.com

The idea first came to me a few years ago, when I started writing a story about a witch and a Charge, who lived long ago in Camelot: Kim and Seth.

That one went into the drawer. It was just a summer thing. A hobby...or so I thought.

A few years passed. I came to Scotland, because I was drawn to the beauty of the highlands, and I stayed because I found love. During a walk along the coast, in my imagination, I saw a modern witch, Julie Evans. Her story started to unfold and I began writing *Blue Diamond*. The plot was linked back to my original Camelot book. The characters were related. Their magic had a history.

I kept getting more and more ideas during hikes

and when visiting old castle ruins. Without noticing it, I had created a universe—that of the Evans family of witches. The plan was set for two trilogies, covering the different generations.

I wrote Julie's story, but at the back of my mind was Kim and her story.

This is that original story!

And after all the tough work rewriting it (and some hard-to-hear criticism from my amazing beta readers and editors), it is ten times what I could ever dream.

Kim and Seth, college students, have only just met. The spark of love between them, beautiful and passionate, has only begun. But they must go to the past, forget their identities and lose one another. Their journey back to each other requires them to make tough decisions in the past that can forever reshape the world of magic.

The History and Mythology Behind *Forbidden Road*

When my husband read through my final draft to do the technical editing, he remarked that when it comes to Arthurian legends, I seem to be extremely knowledgeable but my Scottish history and mythology is a mess. At the time, places and people had random Celtic names and inconsistent origins across both Scotland and Ireland.

So I did my research. That night, I discovered Fergus Mór.

It was love at first sight. The guy was a gold mine of inspiration!

Fergus Mór was king of Dalriada, or Dál Riata, which spread from southwest Scotland to Northern Ireland (including some of my favorite hiking spots).

He is thought to be the founder of Scotland and an ancestor of past and current Scottish rulers. He even claimed lineage to the legendary King Arthur—not something I included in my books, but it did fit perfectly with the correspondence I had written between him and Arthur's father, Uther Pendragon, in *Merlin's Creed*, the second book of this trilogy.

He ruled until his death at AD 501.

Many legends describe him in contradictory ways,

including being exiled to Scandinavia by the Romans, and dying in battle against the Picts.

I chose Domangart Réti as the name for his son, which fit best with the occurrences in *Forbidden Road*. In historic documents, there were different accounts on who was his successor, including Domangart Réti, Dúngal, and Eugenius.

I also looked up the name Áedán, an old Celtic Scottish name, which I had chosen for Kim's father in *Forbidden Road*. I discovered that one of the later kings of Dalriada was also called Áedán—Áedán mac Gabráin. A fascinating fellow, who was notorious for pestering northern Scottish and northern Irish kings, and his army's "exploration" went as far as Orkney and the Isle of Man.

I'm glad I got challenged. The depth that these legends gave to the trilogy, not to mention to my own experience of writing it, is fantastic. I enjoyed walking into the mysteries of the past and adding a setting of myth and legend to my books.

To me, this was magic.

There was, however, one place, where I decided to leave facts and research outside the realm of my story, and take artistic liberty: when it came to castles, especially Fergus Mór's.

I've always dreamed of beautiful fantasy buildings

like the ones depicted in modern adaptations of Arthurian legends, or in Disney fairy tales. So, I let my imagination run freely and in this book you will find Fergus Mór living in a grander castle than what would be historically accurate.

If you are curious what sort of home he did have, I encourage you to look up Dunadd Fort, an archeological dwelling attributed to him.

See the Evans witches on:

www.reutbarak.com/evans

Want to know more about me, what I do, and what I cook? I welcome you to my website:

www.reutbarak.com

I also wrote a cookbook series: RawMunchies, healthy vegan recipes that has a YouTube channel and a blog on:

www.rawmunchies.org

And an experimental, funny collection of fairy tales, with colorful, eccentric characters, written in a special format on:

www.funnyfairytales.org

Prologue

The swirling motion stopped. Everything was still. I opened my eyes.

My first thought was Seth. I called out his name.

A woman said something soothing in a language I didn't understand, as though trying to tell me that he was all right.

I looked at her. She resembled one of my college professors. But she was dressed differently.

Everything was strange. Like a weird dream.

I was lying on a bed. In the middle of the woods. It was broad daylight, and birds sang above me. It looked like a place I saw in a picture, from Ireland.

"Am I in Ireland?" I asked.

"Ireland?" The woman was puzzled.

She didn't know about Ireland! How was this possible? Where had Seth and I been sent? Or...*when?*

There was a loud noise in my head, like a blur setting in. The memories of what had happened right before, in college, and my life until now, began to dim and the voices around me seemed warmer, safer.

Every time I blinked, the colors were more vivid and the people's voices louder and clearer, but other parts of me were shutting down, closing my mind to any thoughts that didn't belong here.

Chapter 1

Western Scotland, AD 500

The day that Kimberley Áedán was kidnapped began with a broken wheel. It was the wheel of the royal carriage of the kingdom of Dalriada, and it fractured completely by chance. There was no magic involved, no road rut, no conspiracy, and not even the hand of destiny, as generations to come would claim. It was just a very old wheel.

The coach raced wildly in the dense forest, shaking from side to side. The driver tried to take control over the panicked horses. But the weight of the carriage, shifting the balance to the side, was too difficult to maneuver between the divots in the road.

The two men inside were jolted in their seats.

As the coach kept racing at top speed, the door flew open, letting out one of the trunks, which fell, spilling its contents.

"Stop the horses!" Seth cried. He was the younger of the two men, in his late twenties, with short brown hair and taller but a little slighter in build than his companion.

He pushed himself through the open door and hoisted himself to the roof, with rare agility, nearly falling as the carriage shook. From there, he joined the driver and with their combined strength, they pulled the reins. The horses whinnied and finally slowed down, but the coach only stopped once its corner fell into the road.

"Are you all right?" the driver asked.

"Fine." Seth turned to look back through the carriage window, at his companion, who was still inside. "Niall?"

"I'm good." Niall caught his breath and opened the left door. "I'll stay with the driver. If you could go look for the trunk...see if the box is still in one piece."

Seth climbed down and let Niall take his place.

Niall was the first knight, the highest mortal rank in any court. He belonged to the court of Fergus Mór, the regional high king. This journey was of great importance. Fergus Mór had secured his throne by arranging the marriage of his son Domangart Réti, the crown prince, to the daughter of King Áedán, the wealthiest of the lesser kings. Niall was delivering the marriage treaty that would seal the alliance between these two kingdoms.

The golden box, containing the marriage contract, was in the trunk that had fallen out.

Seth retraced the path of the wheels, his sharp eyes scanning the road on both sides. Behind him, Niall helped the driver pull the carriage out of the dirt. The driver cursed loudly.

Fergus Mór was a good king and ruled with justice. His knights always felt a duty to serve him well. Some of them feared what would happen when he was succeeded by his son. Much importance was placed on the marriage. The treaty was a complex one, and it took two weeks of negotiations just to get the first draft.

The bride was Áedán's only daughter Kimberley. Seth had heard little of her. Áedán had traveled to Fergus Mór a few times to discuss the terms. From the stories, she seemed no different than other ladies of court he had met. Exactly what Domangart would be looking for, given his exploits at Fergus Mór's palace.

It took a few minutes, but Seth finally spotted the glitter of the box. It was lying on the wet grass.

He walked over to it and picked it up. It was an impressive piece of art, ornamented with floral engravings around the royal crest. To his relief, it had survived the fall. There was one small scratch on the bottom and the hinges got twisted, but in spite of the deformity, the lock was still intact.

He tilted the box and heard the paper move inside. A strong odor came out when he did this. He had sensed it earlier and mentioned it to Niall, who said he didn't smell it. He returned the box to him.

"It didn't break," Niall remarked in relief.

"No, but I think you should smell it. The odor is stronger now."

He handed it over and Niall held it close to his nose. "I can see what you mean. It must be the prince's ink. You're right. It is strong." He wrapped it carefully with a cloth. "The lock looks all right."

The driver joined them, covered in mud.

"How are we doing?" Niall asked.

The driver shook his head. "There's no way she'd make it to the castle, I'm afraid. Not with both of you inside."

"Do you remember the way?" Niall asked Seth.

He had been there twice before. "It would be a little over an hour's ride from here. As long as the same roads are still open since last spring."

"As far as I know, they are," said the driver.

"Good," said Niall. "Seth and I will take the horses. We'll send a few people to help repair the coach once we reach court, and hopefully we'll see you at dinner tonight."

Kimberley Áedán paced the marble floor of her father's palace. *What was taking them so long?* She went to the window and looked out, biting her fingernails. Then, she noticed herself doing it and put her hands behind her back.

Patience was not one of her strengths. Neither was dealing with excitement.

Marriage. She had never really given it much thought before her father sat her down to speak about Domangart Réti. The notion itself didn't surprise her, of course. Marriage was a necessity. Something that nobles did, and she was a king's daughter.

Her father said that it was her right and duty to be married well, and this alliance would be very carefully arranged and made beneficial for her, placing her on track to the crown. The final decision would be up to her, but it was clear that she was expected to go along with it. Enthusiastically.

She was brought to his court a few months earlier, when her year and a half of education was complete and it was certain that she had the necessary skills and preparation to excel in her father's court. It was the richest one in the region, and a high level of sophistication was required to maneuver its politics.

She didn't remember her life before that, not since the accident she'd had. A fact that her teachers instructed her to prudently conceal.

Her mentor had been no other than a fairy queen, Morgan Le Fay. Few princesses could boast that—to be trained by someone with that amount of experience, an immortal who had walked the earth for many years, seeing different courts, speaking foreign languages, and meeting nobles of different ranks. Morgan was a great teacher, too. Harsh at times, as fairy leaders often were, but always fair.

Kim missed her. And the fairy tribe, in their beautiful forest town, built generations ago, with its arched pillars and silver roofs blending naturally with the surrounding woods. She'd lived with them there, in that beautiful paradise, learning everything she could.

No matter how grand or luxurious court life was, or how much she was looked up to by other court ladies, her every wish immediately fulfilled, she'd often find herself glancing out the window toward the woods with a longing. She remembered clearly the last time she saw Morgan, looking back from her coach, before disappearing from view in the dense foliage.

Soon, the royal carriage would arrive, coming out of those very woods. The regional king's first knight. Here to deliver her wedding contract.

She had written Morgan about the marriage, and it was clear from the reply that Morgan was not supportive. She wrote that it was a hasty choice, too early in her court life and that Domangart was not the right one for her.

It didn't sound like Morgan. Though strict, Morgan normally pushed her to excel and take challenges. She looked up to her. It would have been nice to have her support.

Three months till the wedding. She looked out the window, beyond the high walls of her father's castle and the fields outside the gates.

"*Don't stare out too long.*" She remembered Morgan's words and took a step back, into the room. "*It's not ladylike.*"

But she liked to look out, to the distant horizon where she saw the tall mountains that some of the knights had spoken of when they came back from their quests. Beyond them were other kingdoms, some smaller than hers, some larger. Then, after that, there was the sea. Merchants who came to court spoke of a land in the south, where there once was a great kingdom ruled by mages.

Her father said there was nothing of any value beyond the castle walls, except perhaps the nearby marketplace, where he would take her from time to time.

Perhaps it was that way for him. King Áedán was definitely a court person. There was always something on, with knights visiting, to enjoy the feasts and games he'd arrange. They'd bring stories with them, but those were too often about other courts, which sounded all too familiar. Between these, she'd catch the real tales. The things that knights had seen on the journey itself, with accounts of places, dangers, creatures, and people who were very different than the ones in court. Sometimes she'd lay awake at night, imagining that she was there with them.

She was grateful for her father's investment in her, but he never knew who she really was. And she had no mother to talk to, because she had died giving birth to her.

He'd definitely taken every effort to make her happy here, since she came to court. He made sure to surround her with other court ladies her age, hoping she'd enjoy society the way he did, but most of them envied her. Long before it was announced that she was marrying the crown prince, she'd catch them during the endless balls and dinners, staring in that particular jealous way and often whispering to each other afterward. Their gaze would fixate on what she was wearing or at her jewelry, things that her father made it his business to provide at the highest quality he could afford, which was a lot.

They were sure to do it tonight, she realized, as she straightened the light purple dress she wore, which accentuated her blue eyes. Her long blonde hair was raised and tucked behind her ears; a delicate pair of golden earrings was all the jewelry she wore. It might have already been too much. After all, it wasn't the prince himself who was coming, but his first knight. Still, she was expected to make an effort.

That was what she'd excelled at: doing what was expected.

After the wedding, she'd be moving to an even larger court. Everyone said she'd be a good match for it. She could display her accomplishments, her social talent, and her known taste in fashion. They all assumed that she would be happier there. She sighed. They couldn't be more wrong.

She walked toward the mirror. A drawing of the

prince lay next to it. She picked it up.

"They're here." She heard a voice outside her door.

She turned. Through the window, she could see two riders coming in on horseback. She put the drawing down.

The first rider had the shield of Fergus Mór. That would be Niall, the first knight, she concluded. The other must be his squire. He was dressed more simply.

Niall was tall. A man in his early forties with dark eyes and hair as black as coal. She'd heard stories about him. He was a well-known and respected knight, who came from a land across the ocean, in the south. The squire looked about fifteen years younger and had light-brown hair.

There was a knock on the door.

"Come in."

Two maids entered and bowed. One of them walked around her, inspected her from top to toe, and bent down to rearrange the folds of her gown, so that the lacy edge would show first.

"They should be ready in a few minutes," said the other maid in a tone that reminded her of the training she'd received with the fairies. How to walk straight and seem slightly distant, while looking forward with a smile. All the time telling her she was lucky to live life as the king's daughter.

Keep calm. Kim managed to slow her breath.

The first maid readjusted her hair and then both girls helped her go down the stairs.

Soon, she stood next to her father, his chief of staff, and the riders.

"Your Majesty. Your Highness," Niall said.

"Sir Niall," she said quietly.

Niall shook her father's hand. Then, he took her hand and kissed it, bowing for the second time.

"We're sorry for our slightly disordered appearance, Your Majesty." Niall addressed her father. "As I was just explaining to your chief of staff, we've had a mishap on the road just now."

"Not to worry," said the king. "My men will make every effort to have your carriage ready in time for your departure."

"Thank you. That is very appreciated. And, of course, you can rest assured that we've kept the treaty safe at all times."

"Excellent," said the king. "I trust you had a good ride apart from that?"

"Yes, sire. We did."

Her father spoke to both men, and it seemed he knew the squire.

Kim observed him. He gave her a cold smile. He didn't seem too excited to meet her. Perhaps he was tired from the trip.

"I'm sorry." Niall interrupted her gaze. "I realize you have not met my companion. This is Sir Seth."

A sir. Another knight. Clearly the customs of the high court were very different. In her father's court, squires were young apprentices, new to the life of knighthood. This was their opportunity to learn the ropes and sometimes to shine and win the favor of the king when it was time to select new knights to his order.

"Nice to meet you too, Sir Seth."

"Quite the lady for our prince," said Niall. "Talk at the palace has not done you justice."

She blushed. "Thank you."

Seth was still silent.

Her father made a gesture of impatience.

"You must be hungry and tired from the ride," she said quickly. "We wouldn't want to delay you from getting to your rooms."

"Thank you. That is kind, Your Highness," said Niall.

She smiled at him, then looked at his quiet companion. Seth was looking at something behind her. *Rude*, she thought. *Or perhaps just distracted.*

She had to give him the benefit of the doubt.

A servant came and led the two knights to their rooms.

Finally, she was gone. Seth didn't know how much longer he could have endured it.

Court ladies were always a bit of a nuisance, but this one was a pro. It was as if every word, every gesture, every muscle in her face, the very tone in which she uttered each sentence was aligned with court behavior to such an extent that it was mechanic.

How did they get that way, and why? Was it considered attractive?

Of course, he too had once fallen for it, and Niall would at times hint that that was his reason for disliking them. But *that* would never happen again.

He lay down on the bed, exhausted, and tried to forget that he'd have to see Kimberley, or Kim as he heard the staff call her, at dinner too. Niall had left half an hour earlier and the guest quarters were quiet.

"I'm going to check if there is any news about our coach," Niall had said before exiting, "and a letter arrived by pigeon from Fergus Mór. Too bad we got here so late in the day. I would have liked a lesson before the big feast tonight."

"We can do one tomorrow." He liked being Niall's fencing teacher.

Niall was a good student. He had perfect technique and a vast variety of advances. Catching him off guard was a challenge, and Niall liked being his student because he succeeded. Teaching was interesting, and demanded patience and creativity.

But it wasn't anything like the tournaments. He missed them. He'd sometimes think about them, remembering what the sword in his hand had felt like, before he'd damaged his wrist in battle. Everything had been difficult since, but he was still good enough to teach. At least *that*, he still had.

Memories of the tournament hall were often hard to shake: seeing King Fergus Mór looking on; knowing that soon victory would be his. But the hardest memories were not of the sword fights, or the doctors and wizards who worked hard to do everything they could to heal the wound and failed.

The hardest memories were of silk and embroidery and deep, mysterious eyes that belonged to someone he desperately tried to forget.

The sound of footsteps disrupted his train of thought, bringing his sharp senses to focus. They came from the other room. The door in between was half open.

He concentrated. It was definitely not Niall. These were lighter steps.

Whoever was there opened a drawer, then closed it. Then another one. Items were being moved.

He reached for his sword and put it on the bed beside him silently. The golden box was with him, and he placed it carefully on the table next to the bed. Then, he waited, alert, observing.

The sounds got closer to the door, and then moved farther away. There was a shadow of a person.

Seth pulled the blanket to cover himself and his sword and pretended to sleep. The footsteps came closer once again. This time, the door between the rooms moved, and the man stepped inside.

The man crept around the room, as if trying to find something in the dark. He took a few steps closer, to see whether Seth was asleep. Then, he turned. Without making a sound, he picked up the box from the table.

"Put that back down," Seth commanded. He'd been quick. He sat upright, the sharp edge of his sword touching the intruder's back.

The man laughed. "Or you'll what?"

"I said, put it down." He got up.

"I don't think so." The stranger took a step forward toward the table and then turned, quickly drawing his own sword.

Seth smiled. "I don't want trouble and neither do you."

"You talk too much!" said the man and, in a swift movement, he backed toward the window and closed the curtain and darkened the room even more.

It was an advantage, to be in the dark. Seth had fought in almost complete darkness before, and he doubted the man had had the experience. "Again. Put the box back on the table."

"No."

And then, their blades met.

The man was skilled. He had good moves and advances. In a longer fight, he would have won.

But then, that was always the challenge. How to spot and go straight for the opponent's weakest point, catch him off guard. It was what he'd been teaching Niall. Speed was a far better strength than stamina. No one knew that better than a fighter with an injured wrist: a man who had to count on his instincts to serve him where his strength would fail.

His sword flew above the man, who ducked successfully, only to find the weapon approach him again immediately from below, sending his own sword flying across the room.

The fight was over in a matter of seconds, with Seth's sword pointed at the man's neck.

He walked around him to the window, and opened the curtains. The man was dressed in noble attire, but his shoes were worn.

"Who are you?"

The man didn't answer.

"More importantly, why do you want the treaty?" He shifted the tip of his blade, pressing against the man's throat.

The man was motionless, smiling.

"Fine," said Seth. "We can do this the hard way."

Chapter 2

Oxford, Present Day

I never knew my parents as Mark and Julie Ralston. To me, they were always Markus and Julia Taylor. The identities that they had chosen.

I discovered the truth about our family on my sixteenth birthday, when my mom took me to Glastonbury for a weekend and we had *the talk*. Only mine wasn't about guys and safety.

It had convinced me that we were by far the weirdest family at my school. Of course, I had already made that statement many times before.

After all, we had magic.

I was at my final year of college now, eager to graduate and start my own independent life. I was president of the JCR—the Junior Common Room—which meant that I was out in the college quad every day, welcoming the new students and teachers.

This year was more quiet than last. By Wednesday, I was almost alone at my stall, with most freshers sleeping in, tired from the wide range of social events.

"You'd think by now they'd start showing up to the guest lectures," said Jane Omondi, my best friend, who was helping set up the newcomers program.

"It's the beginning of Freshers Week. They're busy meeting people."

"They'll meet a lot of people at the lecture halls, if more of them showed up."

I giggled.

Jane had a unique personality that combined her affectionate, warm nature with strict ideals about how committed people should be at school. You had to know her to get it. Most people just loved her because she was so caring and down-to-earth.

But when you got close, you also saw her sophistication. That, and the amount of effort it took her to get to where she was.

She was raised by a single mom, who immigrated from Kenya when Jane was fifteen, and her dream was to become a literature professor. English was her second language, but it was hard to tell, because she spoke it so well.

She worked hard. When we were in our freshmen

year, she'd organize study groups for exams. Now she was helping the college with hosting guest professors, and was on a first-name basis with some of the leading names in her field of literature.

"They'll come, Jane. They can't party forever."

"Well, they better do it tomorrow. It took me a lot of effort to get the Morganstein lecture set up. I was ready to bang my head on my computer screen."

"I know."

The lecture was with Fiona Morganstein, a world-renowned researcher from Edinburgh, and Jane wanted to make a strong impression. Morganstein's team had a position opening for a masters student and Jane was giving it all she had.

"I'm sure there will be a good turnout this time." I tried to sound more optimistic than I was. So far, attendance to parties far surpassed that of lectures and the two were mutually exclusive, for obvious reasons. People needed sleep. "So, did you hear from the summer conference in Paris?" I changed the subject.

Her face lit up like a Christmas tree. "Gosh! I completely forgot to tell you. I got in. *And* they're paying for me to come!"

"What? Wow. That's great, Jane! It will be a door-opener for you."

"I sure hope so. I've already applied for one of their post-graduate posts. They only have two new positions for next year. It's a drying well over there."

"Don't worry. You'll dazzle them. And I'm sure you'll impress the professor tomorrow."

"You're coming, you know." She gave me a slightly sharp look.

"I'll do my best."

"Kim!"

"I have to run an event tonight. I'll do whatever I can to make it. I know what it means to you."

An alarm went off on her phone, signaling that she needed to go to her shift at the library. She turned it off and looked at two boxes of pamphlets that I needed to take there. "Should I grab one of these?"

"Oh, that would be great! Thanks."

She lifted the heavy box and smiled. "Well...Got to go now. Enjoy your time at the booth." And she was off.

I was actually almost done, and the next person was already supposed to be here for me to hand over some things to. But it seemed nobody bothered to arrive anywhere on time during Freshers Week.

I watched Jane walk away slowly.

Her college experience was different than mine. She knew from day one that she wanted to become a professor. And she was committed to it, finishing every year with an overall distinction and winning scholarship prizes. She had bursaries to pay for her boarding and supplemented those by doing library shifts and working as staff for summer conferences.

Fortunately, she also managed to get serious in other aspects of her life. She was engaged to her sophomore-year boyfriend, Oliver, a Philosophy, Politics and Economics student from a small village in Ireland.

I sometimes felt we were polar opposites.

To begin with, I didn't want to go to college, but my parents had pushed. Only one of my high school friends went—Tilly, who studied art history in Spain, and would speak with the rest of us once a month at most.

The other two, Scarlett and Mindy, started a beauty salon in West London. Scarlett's father, who was an accountant in a big firm, got them set up with a place and helped them hire a manager to run it. They now had a thriving business and a beautiful website with pictures of them working with famous clients.

I wanted to join them, but my parents were dead set against it. Especially my dad, who was always on my side, except in this case.

We were close, despite my constant fight for independence. My mom was caring and strong. Beautiful inside and out and a good listener. But whenever something happened, I'd go to him. I could trust that he would understand. He invested a lot of his time in me and my younger brother, Harley. He was down-to-earth and I knew we could see things eye to eye. Except for this.

I argued that in his previous life, back in New York, it was his entrepreneurial skills that made him successful and not any university knowledge. He said that if I truly felt that way, he'd pay for me to study business.

We fought about it a lot. Eventually, I figured that if I applied and didn't get into the place he wanted, he'd let it go.

He wanted Oxford.

He prepared me for the interviews. He had a natural gift for that type of thing, speaking to people in a convincing way. I was afraid that he would take it personally when I didn't get in, but I had to show him that even with the best efforts, I would still fail. And I didn't use any magic.

I got in with a full scholarship to study literature.

I was miserable all summer. It was Mindy who said that I could be happy here. She still lived at home, while getting the salon off the ground. She said college would be my ticket out of the house. I'd always spoken about how much I wanted to be on my own, away from my family. It was also close to London and we could meet up a lot.

She was persuasive and it actually worked out well. Even for social events here. For tonight's party, Scarlett's boyfriend, the up-and-coming London DJ, Tyler Clash, was coming to do the first hour of music. She was too busy to make it, but we said we'd meet up soon.

I had to text Tyler to ensure everything was good to go with his travel arrangements. Then, I tried to call the volunteer who was supposed to replace me in the stall. She was now half an hour late.

Her name was Veronica Hobbs, a second-year music student who had arrived a week early. I hadn't had a chance to meet her yet, but she seemed keen on the phone. In spite of this enthusiasm, she hadn't answered any of my previous texts today, and her phone rang now without a response.

"Excuse me," said a soft voice.

I looked up and put the phone down. "Sorry." I got up from my seat and smiled. "I didn't notice..."

She was a young girl, with an eager smile. In her hand was the handle of a neat pink suitcase with large wheels.

"Sorry. Yes, how can I help?"

"I can't find my dorm. I've been walking around, but the signs aren't clear. My parents are going to arrive with the rest of my things really soon." She spoke fast. Stressed. "I can't understand this map at all." She showed me a folded sheet with markings.

"Oh, actually, that's close to us. I'll come show you."

"Really?"

"Sure. Just let me leave a note with my number, if anyone is looking for me. I'm Kim Taylor, by the way."

"Zhi Ruo Wang." She shook my hand.

"Welcome to Christ Church college, Zhi Ruo."

I could tell by the look in her eyes that she was already mesmerized by the beauty of it.

I jotted my name and number on a piece of paper, and picked up the box of pamphlets to drop at the library on my way back.

We started walking toward her dorm.

"You don't mind leaving your personal phone number there like that?" she asked.

"It's on the brochures anyhow. I'm president of the Junior Common Room." I had decided to hand over the post this year, but my number was still on the pamphlets, because the next president hadn't been selected yet.

"Wow!"

"Thanks. So, what are you going to study?"

"Physics. How about you? What do you study?"

"Literature."

"Oh, you must read so many books." She seemed impressed, which was surprising considering her major was in science and mine wasn't.

"I just like reading."

"I like equations." She giggled. "But, I do read."

She seemed very nice. We reached her door a few minutes later, still talking about books. Zhi Ruo searched for her keys, and I put down my heavy box and took a breath.

"I'm actually handing over the post this year." I handed her one of the pamphlets. "You should apply, that is, if it won't interfere too much with your studies. Oh, and since you just arrived, there's a party tonight, at the Junior Common Room. You should come. You'll get to meet people from the college."

"Thanks." She smiled, opened the door, and pulled the heavy suitcase into the hall. "I might just do that. I will see you at the party?"

"Sure."

The door closed behind her, and I bent down to

pick up the box. As I turned back, I felt a sudden pain in my side and stumbled forward, realizing that the door had opened when I moved and someone had just walked straight into me. The box fell to the floor, spilling its contents into a muddy puddle.

"Are you all right?"

I turned. A guy stood right beside me.

"Fine," I managed. But my side hurt badly.

He looked around at the mess. Half the brochures were in the mud. "I can help you get them."

"Thanks, but I think it's too late. We'll have to throw those away." I started to pick them up. A soft, warm feeling spread through me as my magic healed the wound. I stopped it. I was always extra careful not to be noticed using my powers.

He joined me, silently picking up the pamphlets.

I kept waiting for him to apologize for having bumped into me, but he still hadn't done it when he handed me the last brochure. He just pulled out a canvas bag from his pocket and put them all into it.

"Here." He handed me the bundle. "You should really recycle those."

He had the nerve! "Thanks. I'll be sure to learn good manners from you."

"What?"

I had surprised him.

"*You're very welcome for the help!*" he said with evident anger.

"Hey, you bumped into *me*." *And still hadn't apologized*, I wanted to add.

"No. *You* bumped into me. You weren't even looking when you moved with that box, standing right outside a dorm entrance."

"I was helping a freshmen. I'm head of the Junior Common Room."

"Oh, you are, are you?"

What was his problem? I took a deep breath. "Okay, I think we got off on the wrong foot here. I'm Kim. I get that this is a hard week for everyone. So, how about I welcome you, uh..."

"Seth. The name's Seth. And I've already been here for a year. Well, not at this college."

A *year?* He seemed too old for a second-year student, but some people came here at a later age.

"So you're a sophomore."

"I'm a masters student."

Oh. He was looking away from me. I had to be polite, though I didn't want to be there either. "So... what do you study?"

"Computer science. You?"

"Literature."

"A Charles Dickens fan?" He looked at me now.

"Yes, actually. My favorite is *Great Expectations*."

The look changed to that of interest. "Mine too. I like what he did with Estella. Showing that the princess femme fatale was really a nut head."

"What? No, she wasn't. She was miserable, because she wasn't free to be who she wanted to be."

For a moment, it seemed my words had impressed him. Though, part of me couldn't help but wonder, from the way he had said the word *princess*, if there wasn't a hidden insult there. I decided not to let this go on any further. "Anyhow...I must leave now. It was nice meeting you." I gave him a short smile.

"You too." He picked up the box, handing it to me, and placed the canvas bag on top of it.

"Thanks." I walked away, trying to put this Seth guy out of my mind.

The college was quiet, and it was easy to find a hidden spot where nobody would see what I was about to do.

I closed my eyes and thought of the wet pamphlets in the bag. *Pamphlets, be clean and dry! Pamphlets, be clean and dry!* I concentrated on the image in my mind, of what the pamphlets had looked like before.

Magic started deep inside me and rushed through me, from my core and through my fingers to the bag. I felt something move, straighten, lighten. Then, I opened my eyes and peeped into the bag.

The contents were clean and dry. I took the risk and let my powers heal my painful side, and then I walked to the library, remembering how much I loved having magic.

"What's in the bag?" Jane asked, when I put the box on top of the one she'd brought.

"Pamphlets that had fallen. Some guy bumped into me."

"Well, then he should have helped you carry it here."

"Good point." Her way of seeing it immediately put me at ease.

She opened the bag to examine its contents. "You're lucky. They're all dry."

For a moment, I felt tense. I'd never told Jane, or anyone, about the magic. "Yes. Very lucky."

"You're okay, right? He was just an idiot." She put a warm hand on my shoulder. She must have sensed my stress without knowing its real cause. "And people are all crazy this week. Can't find a straight head on campus."

"Yes. They are."

"Should I make you a cup of tea?"

"No. Actually, I have to get back to my post. My replacement didn't show up."

"Who is it?"

"Veronica Hobbs."

"The music student?" She opened a drawer and took out a student card. "Someone brought this in a few minutes ago. Said they found it near Tom Tower."

She handed me the card. On it was the picture of a curly-haired girl, almost too young to have finished high school, smiling shyly. "Have you tried calling her?"

"Yes. I also texted her. How could she leave this behind?"

Jane chuckled. "Should I show you the lost and found box...or should I remind you of the time that your own card was in it?"

A few minutes later, I headed back to the booth. When I turned from the library to the quad, I could already see that it was empty. When the next student showed up, almost two hours afterward, I asked him whether he knew Veronica.

He said that he did and he saw her earlier, talking with someone near Magdalene College. He waved to her and she looked at him, but didn't wave back. Then, a car stopped by and she got in, hurriedly. The person she was with just kept walking.

"Strange."

“Do you think something happened to her?” he asked.

“Probably not, but I’ll text her again, and leave a message with security right now.”

There was still no word from her when I was preparing for the evening back in my dorm. Security had said not to worry, that people could often be unavailable during Freshers Week, but I didn’t feel relieved.

Before going to shower, I sent an email to her, and to the welcome booth volunteers – to text me if they saw her.

There was nothing more I could do, so I tried not to think about it too much when I was getting ready, hoping that I would hear from her by morning, or even just meet her at the party and she’d say that she had lost her phone.

Still, I couldn’t stop thinking about it when I was getting dressed.

Jane texted that some guy walked into the library and saw his bag with the pamphlets in it. She said he seemed very nice and had asked her to apologize for what happened. I wondered whether she had knocked some sense into him.

She also wrote that he completely exaggerated the situation, saying that the brochures had ended up in the mud, and she had to tell him that most of them were clean and dry.

It made me wonder how she would have reacted if she found out the truth about my being a witch. I didn't know why I never told her. I guess it was because magic often confused me.

Just because I was a witch didn't mean that I could do whatever I wanted. Magic took concentration and could really tire you.

It was also not completely mine to enjoy. It was in the service of mortals. Your powers were just waiting. Given to you only so that you could protect someone else. Someone you would meet and fall in love with, for life. Your *Charge*. I sometimes thought it wasn't fair that my greatest gift was nothing more than a service for someone else.

To add to it, those born to magic couldn't use it to get ahead, or bestow influence to anyone else. The magic got undone when we tried.

Of course, I also had the added stress of my parents' story that meant that both me and Harley, had to keep magic a secret, so I didn't really have any witch friends to share it with. I often wished that I at least had *that*. Then, I could help people like Veronica.

There was a buzz on my phone. I glanced at it.

"Hi, it's Zhi Ruo. Sorry to bother you, but I was just checking the form for the JCR president."

"Hi, Zhi Ruo. Glad you are applying. Do you have questions?" I texted back.

"No. But I'm having issues with the system. It keeps crashing. I understand you're announcing the candidates tonight."

"Yes." I texted and glanced at the clock. There was plenty of time before I'd have to get going. Maybe my inability to help Veronica put me in a mood to try to help her. "You can use my computer, if you need to."

"Really?" she replied. "Are you sure? I wouldn't want to be a burden."

"It's not a problem at all." I texted her my address. Luckily, my room was very easy to find.

For some reason, it took her awhile to get there, and I was beginning to worry that I might be late.

"Sorry. I got lost on the way," she said when she finally arrived, and I opened the door to let her in.

"Don't worry about it. I have the form open and ready."

She smiled thankfully and took a seat at my desk. "Will you be presenting us?"

"Each candidate will be presenting themselves. But, if you want, I can help you with a couple of tips. We can talk on the way to the JCR."

"Wow! That would be great."

"I'm in a bit of a hurry, so just do your best with the form."

"Of course." She turned to the computer and started typing her answers.

My makeup needed one last touch, and I moved away from the desk to my sink to give her privacy.

With my back toward her, I felt something. Something that completely surprised me.

Zhi Ruo was using magic.

I concentrated. The sensation was clear. She was definitely radiating spell power.

Puzzled, I looked at her through the mirror.

Through a small mirror on my desk, she was looking right back at me.

Chapter 3

Western Scotland, AD 500

It was late when Niall returned to the room.

"What happened here?" was his immediate question.

Seth looked up. He was at the table, examining the golden box. The intruder was lying—unconscious, tied and gagged—on the bed.

"He tried to steal the treaty. I need to know why he wanted it, and who he is working for."

"Why don't we just *ask* him?" said Niall, in a tone that indicated that *that* type of asking was not something he was unfamiliar with.

"You know I don't do that," said Seth. "I gave him a dose of the truth potion instead."

"You had a truth potion with you?"

"Yeah. You can never know." The man was asleep, which informed him that the potion was still working its way through his system. It was how the drug acted, twisting the mind when it dreamed. When the effect was complete, he would wake up and they should have a few hours to question him. It was far fairer than torture. "I might have given him a bit too much. He's been down for a while. Either that, or his mind doesn't give in easily."

"How long has it been?"

"Not long after you left."

"Really?" Niall went to the man and felt his pulse. "Still very weak. Might take a few hours longer."

"We should find a way to open this box and see why he wanted the treaty."

"There could be many reasons. Why don't we just wait until he wakes up?"

He turned to face him. "We've both delivered important documents for Fergus Mór before. None of them reeked. Don't you think it's suspicious?" Niall could sometimes be too trusting, especially when it came to the people of the court. "Who besides Fergus Mór and Áedán has the key?"

"Prince Domangart."

Seth swallowed hard. Niall was normally careful not to mention him by name. For a moment, a painful memory flashed in his mind and once again he saw the woman he was trying so hard to forget. He shook it off.

"In that case, we should definitely open the box."

Niall chuckled. "We've both seen the treaty. It's just a standard wedding contract, with a few special additions."

"There's nothing standard about the prince."

A knock on the door interrupted the conversation.

"I'll check who it is." Niall left the room.

The main door to their quarters opened, and a lady's sweet voice spoke. "Dinner will start shortly. There are hot water buckets ready for you if you want to use your baths."

"Sure. Please leave them in this room. My companion is resting in the other."

A few people entered, and heavy noises indicated buckets were placed near the door that connected the two rooms.

When they were gone, Niall returned. "I'm going to clean up. You should too. The box can wait."

Seth checked the unconscious man's pulse. It was still very faint.

Kim sat in her room, waiting. An empty dinner

plate and a half-empty glass of wine stood on the table beside her.

"Always be the last one to come down to dinner," her maids told her when she had first arrived. "Your father would meet the guests and talk about the court's affairs. Unless you find that type of thing interesting, you'd do well to avoid this part of the meal. It will also make you something for them to wait for. The highlight of the evening."

She'd sometimes wonder what the court affairs talks were about, and whether the men talked differently before they had had their drinks.

At this point, her father would be making a speech about the upcoming marriage that he had successfully secured. He'd talk about the alliance with the high throne and crown prince, along with his hopes that she wouldn't forget to visit her home when she was queen.

What the maid said was definitely true. She was the highlight of the evening.

Her father would see to it each time. Every dinner required a lavish gown. It would take a couple of maids to put it on, along with fine jewelry, and she would come down wearing it. Or, if she were perfectly honest, the clothes were wearing her.

Food etiquette was also important to the king. Her

maids would bring it to her in private, straight from the kitchen, to give her a taste of everything and then bring seconds of anything she liked. It ensured that when she sat at the king's table she would seem modest in her appetite and fine in her taste and be free for conversation.

She had seen a traveling puppet show visit the fairy tribe. Now, she felt that she could relate to those dolls on a string. It seemed that in court, everyone was a puppet.

She remembered the first time she met her father. He came to the fairy tribe, a stout man with ginger hair and beard.

She looked nothing like him. When she mentioned this to the fairies, they said that she took after her mother, who had died giving birth to her. She wanted to know more about her, but kept getting conflicting facts whenever she asked. Once, she was a princess from that land in the southwest. Another time, she was a lady from the east. She even got an answer that her mother was a fairy. In the end, she learned not to ask them about it. Especially not Morgan.

She knew that it was important, and that they were not telling her the truth for a reason. But, there was one far more important question on her mind.

She found the courage to confront Morgan on that final day, before they were going to leave for Áedán's court.

"I have to ask you something."

"We're going to be late. The carriage is ready for us."

"Please. This is important to me."

Morgan looked at one of the other fairies who was with them. "All right. But I can't promise I have the answer."

She took a breath and went right for it. "I really want to know: I don't remember anything except the last year or so, which I've spent here, with you. How is that possible?"

Morgan seemed impatient. "We've been through this, a few times. You had been raised by a different fairy tribe, but you got kidnapped and injured during the rescue attempt that didn't go as planned. When they found you, you had a serious head injury and other wounds which were too strong for them to heal, so they brought you to me. You should be happy not to remember anything prior, because luckily this includes not remembering the kidnapping."

She was lying, Kim knew. A consistent lie, one always told with a warm and kind voice. She often saw regret in Morgan's eyes when she said these words, as if she wanted to tell her the truth, but couldn't. As if it were for her own good not to know.

"It's time." A maid entered the room, her words bringing her back to the present. "Your father is just about to end his speech."

She rose. Time to put on the show.

The maid looked at her dress and was content. The seamstress had stitched the top tightly, to push her bosom upward and accentuate her curves. She was about to get married and all the men in court had to be reminded of what they were losing. Before leaving the room, Kim looked in the mirror and tried not to laugh.

Everyone rose when she entered the hall. By the way the men looked at her, it was evident that the dress was getting the job done. She wanted to roll her eyes at them, but kept a broad, fake smile on her face.

"I present to you, the future queen of the high court of Dalriada, my daughter, Kimberley Áedán," her father said, once she took a seat on his right, his glass raised.

There was a loud applause, and then murmurs. They all made a toast to her long life.

On her father's left, she spotted Seth and Niall. She smiled at them. Seth looked away. *What was his problem?* She decided she didn't want to know. This was *her* night. Well, sort of.

The main course was served, and conversations were minimal small talk, but things picked up again during dessert. Niall told them about a merchant town he had visited on the journey there, where a fortune teller delighted a crowd of spectators, saying that the prophecy of Camelot was about to come true. People laughed.

The prophecy of Camelot. It sounded familiar. She knew that there was once a famous mage called Ivan of Camelot. The fairies had spoken about him and how he defeated the tyrant mage, Harthenon.

It was a few hundred years ago, and the world was ruled by mages then. Harthenon was head of the great kingdom of Avalon. To prevent a rebellion, he created a curse that, in the event of his death, would cause the earthly dominion of mages to end and make them serve as protectors of mortals.

Nobody dared challenge him. But a vision came to a young mage called Ivan, from the small village of Camelot, which Harthenon later burned to the ground. In the vision, he saw that the new world would be a better one. He also saw a human king build a capital city on the ruins of Camelot, and rule the country from there in a way that would benefit both mages and humans.

He saw guardian love and the girl he had just lost in the fire, alive again, and him as her savior. That gave him the courage to risk his life and kill Harthenon, thus activating Avalon's Curse.

She listened more intently to the knights now, but the conversation had moved on.

When the feast was over, the staff cleared the tables to allow space for dancing. It was expected that she'd linger with her friends, watching the couples take the dance floor, doing a few dances herself, and talk about how sad she was to leave, and how much she was going to miss them when she was married. That she would write often and invite them to visit her whenever she could. And they would make her promise to write about all the jewels and gowns and the high court's gossip.

Luckily, her father came after a few minutes, asking her to join him with Seth and Niall. But shortly afterward, he had to leave them.

"My lovely daughter will entertain you," he said to the knights and left the three of them alone.

She gulped. She wasn't sure how they'd like her to act. She wondered what type of small talk would match what they were used to, and whether she could break the ice with Seth.

She directed her attention at him. “It’s very nice of you to have come all this way.”

“We were ordered to do so,” he replied coldly.

Niall’s hand tightened on his drink.

“Well, I am still thankful you did. I trust that, at least, the journey was to your satisfaction,” she said, deliberately ignoring his previous response.

“Yes, the...flowers on the way were lovely,” Seth said, with a hint of irony.

Why was he being like that? She decided to challenge him and play along. “Were they now? Too bad I wasn’t there to see it. Unfortunately...” she paused, smiling at Niall, “I seldom come out of the palace.”

“How very ladylike of you,” said Niall.

“Yes. It is indeed quite a *large* palace,” said Seth in a cynical tone.

Niall choked.

“Are you all right?” she said.

“Yes,” Niall said, catching his breath.

Seth looked at her impatiently.

A lost cause, she concluded. “You’ll excuse me, sirs. I just remembered something I forgot to tell one of my friends.”

She walked back to the women, but paused when she heard Niall’s voice, speaking low to Seth. “You must be out of your mind!"

She turned.

Niall immediately smiled and walked to her. A dance had just ended and a new one was starting. "It's a shame to miss the music, Your Highness. I noticed you are yet to have your first dance. Might I have the honor?"

A true gentleman.

"Of course," she smiled, "and the honor would be mine, to dance with the first knight of the high court."

He took her hand and led her to the dance floor. Everyone made space for them. They reached the center of the hall, and Niall put his hand on her waist. A foreign young knight, who she knew was in love with her, looked away.

The music began. A lively piece that she liked.

Niall was an excellent dancer. He led her well, his movements swift and his lead clear. The floor seemed light under his feet. The crowd clapped to the beat and other couples joined them. She was finally enjoying herself after that long day and the tune ended all too soon.

She and Niall bowed to each other, and then he took her hand and led her to Seth, who had just danced with the daughter of one of her father's ministers.

It shouldn't have come as a surprise, of course. Officially, Seth was her guest too. But an awkward moment passed between them as they stood there, about to dance.

Then, something strange happened.

It started when Seth's hand touched hers, and she felt a tingling sensation on her skin.

It was a strong hand, his left. But then he placed his right hand on her hip. That hand seemed weaker. Curious, she tried to look down at it, but he didn't allow her time to do that, leading her straight into the center of the circle. He glanced at the musicians and they took the hint. The music started immediately.

His dancing surpassed Niall's. And any man she'd ever danced with.

His moves seemed effortless. No, not just effortless, and... it wasn't only his moves.

Despite having danced this dance many times and the fact that the moves were the same, it felt different with him. It felt... perfect. As if there were no two dancers better matched, and that tingling on her hand where he was touching her bare skin became stronger with every step.

Though he had previously avoided her, he now looked at her the entire time, deep into her eyes, but never smiled. She felt as though he were trying to hypnotize her. As if they'd danced together before and he knew exactly what would make her body do what he wanted.

The floor seemed to spin around them, the music beating inside her. She could feel his warm and steady breath, aligning with hers and with the beat of the music.

It was intoxicating and she let it all in, something deep inside her awakening for the first time since she could remember. She closed her eyes and moved, dancing like never before, every step in exact harmony with his.

She didn't even notice that no other couples joined them, and that the court stood still, observing. She didn't care about them, or what they thought. She just let him lead, take her wherever he wanted. And every time she opened her eyes, she was met by his gaze, a deep grey like the ocean on a warm but cloudy day.

She'd never danced this well before. Nobody in court had. It was their enthusiastic applause that brought her back to her senses, back to reality, when the music ended.

For a moment, the two of them stood still. Then, Seth bowed, his eyes still penetrating hers, and she bowed too.

"Thank you," she whispered, her voice quivering.

"Yes..." he said, almost in a whisper, and for a moment he smiled.

Then, he quickly led her back to Niall and excused himself.

Her head started to spin. As though something deep inside her that had so long been asleep had been awoken by a loud bell, and now that Seth was gone, she just wanted to be alone.

She started to walk out of the hall.

"Are you unwell?" Someone had stopped her on the way.

"Tired. I need to go." She didn't even notice who the speaker was.

From the other end of the large gallery, she heard Seth's voice, speaking with Niall. They were next to the musicians, who were playing loudly, but she could hear him clearly, as if he stood right next to her.

"I'm not going to tell Áedán."

"Surely you don't suspect the king."

"I didn't, until he just invited us to stay for a whole week," Seth replied.

"To fix the carriage."

"He can lend us one of his *ten*. You're first knight.

You are needed at court. Why delay us?"

"Is this really about the king, Seth?"

"What do you mean?"

"You know what I mean." Niall paused, and then said in a meaningful tone, "The princess. I saw you. Both of you."

For a moment, all the dizziness was gone and her senses were sharp, alert, tuned in on the conversation.

"She's just like all the other court girls," were Seth's sharp words. "Probably worse."

No, he couldn't have just said that!

"I've seen the way you danced with her just then," said Niall.

"She's a good dancer. But otherwise, she's arrogant, spoiled, and madly in love with herself."

Nobody had ever spoken of her this way. Nobody! But if ever anyone might have dared to say anything against her, anything she didn't like, she couldn't be hurt by it.

Seth's words hit the bottom of her soul like a poisonous arrow.

She was almost too angry to miss Niall's response. Almost. "She just reminds you of *her*. They do look a bit alike."

After that, it all went into a blur. Seth's words,

arrogant, spoiled, and madly in love with herself, echoed through her mind, along with two strong, conflicting emotions. Hurt from Seth's harsh words made her imagine how much he would have to watch his back when she became queen. But far stronger than that, jealousy made her wonder who that other woman was.

She made it to her room on her own, forgetting to call the maids, which was against all the rules she was always following so diligently.

Other rules were more important. Older ones. Ones that felt as though they had been rooted deep inside her long ago.

Soon, she was comfortable in her bed, under the warm blanket. She just wanted to close her eyes and not think. Sleep started to take over.

Right before she drifted off, she saw an image of Seth in her mind and then, though she wasn't sure whether she was awake or dreaming, she thought she saw the light of the moon shining on her blanket.

Right where Seth's fingers had touched her, there was a strange bluish glow. Somehow, she knew that this had happened to her before.

Chapter 4

Oxford, Present Day

The party turned out to be more surprising than a normal Freshers Week one with its small pranks. Everything was overshadowed by discovering Zhi Ruo's real nature.

She managed to maintain that naive new girl vibe while we walked from my dorm to the Junior Common Room, and seemed enthusiastic about getting tips on how to become president. But my first impression of her changed dramatically throughout the evening.

The whole time, I pretended that I hadn't noticed her use magic when she was doing the application. It had puzzled me. You couldn't use magic to gain power, so what *was* she doing?

When we got to the JCR, a few students were chatting outside, and the party hadn't started yet.

A familiar face greeted me at the entrance, and I nearly stopped fifty feet away, when I recognized him.

What was he doing here?

He stood next to one of the younger students and smiled once we reached them.

"Hi, Kim."

"Seth. Good evening."

His lips closed. He seemed amused by my formal response.

"I'm Bradley." The young student introduced himself.

"Nice to meet you, Bradley."

"I understand you're president of the Junior Common Room."

"Well..." I'd miss that introduction soon. "Actually, we're announcing new candidates for the presidency tonight."

"Really?"

"And I'm one of them." I heard that girly voice next to me. She smiled at him coyly, her head slightly tilted.

Gosh!

"Well, I promised I'd bring Bradley to the right place," said Seth. "So, I'll just leave you guys to it."

I felt an inner sigh of relief, but then I remembered that I was going to ask everyone I saw about

Veronica. I had printed a picture of her from the student records and brought it along with me. I also looked her up online and found out that she was new to the university, having transferred this year from Berkeley.

"Wait. Before you go: I'm looking for someone. She's a music student. Maybe you guys know her. Her name is Veronica." I showed them the image.

They all shook their heads.

"Hey, I can ask people at the party for you," Bradley volunteered.

You could tell he was a nice guy.

"Thank you, Bradley."

"Yes, that's very thoughtful of you," said Zhi Ruo.

I wanted to roll my eyes at her, but then I realized that she might be genuinely interested in him, and this was her way of showing it. She might also have had something to drink already.

They started talking about their experience of the first week, and Seth said goodbye and left. I was just about to walk into the JCR when Bradley's words made me stop.

"Do you know who that was? That was Seth Rivers!"

The name was familiar. *Was Seth famous?*

"Our fencing champion. He was on the news last

night." Bradley continued, Zhi Ruo watching him with admiration. "They said he's like nothing we've ever seen before. He's been winning tournaments all year and they think he's a sure Olympic gold medalist, if there ever was one."

A fancy athlete. No wonder he was so full of himself!

"Isn't Oxford great?" said Zhi Ruo. "We get to meet all these really important people."

I decided to leave them to it and entered the Junior Common Room.

Inside, there was already a small crowd, with students near the refreshments and drinks tables. Tyler Clash stood by his equipment, a group of girls surrounding him.

My eyes searched the room for Veronica, but she was nowhere to be found. I spotted two students from the music program who had visited the booth during the week. When I showed them Veronica's picture, they didn't recognize her, and said they didn't recall seeing her face at an event with the faculty this afternoon.

About half an hour later, once the room was full, I asked Tyler to pause the music so that I could introduce the new presidency candidates.

Zhi Ruo gave such an impressive speech that it

made me wonder why she'd asked me for any advice in the first place.

After that, I filled a plate with some food and went to my table, where students could come and ask questions. From there, I also watched Zhi Ruo.

Somehow, she managed to talk with everyone. I tried focusing my senses to detect some of those conversations. She seemed to find something in common with every person she spoke with.

At some point, she sat on the couch, surrounded by guys who looked at her with admiration. Bradley was there, at the edge, ignored and disappointed. My original suspicion about the lack of real interest in her earlier flirt was confirmed.

I heard her mention the lecture that Jane had arranged. "Are you guys coming to hear Morganstein tomorrow?" And just like that, I knew there would be no problem getting attendance in the lecture hall. Someone asked her what it was about, and Zhi Ruo explained it was focused on Arthurian legends, while smiling in all directions. "Some people believe that they are based on true events."

Yeah. Witches.

She was being careless. I would never have gone down any road that could lead into real conversations about magic.

The lecture was mentioned once more when a physics major joined the group. It turned out that Professor Morganstein had a dual professorship – she did physics research as well.

When I listened again later, she was talking about organizing a swimming day.

I even heard her ask someone about how to become the head of Oxford Union, which nobody even dared try, especially not a new student, because it was less likely than winning a lottery.

Something was not right with that girl. This was a strange kind of ambition. Or, perhaps she was one of those people who were just ready to do anything to get ahead. Maybe she wasn't a girl at all. Witches could choose their age by magic. She could well be over one hundred years old.

"Working hard?"

A voice that I recognized all too well woke me up from my preoccupation, reminding me that there were worse things in college than Zhi Ruo.

"Oh, hi, Seth. I didn't see you."

"I can tell." For the first time, he had teased me, but didn't seem amused. "Have you seen Bradley? His sister is looking for him."

I looked at the couch where Zhi Ruo sat. I had been so focused on her, that I hadn't even noticed that Bradley was no longer there. Though, come to think about it, why would he stay?

I couldn't see him anywhere else either.

"Sorry. I don't know where he is."

Seth looked around the room.

"He might have left," I said, thinking of how things had gone with Zhi Ruo.

Seth pulled out his phone and texted something, and then his eyes went back to searching the room. "His sister wrote me half an hour ago that he hadn't called as they arranged."

"He may have gotten distracted."

"How do you mean?"

I pointed at the couch with Zhi Ruo.

"I see." For a moment, he stopped to observe her and raised an eyebrow. For once, watching his critical look, I almost liked him. But his next words brought us back to our usual tension. "She's going to make president for sure."

Was he hinting that this was the needed behavior to win the vote? "I never had to stoop to those tactics when I got elected," I said simply. I didn't want to give him an opportunity to start an argument.

"No?" he teased.

Okay. He had it coming. "It's surprising how much you get done, when you're not busy bumping into people."

He laughed. "I thought we agreed that it was you who bumped into me."

"*You* agreed."

"I still have a red mark."

Just then, a dancing couple crashed into my table. The girl burped, and I could smell a strong scent of alcohol. Seth moved away just in time, but the guy still managed to knock over my glass. Seth tried to catch it, and it slipped from his hand, spilling all over me.

"Sorry."

"Oh for..." I couldn't be seen to curse in front of everyone. I looked down at my ruined dress. "You know, for a fencing champion, your coordination sucks!"

"Hey, I was trying to help you. Blame the drunk newbies."

The couple laughed, and looked at me, then at Seth. "You two need to get a room," the girl told us.

Seth looked at me and suddenly his expression changed. He looked down, and waited for the couple to leave.

"I'm really sorry, Kim." He shook his head. "I haven't had a fight with anyone in months. And now it's twice with you in one day. I don't know why this is happening."

"I thought you were a pro at fighting."

For the first time, he gave me a kind smile. "Actually, I'm an amateur."

Right. He had to maintain the status for the Olympics.

"Look. I'm sorry about your dress. How about...I walk you home and take it to the dry cleaners for you, or if you don't want to be around me, I could pick it up from somewhere tomorrow? And on the way, I'll apologize for not carrying your pamphlet box."

He did not just say that! Was he for real?

I looked at him, confused. Up until that moment, he was all sarcasm and mockery. Now, suddenly he was the nice guy? *Maybe something Jane had said to him clicked just now?*

Or maybe Seth had a personality issue? I wanted to say something about his apparent mood swings, but then I realized that it was not something I'd normally do. I was usually forgiving. I liked to give people a second chance, especially if they apologized, which he did. *It was just that, with him...wait, why did he upset me that much?*

He looked at me with anticipation. I took a deep breath. It was more important for me to be true to myself.

"Okay, yes, I'd like that." It was so hard to say it. But it felt good afterward, because I knew that I didn't let him get to me anymore. "Just give me a moment to tell the organizing team that I'm leaving."

He smiled. "Sure. Should I wait for you by the entrance?"

I nodded and quickly gathered my things.

Right before I stepped out through the front door, I felt the urge to turn. It was like that feeling that comes when you have a hunch that someone is looking at you, and when I looked back, from the couch where she was sitting, I saw Zhi Ruo's eyes fixed on me.

The night was cold, but the moon was shining brightly when Seth and I got out and walked across the quad.

We had to take it slow. The damp fabric clung to my skin, making it difficult to walk. I would have magically dried it, but I was not going to take the risk of using my powers so close to Zhi Ruo, who was sure to detect them.

Seth seemed happy to walk at my pace.

Above us, I could spot a few stars through the mixed colors of the college night lights, which were soft and gave the gothic quad a look of mystery and enchantment. It had also rained while we were inside and the floor we crossed shimmered like marble from the small drops.

Seth looked at me intently. “I’m sorry about before.”

His tone was sincere, which meant that I shouldn’t be mad at him anymore.

“It’s okay,” I said.

“So... How come you’re stepping down as president of the JCR?”

“I wanted to focus on my studies this year. Finish with good grades to open options for later.”

“Smart move.”

I couldn’t help but smile.

“You’d be hard to replace.”

“Oh?”

“I’ve met people who do this type of thing before. You’re a lot more passionate and diligent. Even after three years in the role. Bradley’s sister spoke very highly of you.”

He’d been speaking about me with other people? “How do you know her?”

“I had a tutorial with her this morning.”

“You teach?”

“Yes.”

“How? I mean, with all the time you spend on sports.”

"Just like you, I find study time, even with all the socials."

"I do literature." I was a fast reader, and that was the part that took the most time in my course. "It's lighter in comparison. You have to do a lot of…"

"Coding," he completed my sentence. "So, we each contribute in our own way."

"You are involved with the college?"

"I was helping them fix a computer system this evening."

How *did* he have time?

We reached my dorm quicker than I'd thought. And suddenly, I felt sorry that it didn't take longer.

"Should I walk up with you, or wait out here in the dark and cold as punishment for this morning?"

I looked at him for a second, and then I burst out laughing. I couldn't help it, and I could tell he was satisfied.

"I'm not exactly sure I'm going back there. I think I want to clean up first and then see how I feel."

He glanced at his watch. "It's not that late. You can still make it back."

I thought for a moment. "Okay. But, the only place to wait for me is the kitchen and someone was baking for the first time in their life earlier today."

He chuckled. "I can deal."

"Your choice, then."

I walked with him to the kitchen, where the smell of burnt starches and sugar was still strong. He made a funny comment and then I rushed upstairs to shower and change.

When I returned, he was sitting by an open window. The smell of burnt cookies was hardly noticeable.

"You're not dressed to go back."

I wore jeans and a sweater. "I think it's getting late and I've got a lecture tomorrow."

"Fair enough." He got up. "I'll walk you to your room then."

"Thanks." An idea came to my mind. "Hey, maybe you can help me with something? Someone was using my computer today. I'm wondering if you could tell me what they did."

"Sure. I can't promise anything, but I'll give it a go."

We walked up, together. I was eager to find out what Zhi Ruo had been up to.

When we got to the top floor, I fished inside my pocket for my key, unfortunately sticking my hand in at the wrong angle. It fell to the floor, and Seth bent and picked it up. He handed it to me.

His hand was warm. For a moment, it actually felt

nice. "Thanks." I smiled.

And then he ruined it. "Dropping keys? Maybe we should work on *your* coordination."

I turned away.

"Sorry. I'm really sorry. Look, I...thought it was funny."

It wasn't. It was insulting. *Or was it? Was I getting overly emotional around this guy?* I quickly turned the key and pushed open the door.

He held it for me. "Forgive me?"

"Okay."

"Hurray!"

"Can you wait here for a second?"

I didn't bother turning on the lights. I just rushed to my desk and grabbed my computer. We walked back to the kitchen, where, after careful examination, Seth couldn't find anything special about what Zhi Ruo had done on the form. He pulled out her entries for me to read and I had to admit, they were not any better than average. He looked for other things she might have done, but didn't see anything suspicious.

Why had she used magic? Was it to conceal something so I couldn't find out about it now?

When we were done, he carefully closed the machine and handed it back to me. We walked up again and stopped by my door. This time, the key was ready in my hand.

"Thank you for your help," I said.

"Anytime."

For a moment, we stood there, looking at each other.

Then, he smiled. "I'm glad we got to talk." He looked as though he was going to bend down and give me a hug, but hesitated.

"Me too," I said. "I...should go now."

"Yes. I mean...hey, we should meet again."

"Uh...yeah, sure," I said, not really knowing how to react.

"Good. See you soon then."

And with that, we parted.

Did I want to meet him again? I wondered, when I was finally alone, in the quiet of my own room.

He puzzled me. I wasn't myself around him.

The things that had happened today went through my mind, as I lay on my bed, thinking, still in my jeans and sweater.

The more I thought about Seth, the more agitated I got. His words from earlier this morning were aggravating, and when I recalled them, my blood boiled in my veins. But then, I thought about how nice it was when we just talked and I saw his warm and helpful side, and then I really did want to meet him again.

I turned my face to the wall and tried to hush my chattering mind.

Nobody ever made me feel this confused before. People had said stupid things to me, but it never really got to me. Not like this. What gave him such influence? Was it his bluntness or the fact that he could also be that friendly?

How did he even manage to insult me in the first place? I didn't lack confidence. I knew who I was. I didn't require validation from anyone. I was popular, I was smart. I was...reassuring myself? *What was wrong with me?*

"Love can be confusing." I suddenly heard my mother's words to my brother Harley, a little over a year ago. *Love? What love?*

Harley was seventeen then, and as tall as my dad. He also had his bright eyes and my mom's dark hair.

The memory was completely out of context. It had happened when Harley told us that Amber was the one.

He rushed down the stairs to show me the Moon-Sign. "Kim, you won't believe it," he said, tears in his eyes. I'd never seen my brother cry. He hardly even cried as a baby.

He stood next to the window, in our old house in

Reading, and where the moon shone on his hand, I saw a bluish glow in the shape of fingerprints. "I took Amber out and we held hands. Look! Look, Kim! The Moon Sign! I found her."

Their love was bubbly and energetic. Much like a normal high school love, with raging hormones, but on steroids. It was as though they couldn't sit still.

My parents, on the other hand, were sweethearts at first sight. But my mom, who was the one with the magic, often said that there were many types of love. Of course, I'd never met the rest of the family, so I didn't know what other examples were like.

I got up. I needed to do something that would stop my overactive brain. I brushed my teeth and then put on my pajamas. Routine tasks, which didn't require much thinking. When I was ready to go to sleep, I opened the window and sat on my bed.

The room was too hot, even with the fresh air coming in.

So much had happened in one day. The party, Seth, Zhi Ruo, trying to find Veronica. I hoped she was okay.

I looked at the moon, and its bright light, following the glare down from the window, and onto the bed and my nightwear. My eyes half closed.

Then, I looked at my hand.

Shining clearly, where Seth's fingers had touched me to give me the keys, was a strong bluish glow.

I sighed.

"You've got to be kidding me!"

Chapter 5

Western Scotland, AD 500

When Seth got back to the room, the intruder was still in deep sleep.

"What are we going to do with him?" asked Niall.

Seth went to the bed and had a closer look. "Too bad nothing about him betrays who sent him."

Who would want the contract? There were many visitors that night. Áedán's invitation was extended to any noble in the area, and they could all guess that the treaty would be arriving.

Of course, the man could be acting for someone who wasn't there or even for himself, which would explain why nobody had come looking for him.

A quick check of the man's coat pockets earlier had produced a few items, like the key to their rooms, but nothing to identify him.

There was no harm in trying again.

Seth turned him onto his back. The search didn't take long. Under his heavy coat, the man had a shirt made of rough material. Inside a large pocket was a folded paper. In another internal pocket, a tiny jagged object brushed against his fingers. He pulled it out. It was a small golden key.

"Look." Seth put both on the table and unfolded the paper. It looked exactly like the marriage agreement.

Niall's eyes opened wide. For a moment, he stared at the objects. Then, he picked up the folded page. "What? Why would he have this?"

"He might have been planning to steal the original and replace it with this forgery."

"How could he know what the original looked like? You...don't think he was working for Áedán?"

Seth held up the key and gave Niall a meaningful look. Nobody would have bothered to put gold into a replica. It was Áedán's original.

"Right," said Niall.

"We'll have to find out what's going on. I think we need to open that box."

This time, Niall agreed. The key fit perfectly and the lock opened immediately. When the lid lifted, the room filled with a strong odor. The treaty inside was dry to the touch and the smell came directly from it.

Seth put the original and the replica side by side on the table. They looked exactly the same. Then, he picked up the original, turned it and held it close to one of the candles, exposing it to the light and warmth of the flame, which now revealed invisible ink.

Behind him, he could hear Niall gasp. For a moment, he felt his own blood stop in his veins.

The back of the page was covered with Prince Domangart's handwriting.

Our pact will be complete, as soon as Fergus Mór's men arrive. Detain them as arranged. My assassins will attack in Dalriada on the first day of the equinox.

It was six days away.

"What the devil?" Niall mumbled, taking the page in his hands.

"It was the only way to deliver the message," Seth found himself saying. "The prince had been trying to come down to meet Áedán for the past few weeks, but Fergus Mór needed him at court." Of course, a messenger or a bird would have been too risky, as both could be easily compromised and the message intercepted. But nobody would suspect the treaty itself.

Still, it would be safer for Áedán to send someone to have the original replaced.

"Six days to save Fergus Mór," said Niall. "We must return to court immediately. Áedán and Domangart have conspired against the king."

There was a noise outside their door. Seth turned. Footsteps. Heavy ones.

By now, Áedán would realize that something had gone wrong with his plan, and they both knew that he would try to stop them from returning home.

Outside the window, they could see the high walls and the massive castle gate. Even in the dark, one could make out the soldiers patrolling. And Áedán's moat was a deep one.

An idea crossed Seth's mind. A way to ensure that they didn't meet with resistance. It was somewhat diabolic, but it could have higher chances of working than a direct approach.

He turned to Niall. "How far would you go to save the king?"

Kim turned in her sleep. Her dreams were lucid, but made no sense. There were buildings she hadn't seen before, and people spoke in a strange language.

Then, there were the fairies. When she had first met Morgan, she remembered waking up, not knowing where she was. Someone was saying things she didn't understand, holding a note. She knew the language now. They were saying, "She's the one we've been waiting for," and, "There is a letter in her pocket." Or was it Morgan herself who had said it? Everything was blurry and muffled.

The images of the strange buildings returned. Tall, with too many windows, sometimes with walls made of glass. Then, a mirror where she saw herself, dressed very differently than the garments of her father's court. And there was strong white light in the room. Stronger than a hundred candles.

Then, for a moment, there was Seth, or at least his voice, and his smell, so close, his warm hand on her face.

"Don't make a sound."

Don't make a sound. Kim opened her eyes. There really *was* a hand on her face!

A sudden chill sent shivers down her spine. Her whole body shook, her heart beating fast in her ears.

The room was dark and the large hand covered her mouth.

She froze, unable to move, or scream, or do anything. But then, she noticed a strange warmth coming from that touch.

"There are two of us, and we're both armed."

It was Seth. She recognized his voice. His touch on her face was surprisingly soft. As though he didn't want to hurt her.

"Can you hear me? Nod, so I know."

Her head felt heavy, but she managed to do it.

And then, suddenly, it was as though a surge of power came over her, and her body stilled. Her pulse became cool and strong again. All the heaviness and the fear were gone.

"Get up quietly."

She could move now, easily. She sat in bed and then turned to the side, getting up and taking a step forward.

Seth slipped behind her. He put his hand on her waist.

Suddenly and without thinking, she caught it and swiftly twisted it, taking him off-balance.

He was quicker than her, countering her move. A sharp metal object was at her throat.

"Nice try."

Still, she had surprised herself with that maneuver. She'd never done anything like it before. It had always seemed impossible when she saw the knights perform it in unarmed training. Her move was faster than theirs and different in style.

"If you cooperate, you'll have nothing to worry about. We honestly don't want to hurt you."

He meant it; there was sincerity in his voice. If that was indeed the case, why was he there?

"What do you want? Why are you doing this, Seth?"

There was a moment of silence. She couldn't see the other person with him, but she could easily guess that it was Niall and that a non-verbal message had passed between the two men. She had made them aware that she knew their identity.

"We need to get back to our court and we have to take you with us. It's all you need to know. We'll keep you safe. For now, we need you to lead us to the stables."

"Or...I can just scream for my guards right now."

"Scream, and your father dies." It was Niall's voice. He pulled out a small golden object that shined in the dark. "You know what this is?"

It looked like a compact mirror. But when Niall opened the lid, instead of her reflection, she saw her father's room, with the king asleep in his bed.

She heard herself gasp.

A Magic Stinger. They were rare, created before the Curse, but word was out that Fergus Mór had one. Through the mirror-shaped object, Niall controlled a poison dart. He must have flown it into the king's room through the window. One word and it would kill her father.

"Now," Niall said, closing the lid. "Is there another door out of this room? Or do we take you out the window?"

He was overdoing it. There was no need for further threats.

Seth's kinder approach was far more intimidating. He meant every word, so it was clear that any danger coming from him was real. Not more and not less than he said.

She considered her position. It reminded her of a story her father had once told her of Fergus Mór, that spoke of a similar situation. His course of action then was to cooperate in order to save his people from a battle. She would be saving her father.

"I'll lead you out then," she said. "I know we all stand a better chance of getting out of this without a scratch that way."

She put her hand on Seth's and pulled it away from her neck slowly. He understood. Complied. Trusted her words.

She turned to him. "But, in return, I expect no harm from either of you."

"You have my word," Seth replied.

He said *my*, not *our*.

"There is a closet behind Niall." She deliberately said his name. "I've got a warm coat there. That's also where you'd find the way out."

There were noises, as Niall went to check the closet and inspect the coat. He must have tried to look for any sharp objects she could use. "Clear," he said. "I'll lead the way."

Seth took the coat and handed it to her. Then, he helped her find her footing in the dark and they descended a small spiral staircase that started behind her wardrobe.

They walked slowly and silently, reaching the bottom floor and then heading toward the stables. Once there, Niall surveyed the hall. He found the night guard asleep and hit him on the head from behind.

Kim's heart missed a beat.

There was no need for him to do that. She could have easily talked her way through.

He picked up their saddles and walked to the horses. Seth motioned her to join him as he prepared his own horse.

When they were ready, Niall pulled out a sword and walked to the door.

"Stop!" she heard herself say.

Niall turned.

"My father's men obey me. I can get you out of the castle without violence. But only if you do your part, and not hurt anyone else."

He sniffed. "What exactly do you propose?" His tone was condescending. Still trying to assert power, though there was no need.

She knew that she had caught him by surprise. She, too, wondered at the authority in her own voice. Her whole behavior was strange to her. Instead of freezing in fear and closing down, she was cool minded, choosing what she said. Knowing that every word and the tone in which she uttered them mattered. She had to be strong. She was defending her father. She'd never thought that that could give her so much confidence.

She turned to Seth. "There is a hidden passage that goes under the wall and moat, large enough for a horse. There are usually only two guards, one at each end, but they have ways of alerting others. The tunnel ends in the woods, near a large waterfall."

"I find it difficult to tell if she's speaking the truth," said Niall. Her fists clenched in anger.

"She is." Seth's voice was calm. Confident. "Let's go."

Why was he so much easier to speak with than Niall? Far less brutal. What was his role, compared to Niall's?

He was clearly no squire. They behaved like equals, and sometimes he even took the lead. She'd have to figure this out soon, and use it. Once again, she was surprised at her own thoughts.

She led them to the passage, stopping by the first guard, and he saluted her immediately.

"Your Highness."

"These men are Fergus Mór's knights."

"I'm aware."

"My father ordered a Code Silver tonight. There's been a threat on my life. Two of my maids will follow in a few minutes, to chaperone."

"I have to check this with—"

"No time. Trust me. My father would praise you for letting us through quickly. Every moment matters."

He hesitated, observing them. "Where's your horse?"

"Waiting on the other side," said Seth. "Her safe escape has already been arranged."

The guard looked at him with recognition. With trust. "If you say so, sir. Just be sure to keep her safe."

How did they know each other? Was this planned? It couldn't have been. Seth must have been to her father's court before. Prior to her own arrival.

"You shouldn't have told him that your maids are following," Niall said once they'd put a distance between themselves and the guard.

"He wouldn't have believed it otherwise," she said coldly. "Besides, pretty soon someone will figure out that I'm gone."

They had a similar conversation with the guard on the other end. Again, she noticed that he recognized Seth.

Niall got on his horse. Seth was preparing his to help her mount.

"I'm not going any farther. Not until you tell me what's going on!" she said.

"Oh, really?" said Niall, pulling out the Stinger. "You'll come, willingly or not. You're lucky you don't have any broken bones yet."

Clearly, his knightly conduct didn't extend beyond the halls of court. Seth seemed the opposite.

"Your dart will be discovered by morning, and then what will you do? I'm the crown princess-in-waiting. And not only that. My father has every knight in the area working for him. You can force me on that horse, but there'll be people catching up with you. The birds will be out with the message faster than you can ride."

He laughed. "We should have knocked you unconscious."

She kept her wits. "But you need me alive. Clearly. And you couldn't guarantee that I would survive if you got into a fight. Not if it was against even half of the knights who are my father's guests tonight. So tell me, why do you need me?"

Seth looked at her. His face in the moonlight showed he was deeply impressed. "There's been a conspiracy around your marriage," he said, without hesitation. Niall seemed shocked. "We're not sure about the details, and the only way for us to save the king is to take you with us."

What? A conspiracy against Fergus Mór? How was her marriage related? "Does this involve Prince Domangart?"

Seth winced when she uttered the prince's name.

"And you need me to prevent it? Without me, this conspiracy can't happen?" *Did she have leverage?*

"It still can. But your absence will send a message, an alert that the plan had been discovered. And having you with us will deter knights from attacking, who might fear for your safety."

There was something else, something he wasn't saying.

He walked to her, cautiously. "I don't want to do

this by force. You've been fair, but I need to take you with me. I'm sorry, Kim."

His calmness and his warm voice were terrifying because in that moment she knew that Seth was far more dangerous than he seemed. He was kind because he could *afford* to be. It was suddenly evident to her that Seth never needed her compliance in the first place. She had no leverage.

And yet, something about him made her feel complete trust. It was in his behavior toward her.

She let him help her mount his horse and they rode away.

Seth took the lead, riding down unmarked paths that were apparently well known to him. After half an hour, he and Niall decided to split. Seth handed Niall the golden box of her marriage agreement. *So, the treaty itself was significant somehow!* If Niall were caught, he could threaten that Seth would kill her.

She knew that it would never happen. Another knight might do it, perhaps even Niall, but not Seth. His actions had reasons; something about his ways almost spoke of choosing morals over power.

Once Niall was gone, calmness took over, and she leaned forward, closing her eyes, and fell asleep.

She woke up to a gentle touch on her shoulder. She tried to push it away with her hand and turn her head, but it just resumed.

Something hairy moved under her chin.

"What?"

"You need to wake up."

It was a man's voice. Someone she knew.

Slowly, she tilted her head. The hairy thing moved and gave a soft neigh. Instinctively, she moved back and opened her eyes.

The first thing she saw was the light of the moon shining on a valley below her.

The horse gave another neigh, and then she remembered: Seth, Niall, and the escape in the night.

"Where are we?" she said, turning.

"We've reached the end of our ride. Beyond is the trail to Haven. By foot."

Haven? She'd heard of it. The knights sometimes mentioned it in their stories. It was one of the safest places in the kingdom. It also had a direct road to the high king's court.

Seth dismounted and held his hands out to her. "Come."

She tried to bend down, but it was difficult. Her body was filled with the physical discomforts caused by having slept the way she did. Her back hurt, her legs were sore, her arms felt as though she'd been holding something heavy, and her neck was stiff.

"I can hardly move."

"Lean and I'll pull you down."

She obeyed, hearing herself mumble as he did it, but his movements were careful.

"Just sit here for a bit. Try and rest your legs. I'll be right back," he said.

He approached the horse and took the reins in his hand, leading it away.

She looked around. Everything seemed to be alive in the night. Soft sounds of animals mingled with the rustles in the bushes.

There was a full moon and in front of her, long shadows gave the valley and the scenery an effect of mystery. Between the trees, mist rose above a small stream and in the distance, she could hear a waterfall.

Something moved inside her. It started in her heart. A sensation of warmth. It spread from there, moving through her veins, down to her feet, toward her fingertips, and up to her head.

She closed her eyes. The feeling was a pleasant one. It reached her neck and she felt a release; the pain in her back disappeared, as did the one in her arms and legs. When this ended, there was no trace of her discomforts and pains.

"I wish you could stay with us." She heard Seth's voice, speaking to the horse, and opened her eyes.

He stood a short distance from her on a split in the road, in one of the paths that led away from where they were. He spoke very softly in the horse's ear.

To her surprise, the words were completely clear to her. *It must be the cool night's silence,* she thought.

"We must leave you here. I hope you find the way back safely." Seth gave the horse a smack on the rear, and the horse set off.

"Why did you do that?" she asked when he returned.

"We must walk from here."

"All the way to Haven?"

"It's just a two-day walk."

"You're kidding!"

"I'm afraid not." His voice was impatient. It was very late. "It's a good path, and there'll be places to rest on the way."

There was no point resisting. She was in the middle of nowhere, and she knew the terrible things that could happen on these roads if she were to escape Seth and attempt to go back alone. At least in that, Seth was trustworthy. If he'd had any sinister intentions, he would have acted on them by now.

He took her hand. His grip was firm, but once again, she noticed the weakness behind it.

He led her down a sheep's path, near the cliff's

edge, and stopped by a large bush. Seth removed the foliage and revealed an entrance to a cave.

"After you."

"What?"

"The cave helps us descend to where the path begins."

"That cave?"

"It's safe. I was here yesterday."

"No!"

For a moment, he had that sarcastic look in his eyes again. He took a deep breath.

"What are you doing?"

"Counting to ten slowly."

She gave him a push. "Don't mock me." She moved forward before he could say anything else.

"Walk quietly. You don't want to wake up the bats."

Chapter 6

Oxford, Present Day

I found it hard to sleep that night.

Right after I saw the Moon Sign, my life flashed in front of my eyes. It was the way it worked, but not what I needed after the day I'd had.

After that, I fell asleep but kept waking up with thoughts of what happened the previous day. When I did dream, it was of past memories, stories I'd heard about magic and guardians, my own powers and how I experienced them. My family. And Seth.

When the alarm clock rang, it was a relief. The night was finally over. I rubbed my eyes and sat up in bed. But I couldn't linger. I had just enough time to eat and dress up for the lecture.

I sat in front of the computer, munching on my fruit bowl. Jane had put up some links to Morganstein's videos on the lecture page. I tried to watch them as I ate, but my mind was clouded.

I wondered when I'd meet Seth again. He said he wanted to see me. His hand had been so warm when he had touched me.

The lecture hall was still mostly empty when I stepped in. I looked at my watch. I was early. Somehow, I'd managed to be quick at getting ready. I told myself that it was a result of overexcitement after drinking too much coffee, but I knew the real reason was my hope to see him there.

There was, of course, no reason for him to come. This was mainly a literature lecture, but I couldn't help but wish for it.

"You're all flushed," Jane said when I walked up to her. She had saved me a seat in the front row. It was a disappointment, because it meant I couldn't observe the rest of the hall.

"Bad night," I said.

"Sorry to hear it. What happened?"

"Just... distracted from the day."

"Worried about Veronica?"

"That, and other things. I didn't get any messages from her or from security."

"Strange. Maybe she hooked up with some guy..."

"Yes. But she was seen getting into someone's car hurriedly." I had texted Jane about it after speaking with the other volunteer.

"That is someone else's account. You weren't there. She might be fine. And you did the right thing in calling security."

Something told me that my worry was well founded.

"How about, after the lecture, we go around campus and see if we could find out if people saw her?" Jane suggested.

"What about the professor?" Jane usually had to spend time with our lecturers to check everything went well with their stay at the college.

"I've arranged for her to have lunch with the college dean."

Of course she had.

The door opened and an excited group of students got in and made it all the way to the other end of the front row. I spotted Zhi Ruo in the middle of it, energetic and chatty.

She caught my gaze and smiled.

I looked back at the rest of the room. Seth wasn't there.

Soon, the doors closed and the head of the department stepped up to the stage to introduce Morganstein. His words were similar to the summary I saw on Jane's page.

Her expertise was Arthurian legends. To me, these were witch history distorted. Though, by the end of the lecture, I was forced to admit that her story was the closest I had heard to the truth.

She was greeted by applause when she got on the stage, a tall and slim woman with long, black hair and abnormally pale skin. Her large, almost crystal-blue eyes observed us. She was far more impressive in reality than in any of her photos or videos. She smiled at the room and everyone went quiet.

"When I say to you the word Camelot, what's the first thing that comes to mind?" she asked the audience.

"King Arthur."

"Knights of the Round Table."

"Lancelot and Guinevere."

"Magic."

"Merlin."

Morganstein smiled.

"The National Lottery!" some wise guy shouted and everyone laughed.

"And where was this Camelot?"

The room was silent. A few hands were raised. Zhi Ruo's was one of them, and Jane's.

Jane was chosen. "Glastonbury area. About one thousand five hundred years ago when cross-referencing most literature texts."

"Very good." Morganstein smiled in approval. And then her eyes moved from Jane to me.

For a moment, it was almost as though we were the only two people in the room. In her short gaze, I saw surprise and a hint of recognition. She looked away.

"Anyone else?" She turned to the room.

There were a few more answers. None as strong as Jane's.

Morganstein went on to speak about Arthur and his role in establishing not only Camelot and the Knights of the Round Table, but also a legacy of justice, honesty, and human rights. The quest for the Holy Grail was really a metaphor for finding the truth and the source of everlasting life within ourselves.

The important thing to remember, she said, was that Arthur was a regular human. What he did was possible for all of us, but he took the lead in doing it. He had his many flaws but his dedication outshined them, enough to allow him to make his impact and create his legacy. She also quoted some texts that showed the negative sides of the king, and what brought Camelot to eventual ruin.

"She's so amazing. Don't you think?" Jane said during the break. Her eyes lit up.

"I'm actually positively surprised," I admitted. I

reached down for my phone and opened it to see a voicemail from security. "Sorry. I have to get this."

I quickly stepped out of the noisy room and dialed the number. The message was about Veronica. Her phone was traced and discovered at the edge of South Park. The police had been informed of her absence, and security reassured me that most missing people were found within a day or two. They asked that I call if I heard anything new.

I walked back to my seat, to tell Jane about the message, when a familiar voice stopped me, right before I entered our row.

"Hey."

It was him.

I turned, smiling. "Hi, Seth."

He wore jeans and a dark T-shirt that highlighted his grey eyes. I hadn't noticed their color before.

"What are you doing here?" I immediately regretted saying it. But then, it was probably clear that I was glad to see him.

"Should I leave?"

I laughed. "I just didn't know you were into literature."

"Are you kidding? King Arthur, sword fights, knights in armor..."

"I see."

"I was also hoping you would be here so I could ask you something. Ah..." He looked around.

Almost everyone else was seated again. On the stage, Morganstein was arranging her papers on the speaker's lectern.

"To be continued," Seth said in a low voice, and I felt butterflies in my stomach as I returned to my seat.

Jane gave me a meaningful look.

The second part of the lecture was about Merlin, the mage at Arthur's side.

"What do you think this means, that Arthur was supported by someone with far more power than him?"

"Some would say it was a show of Arthur's leadership to be able to gather strong people by his side, but I think that Merlin was not given a real chance to lead." I heard Zhi Ruo's girly voice. She didn't even raise her hand. "He was discriminated against, like many capable people today. The whole world would have been different if it were Merlin who ruled."

Morganstein's eyes narrowed. "That's one way to see it." It was not the answer she was expecting, to say the least. "Others would say that Merlin helped and mentored Arthur throughout his life, like biblical prophets did."

"But is that what Merlin truly wanted? To be second?" She was persistent, and Morganstein smiled impatiently. "And maybe it wasn't up to Arthur and Merlin at all. Maybe something else happened that forced magical people to serve humans."

I froze in my seat. She was referring to Avalon's Curse!

Was she out of her mind? There were some things that humans should never know about us, not even as a legend. The Curse was what changed the world and made mages guardians to humans. This was one of magic's greatest secrets. There were even witches who never heard of it. When my mom first told me about Avalon's Curse, she warned me about ever mentioning it.

"It's... to establish democracy," I said, loudly.

Morganstein's attention immediately shifted to me. I could see a look of contempt in Zhi Ruo's eyes. It was time she got challenged.

"One of the key elements of a fair rule is separation of power," I said, glad I had paid attention in civics. "If Merlin were to rule instead of Arthur, he'd be unstoppable."

Morganstein looked more content. "But, do you think that Merlin would have wanted the throne?"

"I know it's what I would do," said someone in the

front row, sitting next to Zhi Ruo. There was laughter in that area of the class.

I knew it didn't matter what Merlin wanted. Magic wouldn't have allowed it.

"And use magic for everything?" Morganstein said to him.

"Sure."

She turned back to me. "But what would be a reason not to?"

"If you used magic for everything, people would become irresponsible, because with a flick of a hand you could fix anything you did wrong. Without it, you need to think twice before you do something bad."

Morganstein looked at me approvingly. Zhi Ruo glared at me.

"Actually," I straightened in my seat, looking straight at Zhi Ruo this time, "some would say that magic in Camelot was just a metaphor to describe the good versus evil forces of those dark ages." I was improvising here, but I did take part in a few literary debates, so I was used to making an argument without preparation. "The story of Merlin and Arthur is that of... reshaping society. Creating justice. Making people more responsible."

"Well done!" said Morganstein.

I had over-aimed. But it worked, and Zhi Ruo was quiet the rest of the lecture, done exposing my world.

The class moved to discuss the forbidden love story between Guinevere and Lancelot, and I sat back, sighing with relief.

Jane scribbled something on the last page of her notepad. She turned it to me. "Nicely done!"

And then another note. "He's been smiling at you ever since you started talking."

Seth. Jane's words made the butterflies return, and I found it difficult to concentrate after that.

When the lecture was over, Jane walked to the stage to speak with the professor.

I stayed in my seat.

"Great debate."

I turned, to see Seth enter the row. He sat next to me.

"Thanks. Just doing my best."

"It would have been worthy of the debating society."

"Oh, stop it!"

He chuckled. "So..." He suddenly had a funny look on his face, and he moved his hand through his hair. Then stopped, noticing he'd done it. "Um, about before...Do you...want to maybe grab a drink later?"

He was asking me out! "I thought you saw me as a preppy sorority queen with nothing but a social calendar."

"Who also debates in class." He took it as a yes. "It's a whole new world for me!"

I looked at him for one moment, and then, I just started to laugh. I couldn't help it. I could see a winning smile on his face.

"I think it would be really nice."

"Good. I'll pick you up at seven thirty?"

I nodded.

"Right then," he said, excited, and turned to leave.

"Wait. Don't you need my number?"

He pulled out one of my pamphlets. "Got it."

"And what about yours? What if something happens and I need to cancel?"

"You can't."

It was almost time for lunch when Jane and I had finished walking around the college, trying to see whether we could find out anything about Veronica. We thought it was still a good idea, even though security and the police were already involved.

It turned out that Veronica had chosen to rent a

room in a regular flat, outside of campus, so she wasn't staying with any of the students. She also didn't seem to have participated in any Freshers Week activities. We met only one other person who knew her and said they'd seen her once, at a party that she left early.

"She likes to keep to herself," I said when we were done. None of her flatmates had seen or heard from her since she disappeared.

Jane now shared my worry, but tried to be encouraging. We made a quick call to security and learned that there was still no news. They requested we didn't do anything else.

Jane suggested I come over for lunch and relax a bit. Speak about other things. I assumed she meant Seth. But I wanted to tell my family about him first. After all, it wasn't as if I could say to her that he was my Charge. I said I needed to stop at my dorm, and would come over afterward.

When I reached my room, I carefully locked the door and I took a seat on the old couch, leaning on my favorite heart-shaped pillow. I had to think hard before making that call. I wanted to tell my folks about Seth, but they were under a lot of pressure.

My family had a great secret to hide.

Shortly after they met, my mother did something

that had resulted in my parents getting threatened. The only way that they could protect themselves and my mom's pregnancy with me was, incredibly, to travel back in time and live in the past, hiding their identities.

They never spoke about what had happened, and I only found out that they were from the future when I was sixteen. And they didn't share details on how they managed to achieve something that, to the best of my knowledge, mages couldn't do.

Hiding who we were had a huge influence on our lives. A lot of things were forbidden in order to keep a low profile. I couldn't practice magic openly, even amongst other witches, and I couldn't join a coven. This was because members of the same family left similar magical traces, so if a witch by any chance knew any of my mom's family, they might recognize my trace.

Somewhere in this world there was another Julie and Mark—Ralston, not Taylor—who didn't know that I existed. And there was a whole family—a large one, on my mom's side—which, from her stories, was close and warm. They knew nothing about me either.

But not for long. I looked at the calendar. Monday was marked, "Parents Travel." The day of their return to their older lives to replace the Ralstons, who would be traveling back in time. It was *the* date.

Edinburgh was where it had happened. Where they had been sent back in time.

We had talked it through over family dinners during the past year. I was going to stay behind and finish college, visiting them in New York or Edinburgh on my breaks, as a long distant relative. Harley and Amber got into an exchange program abroad. They would also move in together, though Amber's parents didn't know about that part of the plan.

As a cover story, my parents would say that they were taking a sabbatical, to be close to Harley's school.

There was a lot going on. Especially for my dad. He was about to leave the small and comfortable life that he and my mom had built as teachers in private high schools, and return to the known businessman he was before.

I wondered if, despite the excitement of finally going back, they wouldn't miss the easy and serene life they had built here. Or how much difficulty they would face when they went back to deal with their unresolved problems. At least, they succeeded because they saved me and Harley.

There were instances when I wished they could

tell me what had happened to them that made them do something that drastic. Or why they would go away every few weeks for a four-day weekend, which Harley and I were not allowed to join. And then come back exhausted, as though they hadn't had a moment's rest.

I learned not to ask too many questions about these things. I knew that once they went back, I'd have my mom's family to talk to. And hopefully finally learn the truth.

I hesitated before calling my parents now.

Was it the right time to tell them about Seth? But I was certain they'd be happy for me. I decided to just go for it. I picked up the phone and tapped their contact. It rang twice and my dad picked it up.

"Hi, Dad."

"Kim. Hello."

There was a noise on the line and my mom was with us. "Hi, honey. How are you?"

"I'm good."

"How's Freshers Week?" said my dad.

"Going well."

"Did they elect a new Junior Common Room president yet?"

He liked that I had been involved with the college in that way. He'd say that being in a position of leadership and organization built character and taught responsibility. Harley had been captain of the basketball team twice.

"No. Not yet, but we've introduced the candidates. How are you guys?"

"Busy, but we got some good news."

"Yes," said my mom. "We found a family to rent the house to."

"That's wonderful." I knew that they would have preferred to sell, but that wouldn't have worked with their cover story.

"How is Harley?"

"Still traveling. They emailed yesterday. Their school is being very flexible, letting them do remote work."

"Sounds good," I said and waited, hoping for a pause on the line.

It worked.

"Honey, are you there?" said my mom.

"Yes. Yes, I'm here. I have something to tell you too," I started and realized I was speaking more quickly, animated. "Yesterday, I met a guy. Someone special." I had to be discreet, even on the phone.

"You mean...?" My dad got it immediately.

Then, my mom spoke, in an excited tone with a voice higher than her normal. "That's wonderful news!"

"When did you find out?" said my dad. He meant the Moon Sign. I was almost certain he was smiling on the other end.

"Yesterday. Right before going to sleep."

"What does he study?" It was my mom again. Still excited.

"He's doing a masters in computer science. Got transferred to my college this year."

I could hear my dad chuckle. Of course, I'd missed the obvious. Back in their old life, he was a big shot in the software industry.

"What's his name?" he asked.

"Seth Rivers."

There was a pause. "The fencer!?"

"Yes, Dad. How did you know?"

"I read he had come to your college." He had an alert on his phone for all news relating to Christ Church and to Oxford. "Nice fellow. A bit shy on his interviews. Will be great for you."

"It's not like I have a choice."

He laughed. "So, has he married you yet?"

"Mark!" my mom exclaimed, and then she laughed too. It was the sentence that my grandfather had asked her right after they'd met. He and my grandmother had tied the knot after five days.

Again, I was reminded of the fact that I would soon meet the rest of my family! "We've just met," I replied.

"That's what we said," answered my mom. She and my dad got magically handfasted after a week. Harley and Amber were secretly engaged. It was how guardian love worked. Fast. Intense.

Not the way I liked it.

"Kim, honey..." My mom's voice was suddenly serious. "Remember what we said about telling the truth as soon as you can. It's important that he knows."

"I'll tell him when the time is right."

"The time is always right." She once told me that she had waited to tell my dad, and it complicated things for them. "Remember, he's bound to accept it well. It's how it works."

"Thanks, Mom," I said in a stern tone. I was going to do this *my* way.

They got the hint. We went back to talking about them.

The new tenants were going to move in during the weekend. And my parents were coming up to Oxford to stay at a hotel so we could have some time together before parting.

"We thought we would arrive on Saturday

morning, leaving Sunday."

"You could stay longer." I surprised myself. For such a long time, I'd been busy building my distance and establishing my independent space. But now that they were leaving, I suddenly missed them.

There was a pause. "How about we decide when we're there with you?"

"Sounds good."

The conversation ended with them saying they'd love to meet Seth.

It went well. Better than I'd expected. After the call, I texted Jane to see whether there was anything she wanted me to bring to lunch. She said she was making spaghetti and asked whether I had basil. I stopped by my kitchen to get a bag from my fridge shelf, along with some mushrooms, herbs, and white wine to make a side dish.

Then, I went to her flat, which she and Oliver shared. It was paid for by scholarships and bursaries that they worked hard to get.

Her apartment was neat and warm, as usual, with a pile of library books with Post-it Notes sticking out of them, carefully arranged on the coffee table, next to a framed photo of her mom with the family back in Kenya.

"Did you read all night?" I asked.

"No, but I worked like a plow horse most of yesterday." Jane could sometimes get creative and utter really funny things when she was passionate about something. She smiled now, taking Professor Morganstein's card out of her wallet. "It paid off."

"Nice!"

"She said she'd interview me while she's here, so I don't have to travel to Edinburgh, and that there is another position coming up that I might be even more suited for."

"That's amazing. I don't know how you do it!" I took the ingredients out of my bag.

"Just keeping their bellies full while they're here."

I laughed. It turned out the dean had taken Morganstein to one of the fancier places in town.

Jane placed the card into an index box, where she kept business cards from the people she'd met. It stood next to her go-to books, *Get Your Next University Job* and *The Beginners Guide to Networking in Academia*.

I started to wash the basil and marinaded the mushrooms in the wine, with herbs and soy sauce.

"So...the guy from the library?" Jane started working on the pasta sauce.

I blushed. "His name is Seth. He's a second-year masters student in computers. And he's also an

Olympic fencer."

"Interesting." Jane looked down and smiled to herself. "What happened?" she teased.

"What do you mean?"

She raised her eyebrows, indicating that I knew very well what she meant. She must have noticed how much Seth was different from the type I normally ended up with. She called them the playboys from London. They were usually Scarlett's friends. "Your bad-boy fuse must have finally burned. I thought we'd never see the end of it."

"Oh, come on! They were not so bad." They were. I couldn't count the amount of times I spent sobbing on her couch.

"Don't make me remind you! But, at least this one, well...I thought he was nice." She got back to Seth. "Back at the library."

I put down the chopping knife I had been using. "You said something to him."

"Nope. But I sure as hell would have if he hadn't apologized to you. I wasn't going to stand by and let him be an ass."

"Rest assured, his bad ways are now mended." I chuckled, thinking of guardian love. "He was very nice when he asked me out."

"Good. And where is he taking you?"

"Actually, it's a surprise."

"A surprise? No fancy party or gourmet restaurant opening?" She knew my playboys well.

"Nope." I shook my head. "I don't think that's his style."

"Down-to-earth. I like him."

"That makes two of us." I blushed again.

She stopped. "Ooh. You're all smitten already!"

Yes. It was definitely going fast.

When we sat down to eat, the conversation drifted to other things: my plans for the year, stepping down as head of the Junior Common Room, my parents moving away.

But Seth came up again toward the end.

"Text me when you get to where he's taking you." Jane took the last bite from her plate and lay down her fork. "I know he's a good guy, but you can never be too careful."

"It's fine. He's my Char—" I closed my mouth mid-word and almost bit my lip.

Chapter 7

Western Scotland, AD 500

She wasn't what he had assumed, Seth had to admit.

He'd expected panic, shouting and screaming, but Kim had reacted in the opposite way, far stronger in mind than some of the knights he knew at court. She was even able to doze on the horse!

Maybe Niall was right. Maybe he had read her wrong initially, because she reminded him of someone else. The resemblance was there. He saw it when she was asleep, and the memories came, the pain in his wrist suddenly strong.

He remembered lying on his sickbed after that battle. Seraphim, Fergus Mór's head mage, was by his side, trying his strongest spells. His body was almost cured, but the wrist wouldn't heal, and he was weak from all the spells and treatments. He felt like a shadow of his former self.

"Don't despair," said Seraphim. "I know other mages I can write to."

These were kind words, but empty ones. If Seraphim couldn't do it, nobody could.

Niall would come often. A true friend. "Everyone in court is waiting for you to return."

"I think we both know I won't be coming back."

"Seth, you'll heal."

"No. Not completely. Someone will have to replace me."

"Fergus Mór said you're keeping the title. So, any replacement will be temporary. Now, you work on getting yourself better. You've got a wedding to go to. Won't happen without the groom."

That was another problem. "She's been coming less and less."

"She's a woman. They need encouragement. Surprise her. Bring her flowers in the night."

He decided to do that. A few weeks later, when he could walk again. He went to her, excited, expecting she'd be happy to see him, and that the ice that had formed between them would melt.

But her quarters were closed, locked, and the noises coming from inside were all too familiar. She wasn't alone.

He waited. He wanted to see who it was. The door opened early in the morning, and Domangart came out.

He couldn't challenge the crown prince. They quarreled, but the part that hurt remained the look in her eyes that showed no regrets.

"Don't bother explaining," were his last words to her and the last time he ever spoke with her.

Now was his opportunity to get back at the prince. Give Domangart what he deserved. He wondered how far the treachery went.

Getting the warning through was the challenge. Domangart might already be monitoring any pigeon stations around the palace. If that were the case, Niall would have to reach court in person to deliver the message.

There was one other way to get a letter to the king. Haven. The king's sister lived there. Her pigeons were received directly by the king.

The walk there went through one of the most beautiful crossings in the woods, going by the streams of Haven. After passing through Haven itself, the road led to the high court.

He didn't expect Kim to like the idea, especially not the cave. That seemed to bring her princess side out, and he was too tired to be patient.

It was a small cave, easy to navigate, but she had to stop all the time, to adjust her skirt or her shoes. He wondered whether she was also adjusting her makeup.

"I can't see anything. How do you know we're going the right way? What if we get lost?"

"It's a very small cave and I know it well."

"Okay. What if *I* get lost?"

"Just hold my hand and stay close."

"What if I fall?"

"Try not to!"

On the other end, they stopped so that he could make sure that nothing awaited them outside.

"Wait here, Your Highness." It took a lot of effort not to stress the word *highness* in the tone he felt it deserved. He left her leaning on the edge of the opening wall.

Outside, everything was clear. There were no sounds, apart from a fox's cry or a waking owl.

"Sss... Seth?"

Her voice came from inside the cave. Another noise accompanied it.

He turned to see a large wildcat bearing its teeth at her.

"Come out!" he yelled.

But she froze. Her eyes were wide open in horror.

Now she would panic?

He rushed to her and the animal ran off.

She was still shivering and he hugged her. "They're not dangerous. He was probably just hungry. He'd be more scared of you than you are of him."

She nodded, shaking. And then something happened. It was as though a wave of energy passed through her, after which she was calm again, looking around her with serenity, her eyes curious, at where the animal had been. Strange.

He let her dose for a bit, as he prepared something for them to eat from a food pack that he and Niall had put together before leaving.

He was careful when waking her up, and when she opened her eyes and saw him, she immediately moved back.

"It's just me."

"That's not exactly a relief." But she was smiling.

He found himself laughing. "There's food. Here, try this." He cut a bread roll in half.

She held it in her hands, waiting for him to take his first bite, and then nibbled on it hungrily. "Not too bad. Lacks some taste, though."

"It's from your father's table."

There were still a few hours until morning. At least it seemed that way from how dark it was.

Kim looked at Seth, marveling at his stamina. She had had some sleep that night. It appeared he'd been up the entire time.

They were headed to a safe place, a man-dug cave that was built as a shelter for the people of Haven. A good place to rest for a few hours.

The walk was easy, leading them through woods now, far from the cliffs and the beautiful view of the valleys. But the sky was clear, and the moon provided plenty of light.

Some of the court ladies might have even called it romantic. That is, if she didn't tell them about the mud, the spiders, and the sore feet. Or maybe she would not tell them about any of it.

They could never understand that there was something else beyond the toils of the journey. A sense of being alive. And perhaps this was enhanced by the very hardships and danger. It was like being in one of those stories that the knights were telling, and with one of those knights.

Seth was quiet, helping her move through the ferns and stones on the path.

She couldn't figure him out. The knights she'd met at her father's palace were normally easy to decipher. They liked court life. It seemed that their focus was on trophies of different kinds: tournaments, money, titles, court women.

Something else drove him.

"How long have you been in Fergus Mór's court?"

"Almost two years," he answered, glancing at her, and then back at the path. "I've been Niall's teacher for a while."

A teacher? Not a knight? "Were you always a teacher?"

"No. Not always. I was a knight first."

He still had the title. "So...this was a sort of promotion."

He sniggered. "Not really." Something about his tone said he didn't want to talk about it.

"Where were you before?" She tried to shift the conversation a bit.

He stopped. "You're full of questions, aren't you?"

"Just trying to get to know you."

"Why?"

"'Cause we're in this together."

That made him smile.

He resumed the walk. "If you really want to know, I don't remember where I was before." He turned to see her reaction.

She gave him a look filled with all the curiosity she could muster. There was no need to fake it, of course. This was the first time she met anyone who had trouble remembering their past, as she did.

It worked.

"I woke up one day," he continued, "alone on a road. A few minutes later, a carriage passed. Then another one, chasing it. They crashed and soon I heard screaming. A bandit was threatening a finely dressed woman with a sword. Somehow, although I was unarmed, I knew how to take him down and it turned out that the woman was King Fergus Mór's daughter."

"And the rest is history."

"You could say so." He chuckled.

"I..." She stopped. *Should she tell him?* It wasn't exactly common knowledge that she didn't remember her past. Though, it would be such a relief to tell someone, and he had been honest. *What harm could it do?* "I... also don't remember anything except for the last two years of my life."

"What?" He stopped. Then looked at her, confused. "You mean you don't remember growing up in court or being a princess?"

"No. I was trained by fairies. Morgan Le Fay, in

particular. She said I had had an accident, and I stayed with her tribe until I was ready to be presented in my father's court."

He glanced at her with sincere interest now. "We have a few cases in court where princesses were sent abroad to be trained before they came into society."

"There was one other in my father's court."

"Did you ask the fairies about your past?"

"Many times. I never got a straight answer. I sometimes think that they, too, didn't really know. But they knew more than they were telling me."

He took her hand again to help her during a rougher stretch of the path. Once more, she noticed that warmth that she had never felt from anyone else's touch.

After walking a bit further, a strange sensation suddenly made her stop and concentrate. Something was paying attention to where they were. It was behind them. Not far. And not human. It walked like it was big and heavy.

"What?" said Seth.

"I... think I can sense something following us."

"There are lots of creatures around. People who walk here often get overly alert."

That wasn't it. She knew she sensed something threatening. It was in her mind's eye now. A nocturnal creature, a beast, treading the ground, its steps interrupting the other sounds of the night. They had passed a bend in the path a few minutes earlier. It was now there, going right through it, its sides crashing the branches around it and its sharp tail banging against the trunks.

"We can't stop here," said Seth.

"How much longer till we reach the shelter?"

"About twenty minutes. We'll be passing through a large clearing soon. It's after that." He held out his hand. "Come. Don't worry too much about noises you hear. Not many people would walk any of these paths at night."

But he would. And walking with him was almost like walking in daylight.

They continued. She didn't sense the creature anymore. She wondered whether Seth was right before. *Was it just her over alertness, mixed with everything that was happening tonight?*

"You know, Seth..."

"What?"

"You're not like the other knights I've met. I must admit, a few hours ago, I was half ready to send you to the gallows the minute I'm queen."

He laughed. "The gallows! No, not the gallows!"

"I was being merciful."

"Were you, now?" He turned, a smile on his face. "What's changed? You discovered my charming personality?"

She laughed. "Well... you kidnapped me and took me to filthy forests with wildcats and mud."

"Clearly, I made a strong impression." He snickered.

"Clearly."

"You're not what I thought either. Not exactly the typical court lady. Though most of them would envy you, of course."

"What's to be envied?" She sighed. "The main goal of my life is excelling at being a king's daughter, so that one day I could be a king's wife."

He raised an eyebrow, surprised. "I can't believe you just said that."

"What? It's the truth." They resumed their pace. "And I don't think that Fergus Mór's court would be any different."

"The women there are younger and prettier."

"Excuse me!"

"I didn't mean more than you."

"Yes, you did."

"No. No. It's strictly present company excluded."

She giggled.

They'd just entered the clearing, and it was easier

to walk, the ground more visible. They walked side by side.

"The ladies of the high court are more ambitious than in other courts."

His tone had betrayed that he was trying to say something more. What did he mean by *ambitious*? "How so?"

Seth was silent for a few moments, hesitating. "Well, I guess you might as well know. They... like to entertain your future husband."

"Entertain?"

He nodded.

"I see. But surely, this...entertainment would stop once we're married."

He looked her straight in the eye.

"Right. So he's... marrying me for the politics and my kingdom's wealth."

But her words were hardly audible to herself. Somewhere behind them, she sensed it again. The creature.

It had gotten much closer, without her noticing. And they were now exposed, walking in the middle of the clearing.

She turned and looked toward the woods. "The creature. It's back."

And then, in that moment that she didn't look

where she stepped, something caught her foot. An instant later, she was on the ground, pain spreading.

"Are you all right?" Seth bent down, moving the hem of her dress.

Her teeth clenched from the agony. And she held her ankle, shocked at the level of ache.

Behind Seth, the trees moved sideways and into the clearing stepped a massive creature.

All she could hear was the sound of her own screaming.

Seth drew his sword and looked at the scarred, disfigured, and scaly beast emerging from between the trees, its jaw open with saliva dripping. A deranged dragon. It was his one fear. He had faced one before. This was how he'd broken his wrist.

Behind him, Kim was still screaming, and the dragon eyed her.

"He likes it when you scream."

She stopped. That made it easier to concentrate. Not that concentration was the problem.

Of the ten dragons that the mage-king Harthenon had burnt to create the Curse of Avalon, two survived. He himself had killed the other, and at a terrible price. The wound had magic in it that even Seraphim couldn't undo.

The beast in front of him was larger than that one. Was this his kin, now coming for revenge?

It stood high on its hind legs, blocking the sky, casting a large shadow on the ground, its eyes observing him with hunger. It pulled its head backward and sniffed, then exhaled, spitting fire into the sky.

He needed a poisoned dagger. But all he had were two boot knives and his sword. With the princess too wounded to make a run for it, the only chance to survive was to try to blind the beast.

The dragon advanced, poised to attack.

Seth breathed in, filling his lungs with air, and reached for one of the knives. The dragon's tail came at him with lightning speed, wrapped around him and raised him off the cold earth.

"No!"

He heard Kim's voice behind him.

But the dangerous move was also an opportunity. He was now closer to the beast's face. He threw his knife straight toward the dragon's eye.

The moment that the weapon left his hand, the dragon jolted him. But somehow, almost as if guided by magic, the knife hit the target.

The beast shrieked, its tail releasing him, and he fell backward. Instinctively, he pulled out the other knife and thrust it into a scar on the beast's skin, holding onto it as the tail swung left and right.

The dragon roared. It started to move erratically, both its head and its tail shaking.

In its rage, it brought Seth close to its mouth.

Seth focused. His next move, if they were going to survive, would be to thrust his sword into the other eye. But with the dragon thrashing about, it would be difficult.

He waited for the right moment. Just when the dragon brought him close enough and at a good angle, he drew his sword and plunged it toward the beast's eye. He hit the dragon beside the eye and caused a smaller injury than he'd intended. But then, the sword suddenly shifted and sank again, straight into the beast's head – a fatal wound.

"What?!" He couldn't believe his eyes.

The dragon stopped, frozen, as death took over. A stifling darkness spread instantly from its chest in every direction. Its skin started changing, turning stiff and becoming solid.

The creature tilted forward, as it turned into rock.

Seth held onto the knife until the tail neared the ground and then ran, moving away from the falling dragon-shaped mass of rock that had once been a living beast. It crashed into a thousand pieces.

He rushed to Kim. “Are you okay?”

She nodded. Her eyes were bloodshot, open in shock.

“It’s over. He’s dead.”

“I thought dragons were nice,” she managed.

“Not this one.” He looked at her foot. “Can you move?”

“I think so.”

They needed to keep going. Someone else was there, someone with magic. It was the only explanation. There was no other way that battle could have gone the way it did. Especially that final bit when his sword tilted and went into the dragon’s head. Whoever was there might recognize both of them and start asking too many questions.

“Ready?” He held out his hand.

She took it and stood. She seemed stable.

“I’ll be right back. I need to go collect the weapons.”

“Okay.”

He went to the middle of the clearing, walked between the rock and dust left from the beast, and picked up his knives and sword.

“How are you doing?” he asked when he returned.

She smiled. "I think I'm fine now." She was being optimistic.

"Do you need me to carry you for a bit?"

"No. I'll walk."

"Are you sure?" There was no way she could do it easily after that injury.

"I think so," she said with certainty. "Is it a long way still?"

"No. We're very close. But... how about you try a few steps first?" He offered her his hand again, expecting a cry of pain once she started walking. "Careful!"

"I'm all right." Surprisingly, she managed to move her weight from one foot to the other and walk back and forth. "I can do it."

"If you say so..." It made no sense.

"I'll manage. Really."

And she did. Her walk was slow and cautious but she didn't limp, and she didn't need help making it all the way to the shelter.

It was empty when they reached it. A quick scan of their surroundings told him that they were safe. He lit a small fire and mixed some healing herbs for her in a tiny pot.

She sat close to the cave wall, leaning her head backward. "It was bigger than the beast I had sensed," she mumbled, before closing her eyes.

That was right! She had said that she sensed something before the dragon appeared. Of course, it must have been a coincidence. She had clearly sensed something else, because nobody could sense a dragon, not even mages. But her timing was accurate.

"Try this," he said when the herb mix was ready.

She opened her eyes and took a small sip. "It's awful."

"Too much pepper?"

She looked at him for a second, and then burst out laughing.

Laughing, in all the pain she must be in!

"I appreciate the effort, Seth, but I really don't think I need it."

"It's a pretty bad injury you've got there."

"I was able to walk."

"All the more reason to take the herbs now."

"Really. I'm fine."

He looked at her in disbelief. "Mind if I have a look?"

She agreed, taking off the shoe and sock and raising her skirt.

In the light of the fire, he could clearly see that there wasn't even a scratch there.

Chapter 8

Oxford, Present Day

Seth was waiting for me outside my dorm. He rang the intercom, and I allowed myself a quick glance out my window, before heading down.

He wore a pair of jeans and a buttoned shirt that accentuated his athletic chest. For a moment, I stopped and looked. I hadn't noticed his physique before and I had to admit, he was actually really hot.

When I had reached the ground floor, I stopped myself from opening the door too quickly. *When was I this excited about anyone?* I had been on edge all afternoon. So much, that I forgot my towel when I went to shower and had to rush back to my room, with my hair dripping.

Dressing up took time too. I'd never been on a date with someone like Seth. Something told me that pink and tight with a low cleavage was not his style.

Conjuring a new dress was out of the question, of course. This particular type of magic was too easy to detect. I decided to go with a knee-long skirt and a patterned black sweater.

I was just done with my makeup, when the intercom rang. Seth was right on time.

He seemed excited, too. His eyes were shining, and he observed me with a smile as I walked out toward him.

"You look great," he said.

"You too."

"I brought you something." He had a white rose in his hand.

"Thank you," I heard myself saying in a sweet voice that surprised me.

He handed me the rose and held out his hand.

"You want everyone to know I'm on a date with you," I said, before taking it.

"Yup."

I thought I saw a bit of flush in his cheeks. "It's a first date." I left out the word *just*.

"You're very good at counting, Kim."

It made me laugh. Yesterday, I would have been offended by the sarcasm, but everything was different now. I took his hand, which was strong and warm, and let him lead the way.

He took us to the city center, and he kept looking at me, smiling, all along. He was so different than the guy who had bumped into me.

"I hope you like Chinese," he said as we turned into a narrow street near the Covered Market.

"Of course."

"Good."

We reached a small restaurant that looked new, or newly redecorated. He opened the door for me, and soon we were seated at a round table, near the window, where we got a little bit of privacy from the other diners.

Seth said that the place had just opened. He'd eaten there last week and would never eat out anywhere else. He added that if I didn't order their stir-fried rice, I would regret it for as long as I live.

He kept making me laugh.

"So, how come you transferred to Christ Church?" I asked when we were waiting for our food to arrive.

"I heard it was the place to meet great girls."

My cheeks blushed. "Where were you before?"

"St Anne's College."

"I'm sure they have great girls there too," I teased.

"Yes, but I wanted a literature major."

I giggled. "So, Christ Church gave you a good

scholarship."

"Yes." His expression became serious. "They also offered more flexibility, so I could train."

"How many hours do you train?"

"As many as I can get. It's been competitive this year and I don't have many years left. I wish I could continue all my life." He was genuinely sad when he said it.

"You must really love fencing. You know, you could always teach."

"I was thinking about that. I'd have to win the Olympics first."

"No. That doesn't matter. That's for you. As long as you're good, that's all that counts for your students."

He stopped and looked at me with softness in his gaze.

"What?"

"That was a really nice thing to say. You're great to talk to."

"Thanks." For a moment, I wondered whether it wasn't guardian love that caused that sudden moment of affection. "So how did you start? Fencing, I mean."

He paused, hesitating. "Well... I got beaten up at school. I guess it was the fate of us computer geeks."

I put my hand on his. It felt warm.

He smiled. "So I started learning martial arts. At some point, I tried the bokken swords and liked it. Then, I thought I'd give fencing a go."

"Do you still do martial arts?"

"Yes, it helps me focus. It's a different way of looking at combat, especially with the bokken."

"Which art did you learn?"

"Ninjutsu."

"I did karate." My dad had insisted on training both me and Harley, in case we ever needed it for self-defense. My dad had two black belts. One in karate and one in aikido. I still practiced in a local club.

I had never told that to a guy on a date before. Well, actually I did once, and he said it was too aggressive for women.

But Seth seemed excited. "Really? I would never have guessed! You're full of surprises."

"I don't think I can claim the level you're at, though," I said humbly.

"How far did you go?"

"Black belt. Dan-two."

"Wow. That is no level to be ashamed of."

A waitress arrived with our food. We thanked her, and I picked up the wooden chopsticks, and broke them in two.

"So you're beautiful *and* dangerous," he said.

"Just working on the charm," I said coyly.

We dug into our food, and I was surprised at how hungry I was.

I'd followed Seth's suggestions as to what to order. He was right. It was the best Chinese I'd ever had. Even just the rice. I kept telling him that, and he smiled at me between bites, when he watched my satisfied face.

The meal was large, but we managed to finish it, and by the time we were waiting for the bill, it was dark outside.

"So, what are your plans after college?" he asked.

"I'm not sure," I confessed. "I've had a couple of ideas. Like becoming an editor."

"You have time to think. Things might change."

If only he knew. By the time I graduate, I'd no longer be just Kim Taylor, a literature major raised by teachers, with only her parents as family. I would also secretly be Kim Ralston, the daughter of one of the most famous men in the world, and I would have relatives with magic similar to mine who would know the truth and could practice with me.

"How about you?" I was eager to know more about him. "I mean, is it just the sport, or maybe also something with computers?"

He clearly liked the question. "Both, but not that much with computers this year, since I've got all that extra training."

We talked a bit about his curiosity around new trends in social media. The bill arrived, and he paid in cash, leaving a nice tip. Then he got up and offered me his hand.

We walked out of the restaurant and down the narrow street, which was beautifully lit by small lamps.

On another night, I would have felt warmth, as I often did, walking down Oxford's small stone paved alleys, with their soft lighting. I felt safe here at any hour.

But somehow, tonight the darkness sent a chill down my spine, like a foreboding sensation. I felt alert, looking behind my shoulder.

And then, right in front of us, I sensed someone use magic.

I stopped. "Can we go the other way?" I said quickly.

"Okay." Seth turned, responding more to the tension in my voice than to my request. "It would probably take a bit longer," he said simply and we walked down in the other direction.

"Hey there!" someone called from behind us.

"Don't turn," I whispered.

"Kim! Stop!"

A streetlamp exploded right in front of us. Traces of magic leaked from it.

There was no choice. I stopped and turned.

From the shadows, a figure approached, whom I recognized as one of the young students from our college. He had been sitting with Zhi Ruo at the party and during the lecture. He walked straight toward us.

"Good evening, folks."

Seth stepped in front of me. "Look, we don't want any trouble." Something in his body had changed. A subtle, but vital difference. It was as if he stood almost just as before, only his muscles had tensed, ready to fight.

"If this is about presidency of the JCR..." I started.

The student laughed. "Presidency. Right."

I saw Seth's hand move in his pocket.

"You know what this is about," the student continued. "You were a bit too obvious this morning, Kim. In Morganstein's lecture. Only someone who knows the truth would try to cover it like that."

Was he testing me? Did his friend, Zhi Ruo, suspect I had magic?

"You're drunk," I said quickly.

"Ah! Still at it, still hiding the big broom secret." He grinned like a crocodile.

Yes. He was testing me.

From behind us, two people entered the street. I turned and immediately noticed, to my relief, they were dressed in police uniforms.

"Help!" I shouted.

"What's going on?" one of the policemen asked, once they arrived.

"My girlfriend and I were threatened by this drunk student."

"Is that so?" the cop asked me.

I nodded.

The student had a furious look in his eyes.

"Come. All three of you," said the cop. "Let's go. Get out of this street."

Reluctantly, the student complied, and the cops took us into the well-lit Cornmarket Street and then back to the college.

At the gates, the policemen stopped to speak with the porter and register our details. I learned that the student's name was Adam.

After that, Seth and I were free to go, but they insisted on escorting Adam back to his dorm.

Seth walked with me to my building's entrance.

"Do you have any idea what he was talking

about?"

I decided to be honest with him. "Yes, but I don't feel like talking about it tonight."

"All right. Tomorrow then? I'll pick you up for breakfast?"

He was eager to see me again, so soon! He had also called me *girlfriend*, before, with the cops. "A second date?" I said.

"Yup."

"And what happens on the second date?"

"Well," he looked down, "I was...hoping for it to happen on the first."

He wanted to kiss me.

I took a step toward him. He looked at me, surprised. *He didn't think I'd do it.*

I stopped with my body inches from his, and slowly moved my hand toward his chest.

There was a mesmerized look on his face.

I closed my eyes.

He bent down toward me, and I was suddenly aware of his aftershave. The smell was intoxicating. I felt his breath...close, warm. His hand moved to lift my chin, and his fingers brushed against my cheek.

Then, his lips touched mine. It was a soft touch at first, growing stronger. Something ancient inside me awoke. I felt my body get excited like never before.

Both my hands moved up and my fingers gripped his muscular shoulders.

His lips arched into a smile and his hands grabbed me with force.

Too much, too soon. I suddenly heard a tiny warning voice in my head, and I broke the embrace.

"What?" he said, surprised.

I had to think fast. "Leave some for tomorrow."

His expression changed to a smile, and there was a hunter's gaze in his eyes. "As you wish. Bright and early then."

I smiled. "Yes, sir."

"Eight?"

"I'll be ready." I quickly pulled out my key and opened the door, turning only to send him a kiss through the air.

He laughed, shaking his head.

Once the door was closed between us, I allowed myself a silent sigh of relief.

That was incredible. I'd never had a kiss like it before. Slowly, I went up the stairs. When I reached my room, I had a message from him.

"Saucy minx xoxo."

I replied with a kiss.

There was one other text waiting for me, from a number I didn't recognize. It had arrived during the date.

The blissful feeling I just had disappeared and my mind went back to the incident on the street.

But then, anyone in the college who had the Freshers Week pamphlet had my number. It could also be from security with news about Veronica. That thought calmed me, and I opened the message.

"Hi, Kim. This is Fiona Morganstein. I must speak with you urgently. Please call me at this number. You might be in danger."

What?

I looked at my phone, staring at her text. The message was from before the incident with Adam.

It was time to find out what was going on.

"Hi, Professor. It's Kim. Sorry about the hour. I just got your text." I hit Send.

The answer came almost instantly. "Are you in a safe place to talk, where nobody could overhear?"

A safe place to talk where nobody could overhear.

Surely any person would assume I'd be either in my room right now, or out doing Freshers Week activities.

"I'm in my dorm," I typed.

There was a pause. "Is that a safe place for you to cast a tent spell?"

What?! My heart missed a beat.

It had struck me during the lecture that she was unusually knowledgeable about my world. But to know about the tent spell?

It was a spell that created a small, magically isolated area which didn't transmit any sounds or any magic, and those in it were invisible to the outside world.

How could she know this? Was she a witch too? Or maybe, she was someone's Charge? It was also possible that she was trying to test me. Get information about me, or about mages.

I put the phone down. Anything I would say now would be confirming to her that I had magic. Tonight's incident was still fresh in my mind. Something awkward was going on.

She didn't wait for an answer and two minutes later, another text arrived. "We could meet somewhere. You're not safe tonight."

I already knew that, but how did *she* know?

What happened on the street shocked me. Being approached about magic openly in front of a mortal was unthinkable.

"I think you might have the wrong idea about me," I texted back.

Then, I quickly changed into comfortable clothes, took my coat, and made my way out of the room and down the stairs. I didn't trust Morganstein but she might still be right, and I knew just the place where I'd be safe.

I rushed across the quad toward Christ Church Cathedral. We'd done a fundraising event there in the winter, and I still remembered how to make my way around to one of the small side entrances.

A large poster stopped me on the way. It was a missing person sheet. In the faint light, I could make out Bradley's face, and Veronica's.

Bradley too? What was going on?

My heart started to beat fast. I walked more quickly, and didn't stop until I reached the door I was going to enter through. A quick glance showed me no one was around. I put my hand on the handle. Then I closed my eyes.

My mom had once said that telekinesis was one of my aunts' favorite types of magic, though I couldn't remember which aunt. Through the handle, I could feel the connection to the lock, the cold metal and the slight rusting. I focused on that and imagined it turning. There was a click. I pushed the knob, got in, and locked the door behind me.

Inside, it was quiet. I took a step, and my movement echoed in the empty cathedral. I stopped and held my breath. There were no other sounds.

The bottom end corner seemed like the best place to cast the tent spell, considering it was away from any benches. I got to it, closed my eyes, and thought of safety and warmth. The magic moved deep inside me and then out of my hands and feet, along the floor tiles that surrounded me, a few feet outward, and then upward, sealing me in an invisible capsule.

I made a tap with my foot. There was no echo this time. "Hello," I tried. Nothing. My voice was trapped inside my magical shelter.

I bent down and magically heated the floor with my hands. Then I took a seat.

The concentration these spells took was not high, so I didn't feel tired. In fact, I was alert, adrenaline pumping in my veins.

A buzz in my pocket informed me that my phone was ringing. I looked at it to see three missed calls from Morganstein. It was her again. I decided to pick up.

"Hi, Kim."

"What's this about, Professor?"

"Please, call me Fiona. I'm assuming you're somewhere safe."

I didn't reply.

"Look, we don't have much time, so I'll get right to it. You don't have to say anything. I realize you are protecting your secret, which is why you've been safe so far. But two witches were kidnapped from your college in the last twenty-four hours."

Did she mean Veronica and Bradley? They were witches?

"I think you might be a target too." She continued, not waiting for me to reply. "I've seen this happening somewhere else. Someone is trying to gain a large amount of power, and they're going to be looking for anyone who's using spells. It already started in Edinburgh. There's a relatively large concentration of witches in Oxford. Some practice together, though clearly you've been wise to conceal your gift. On the other hand, you don't have other witches to help you."

"I'm sorry," I had to think quick of what a normal person would do in this situation, "I think you might have a certain belief system where—"

"Kim, I know you're a witch. And I wanted to warn you so you are safe. I know you're not going to say anything, so I'm just going to say goodnight. We can speak again when you're ready. Come to me if you need anything. I'm staying at the Old Bank Hotel."

I sighed. "Goodnight, Professor." I hung up.

I had done the right thing, but it felt bad. She

genuinely wanted to help me. That much was clear. The entire conversation had been one-sided. She was definitely not looking for information. She already had some knowledge of what I was, and I was left wondering how.

At least I was in a safe place. I looked around at the cold cathedral. Nobody would ever guess I'd be here. Inside the tent spell, I could conjure a mattress with warm blankets and pajamas. It would be as good a way to spend the night as any. I closed my eyes and concentrated. *Give me a comfortable bed and pajamas; give me a comfortable bed and pajamas.*

The hard floor disappeared from below me, seconds after the images were clear in my mind, and I sat on a fluffy and comfortable bed.

After changing and getting under the heavy duvet, I lay awake, thinking about Morganstein.

Why did she warn me? More importantly, what was she —a witch or a Charge?

A Charge would have her knowledge, but wouldn't take the risk unless the guardian was with them. So, if she were a Charge, who was her guardian? I took out my phone and looked her up online. She wasn't married. Most Charges were. Nor did she seem to have anyone consistently with her in photos, and there were so many of them. It was possible that she was keeping her personal life private.

If she were a mage, maybe she just hadn't met her Charge yet? It was possible. Some of us met our Charges later in life. Somehow, I intuitively felt that that wasn't it. But then, if she wasn't a mage or a Charge, what was she?

As I drifted into sleep that night, Fiona Morganstein came into my dreams. Her face was clear, but it was different than the one of the celebrated professor in a black suit. Her hair was loose and fell down to her chest in long black curls, resting on a white chiffon-like dress, her bright eyes shining. A delicate silver tiara decorated her hair. She stood in the middle of a forest in the dark, bathed in the light of the moon, her skin glowing.

Chapter 9

Western Scotland, AD 500

A warm morning sun shined over the valley and Kim sat outside the cave, looking at the view. In the distance, something glittered through the trees. The roofs of Haven.

Seth had woken her once in the night. She was in the middle of a strange nightmare where her father, furious that she had left with Seth and Niall, was with her in a small room. She was trying to have dinner, and he was yelling at her and shaking the table.

She woke up to the touch of Seth's hand on her shoulder. He said they must get up quickly and step outside the cave, because the ground was shaking. He thought there was an earthquake. She felt it, but when she sat and looked at him and the images of the dream disappeared, the ground became still.

Breakfast was a dull stew with some herbs and hard bread. During the meal, she missed home, but when she sat there, looking at the spectacular view, there was nowhere else she wanted to be.

Seth had asked about sensing the dragon.

"I... He seemed smaller when I felt him, but it was definitely him." It was the best she could describe it. She didn't really *see* the beast, but she was certain that she knew where and what it was.

He seemed confused. "For one, dragons transform when they enter battle, but sensing is a magical ability. And even then, mages don't sense dragons."

"I'm no mage. At least not to my knowledge."

It was possible, of course. If her mother was indeed a fairy, she would be a witch, but then she'd never had any powers, so it was unlikely.

At court, they said her father was only married once, for a short time, and the woman died giving birth. Fairies were immortal, and could only be killed using the forbidden spell of death.

She would have loved to speak with her father about all this, but that would have been unthinkable. There were no portraits of his wife anywhere, no mention of her name. It was as if she'd never existed. The obvious conclusion was that his pain was too great and that it was best not to raise the subject.

She'd tried to dig out some information with a few of his trusted ministers, but they knew even less than the fairies did.

Her new sensing ability came again when she and Seth were clearing the remains of the meal. This time it was a person. Someone approached them, entering the cave from the other side.

"We're not alone." She got up and tried to focus.

Seth stopped and listened. "I can't hear anything."

"There's a person, coming into the cave from the other side. Tall. Moving slowly."

For a moment, he considered what to do. Then he got up quickly. "We should move away from the entrance. That way, we'd see him before he sees us." He believed her. A prudent decision after the previous night. But still, somewhat unexpected.

He led them a few feet down from the cave entrance. Then, he bent towards his boot and took out the knife.

"You'll need to look scared," he said, placing the sharp metal at her throat and standing behind her.

"If you say so."

He chuckled, but spoke seriously. "Focus, Kim. Appear threatened." He placed his other hand around her stomach.

Again, she surprised herself. Instinctively, she

made a movement with both her hands, twisting and getting freed from his grip. It felt like second nature to do that maneuver—one that she couldn't recall ever doing or even seeing someone do before.

"Sorry."

Seth was quick. In a moment, he had her back under restraint. "Just stay with me, Kim," he whispered.

His touch and the sound of his voice had something in them that was difficult to recognize at first. It was warm, but it also felt rough at the same time. Heat was a better word. Like that edge that fire had if you stood too close.

She tried not to move.

As they waited for the stranger to arrive, memories of the previous day came to mind. At first, she'd hated him, then there was that dance, then she found him trustworthy, then funny, and now it was almost as if he was...what was the word for it?

The word came to her thoughts for a moment. *Seductive*. She washed it away with all her strength of mind. There was no way she was going to think *that* of him.

A figure appeared at the entrance to the cave, walking slowly.

"You can let her go, Seth."

He had a deep, low voice and at first glance, one could tell that his combination of features was a rare one. He seemed middle-aged, but the power of youth surrounded him. His garments, though made for travel, had high quality and design and spoke of wealth. On his shoulder, he had the symbol of Fergus Mór's court sewn in, but not with a sword in it.

He was a mage, Kim thought, or perhaps it was more accurate to say that he seemed to almost reek of magic.

"Seraphim!" Seth breathed in relief and let her go.

She knew him only by rumor. King Fergus Mór's first mage. Five hundred years old. A man who was born before Avalon's Curse.

"What are you doing, kidnapping Áedán's daughter?" His voice resonated, a broad smile on his face. It was clear that he knew Seth well, and that the two liked each other.

"So the word's out? How did you find us?"

"I didn't. I'm just out for a morning walk. Good day to you, Your Highness," he said, turning to her.

She paused. Something was not completely right about his tone, or how he observed her.

His piercing brown eyes met hers and made her feel uneasy. She managed a small curtsy and tried to look away, but she couldn't. He had her locked in his gaze, caging her as his pupils seemed to attempt to look into the depths of her soul.

Close your eyes, she told herself, and her eyelids shut.

"There's been a conspiracy," said Seth.

"A conspiracy?"

Now that her eyes were closed, her senses were more tuned on the sound of Seraphim's voice. It was not natural. It was too strong. It penetrated through her and made her want to listen too intently. It was almost hypnotic, but not in a pleasant way.

"The marriage contract had a hidden message in it. A threat on the king's life during the equinox."

She opened her eyes and looked at Seth. *What!? The contract was a plot against the king?*

"I've seen it myself. Niall's got it," he continued.

"Where is he?"

"I don't know. We split so he could ride towards Fergus Mór. He might already be there."

"Is prince Domangart in danger too?"

Once again, that shadow passed over Seth's face. The very mention of the prince's name was hard for him.

"He's the one who wrote the message," Seth replied coldly.

"What? Are you certain? To whom?"

There was a pause. Seth looked at her, and the hint in his eyes was unmistakable. She knew what he was about to say, and her head shook from side to side. *No. No. No. It couldn't be!*

A black veil spread in her mind, covering everything she was seeing, as she awaited Seth's inevitable words.

"King Áedán."

There was movement behind her, and she felt Seth's strong hands supporting her. "Are you all right?"

She had fallen backward. Her breath was quick now, her chest rising and descending rapidly.

"I'm fine," she said. But she wasn't. *She was the daughter of a traitor.* Her own father had conspired against the king! "It's a... shock."

"It must be." Seraphim walked toward them now, his voice condescending. "Poor thing."

She took a step back.

He kept approaching. "My dear, none of this is your fault," he said in a tone of voice that might have been meant to be soothing, but it was irritating instead. Patronizing.

"I know that." She didn't need his compassion. And this wasn't about her. *How could her father do such a thing?*

Seraphim stopped, smiled again, and observed her. Once more, he had that penetrating gaze.

It made her angry now. "I don't believe we've been properly introduced," she said, facing him directly.

He broke the intense eye contact. "I assume you haven't met many mages."

"She doesn't get out much," Seth said, and Seraphim laughed.

Despite being used to Seth's sense of humor, she didn't respond this time. Seraphim's lack of boundaries was putting her guard up. Though head mage, in essence mages served mortals. His conduct suggested that he outranked her in some way. It was unusual for a mage to do that, especially with royalty. It would be considered arrogant, at the least.

"I've met fairies and spent a long time with them," she said.

"Fairies are not mages," he said coldly.

"Of course not." She looked him straight in the eye. The emotional turmoil she felt from learning about the betrayal unleashed itself on this coldhearted man. "They are stronger and wiser and also immortal. They choose when to help humans. They are not bound to us and don't *serve* us like mages do."

Seth looked at her in shock.

Seraphim laughed and looked away from her. "Stop at Haven," he said to Seth.

"That's the plan," said Seth. "We were going to send a message to Fergus Mór. Through Ealga."

Ealga? The king's sister?

"I'll send a bird myself," said Seraphim.

"The prince would be monitoring that."

"In that case, I mustn't waste time. I should get to the king. He will need my protection." And then, uncharacteristic of his previous conduct, he left them without another word.

"Are you out of your mind?" Seth's voice was somber. "I've never heard anyone talk to Seraphim the way you just did."

"Perhaps they should, if this is how he behaves to them."

"Seraphim has his ways. He was being kind."

"You mean condescending."

"He's just accustomed to his high rank and he speaks in his own style, which is no surprise. He is head mage! Everyone respects him."

"Sometimes, even people of nobility need to amend their ways. And respect must always be earned."

He looked away, angry.

But he still took her hand in his to help her on the

path when they continued on their journey toward Haven.

✧

They reached Haven shortly after sundown.

Seth could hardly believe that they made it there before nightfall. It was good speed, even for an experienced traveler.

It was hard for her physically, and she didn't want to talk much. But she didn't ask for many stops. As if she didn't want to be treated as weak. That kind of pride was surprising, and made him recall how different she was from other court ladies. And she bore with silence what she'd just found out about her father.

At the gates, they stopped by the sign that welcomed them to the small village.

Dear Passenger,

You are entering a territory of peace. Be prepared to surrender any weapon you carry with you, or choose another path.

Two guards were ready to receive his sword and knives. He'd met them both before and they immediately recognized him.

They seemed eager to see him again and provided some news of the town, along with information on where to find Princess Ealga. She would be dining at the inn that night. To the best of their knowledge, the place had vacancies for the night.

He looked at Kim. She needed rest from the long journey, though her eyes looked about keenly as they walked through the village, observing the incredible beauty of Haven and reminding him of the first time he'd seen it.

"Haven the pearl" was what travelers called it and it lived up to the saying. It was small. Built by the fairies before the Curse, it looked like a place from a dream. It had ornamented arches and pillars carved of marble. Delicate fountains with small statues decorated the public squares. It felt like it was part of the woods, and the woods were part of it.

It was no wonder that Ealga chose to live there.

He had met her on previous visits. She was a unique, unassuming person and preferred a simple life, away from court. She'd been married young, to her brother's best friend, and both shared a love for travel. When it was time to settle down and start their own family, they chose Haven. She once told him that no palace or court could ever compare to its pure beauty and to its peace. Fergus Mór's castle often felt too ornate to her.

After a short walk, they reached the inn, which was right at the center of the village. He got them a room upstairs, where Kim could rest. He asked whether she was hungry, and ordered her some baked goods from the kitchen.

Once in the room, she immediately lay on one of the two beds.

"If anything happens, pull this cord. It will ring the innkeeper. He knows me," he told her.

She nodded and closed her eyes.

He put the plate of food beside her and closed the curtains, again surprised by her serenity and how easily she was willing to just go to sleep.

Could it be that he had won her trust? Or was she just feeling physically confident in general? He recalled the combat maneuvers that she had demonstrated. Twice now. No princess he'd met before was taught to fight. Not one.

He locked the door and went back down to look for Ealga. The innkeeper said she was dining with a friend in a private room.

"Tell her Seth of Fergus Mór's court is here and needs to speak with her urgently."

That had an immediate effect. A few minutes later,

they were speaking alone, with Ealga asking lots of questions. She was concerned and said something about how she'd always thought the king needed to keep a closer eye on her nephew to keep him from trouble. It didn't mean she believed it. Nothing in her words hinted as much, but she did have a bird sent straight to her brother to warn him.

It was what he had hoped for. Ealga's route of communication to the king was a direct one. Even his son wouldn't be able to stop that.

After delivering the message, he went back upstairs. He turned the key in the hole quietly, so as to not wake Kim, but the door was already unlocked. Her bed was empty.

A quick scan revealed nothing. The plate stood with the food uneaten.

Had she gone down to look for him? Perhaps she needed something. But it was now late and very dark.

Did she try to escape?

He went back downstairs, where the place was full and the innkeeper was busy with orders of food.

"Did you find Ealga?"

"Yes. I need your help with something else. I'm looking for the woman I am traveling with."

"She went out about an hour ago."

"Alone?"

The innkeeper raised an eyebrow. He ignored him.

Just then, the door opened and she walked in.

"Kim!"

She seemed different. Her eyes were bloodshot and her hair was wild. She looked around her, but she didn't appear to see much.

Was she sleepwalking? She started to move toward him and for a moment looked straight at him, but then her glance went through him. She mumbled something.

He rushed to her. "It's okay, it's just a dream," he said in the softest, most soothing voice he could use.

"Igraine," she mumbled.

"Grain?" he asked. "We've got pie upstairs."

She didn't answer. She looked at him, seeing him again, but then kept walking toward the stairs. He held her hand as she slowly made her way back to the room.

She opened the door herself, and he made sure to lock it once more. "Igraine," she said again.

"It's all right. You're going back to bed now."

She climbed between the sheets on her own, ignoring him. "Must tell Seraphim," she mumbled and then, "Igraine" again.

Then, she closed her eyes and was silent until morning.

Chapter 10

Oxford, Present Day

I woke up to the sound of footsteps. It took me a few moments to realize where I was.

The church was softly lit. I turned, moaning, and had a look at my phone. Six thirty in the morning.

Crap, the morning prayer.

I quickly sat up. The footsteps were at the far end of the cathedral. By the uniform, I could tell that I was looking at a security guard. He was walking down the aisle toward me, but then turned and continued to the Peace Chapel, and finished his round, going out of the main exit.

I got up before anyone else could come in, reversed all the spells, and got out of the cathedral.

"Where do you think you're going?"

In front of me was another guard. He observed me with a suspicious look on his face.

"We saw someone got in last night. There's a camera right behind me."

Damn. I hadn't thought about it. Though upset, he seemed a sympathetic man. I remembered something I'd once seen Scarlett do and wondered whether I could fake anxiety and play damsel in distress the way she had.

"I left my phone. Yesterday," I said, presenting my phone. "I came back for it. The door was open. But then... I got locked in!" I spoke in a hurried voice and tried to seem anxious. "I was so scared. I tried everything. I screamed, but nobody heard me."

"So, you were in there all night?"

I nodded, trying to add some panic to my facial expression. "I was all alone. And there were weird noises. I didn't know what to do."

He smiled. His distrust seemed gone now. "It's a large place. The noises are just part of the acoustics."

I could see my emotional show had distracted him from the cold facts about my being there, or how I had managed to get out.

I nodded, looking down. "I guess that makes sense."

"Why didn't you call anyone? You had your phone."

"My battery was dead."

He put a hand on my shoulder. "All right, you're safe now and that's what matters. I'll talk with maintenance about the door. Come, I'll walk you back to your dorm."

I followed him, turning once, when he wasn't looking, to use telekinesis to make a crack in the door just above the lock.

We got to the quad and once again, I saw the posters of Veronica and Bradley. My heart missed a beat, as Morganstein's words of warning echoed in my head. I hardly heard the guard when he gave me his parting scold.

"Next time, come to us. Don't do things like this on your own."

I gave him my word, and rushed to my dorm. There would have still been plenty of time to get ready for the date with Seth, if "ready" had just meant getting showered and dressed. But I had to think of how to bring up the conversation about magic. Now that witches were in danger, I knew I couldn't wait. I had hoped I'd have more time.

Unfortunately, this was often how it worked. Many times, witches met their Charges when the Charges needed protection.

Ironically, I myself was a risk for Seth. Charges could be used as bait to expose us, forcing us to use our magic to protect them.

I tried to recall what I'd heard about how others had revealed the truth to their Charges. I only knew my own family. My dad had seen my mom and my grandpa use magic, and then talked with both of them. Harley invited Amber over when my parents were at the cinema, cooked her dinner and told her the secret. When they returned, she was still there, beaming, and curious, asking a thousand questions. In both cases, the response was very positive, and that was how it was supposed to be. But then, things in *my* life didn't always work the way they were supposed to.

After showering and dressing up, I still had no idea what I was going to say to Seth. I decided to just see how our breakfast date would go, and then think of how I'd want to bring it up. I would give him the minimum information and let him ask the questions. There was no point bombarding him with it all at once.

Like yesterday, I got stuck in front of my closet, debating what to wear. I was sorry I hadn't thought of it when I could conjure clothes back in the cathedral, under the safety of the tent spell.

In the end, I decided on a thin green sweater with a short jeans skirt and dark tights. I had to suppress my laughter when Seth arrived, and we were matched. He was also wearing a green shirt and jeans.

Once again, I found myself stopping to admire his muscular physique. It kept surprising me how physically attractive he was, though I did know that the guy was very athletic.

"Good morning," I said, holding the door.

"Is it?"

Then, suddenly, he caught my hand and pinned me to the wall.

I giggled.

The door closed behind him and we were alone in the dark corridor. His fingers knit into mine, and his body pushed against me. He moved one of my feet gently to the side and put his there, leaning.

"Seth!"

"Yes?" He whispered in my ear, his voice suddenly husky, seductive.

I couldn't find my words. I breathed hard.

"You're panting. I like it." His other hand moved to my face and caressed my hair. He leaned and then stopped, with his lips almost touching mine.

I gasped, excited.

"I think we've got some unfinished business here, Kim."

"We do?" I managed.

"Mmhmm," he affirmed, and the look in his eyes made me feel sparkles all over. His hand moved down to my chin, and he opened my mouth softly.

I closed my eyes.

"No running away this time," he whispered, and I sighed.

His lips touched mine softly, and then hard, demanding. I let out a moan, and immediately held my breath. This wasn't exactly a private place.

Seth made a sound of satisfaction, his lips still on mine. Unfortunately, his reaction made me lose my guard even more. I moved my free hand to his back and pulled him toward me, the fingers of my other hand grabbing his tightly. His mouth opened and I felt his tongue. I tried to respond, but he pulled it back. Teasing.

Where did he learn to kiss like *that*?

Seth's lips made one last attack on mine and then he let me go. I was panting and dizzy. *Wow*!

He smiled, catching his breath. "Kim, Kim. You make me think of...anything but breakfast."

"Hey, hey, this was your doing!" I said, between short breaths.

"I could tell you liked it."

"I never said I didn't," I said, coyly.

He paused, a look of delight on his face.

I smiled.

"How about some food?" He took my hand. "I know a place with the best breakfast salads and I booked us a table. Are you hungry?"

"Starving!"

"Good." He opened the door, letting the sunshine in. I could hear his pulse racing.

We started our walk to Canterbury Gate, heading east, smiling like two guilty teens.

Right next to the gates, we paused. There was another poster of the missing students there.

Seth looked at it with worried eyes. "I hope they find them soon."

I knew he was concerned about Bradley.

The porter must have heard him, because he stopped us when we reached him and tried to exit. "You're from the Junior Common Room, right?"

"Yes," I answered.

He took out a piece of paper that was lying on his desk and showed it to me. It was a colorful printout of an email. On it was a photo of another young man. The face seemed familiar. One of the juniors or sophomores.

"He's been reported missing since last night," said the guard.

Another one?

"He was last seen at a party near the Covered Market."

Next to the image was the address where the party was, with a map and an arrow. It was right next to where we'd had dinner. I showed it to Seth.

"Have you talked to the police?" I asked the porter. My voice was uneven when I spoke.

"My supervisor did."

"Did they tell him that there was another incident on that street last night?"

"I don't know. I wasn't on the call."

"We were approached there by a drunken student," said Seth. "The police came to our assistance."

"Oh. Did you give them a description?"

"They saw him when they came."

"Thank you for letting us know." The porter wrote it down. "I'll tell my supervisor."

We walked out of the gate, silently.

The back alley behind the college gave us some privacy. Seth's warm hand was a comfort after the talk with the porter. But my mind was with the missing students. Missing witches.

"Don't worry," Seth said after we'd walked silently for a while. "They'll find them."

I hoped so. It was concerning that they were gone

this long.

We turned the corner on High Street and then headed east toward Cowley. The noisy traffic and people were a welcome distraction. Slowly, I felt my mind tuning into the reality around me and to Seth's presence. I looked at him, and he smiled.

In the end, we arrived at a small, quiet cafe with white tables and the smell of freshly chopped fruit and bread rolls.

Seth held the door for me, and we got a table right in the middle. He helped me out of my coat and we took a seat.

"It's really nice," I said. "I've never been here before."

"Great. Then I get to surprise you."

That was a given.

"Is it a new place?"

"Relatively new. I was here a couple of months ago with a large group on the opening day. We tried everything on the menu."

"Then you'd know what's best."

He paused, and hesitated. "I can...order for you, if you like?"

Nobody had ever done that for me. Or, probably for any woman in the past fifty years. The thought made me almost giggle. It felt romantic in an old-fashioned, slightly backward way.

"Sure. Let's give it a go."

"Great, I'll be right back." He gave me a quick kiss.

I watched him approach the counter and speak with the staff. The girl behind it blushed and spoke in a soft tone. Seth didn't respond. He just placed the order and came right back to me.

"So, how was your night after I left?" he asked when he was back in his chair.

"I went to sleep a short while afterward."

"So did I." He looked down. "I dreamed about you."

"Really?" I thought I'd sensed a bit of positive tension in his voice.

"What?"

"Nothing," I said, saucily.

"It...wasn't like that."

"Of course not! Not judging by that kiss in the hallway."

He shook his head. "If *that's* what's on your mind, I'm more than happy to do a takeaway."

"Nice." I laughed, surprised at how much I was enjoying this game. Perhaps because it was such a contrast to my first impression of him. "You are very sophisticated, sir."

"Doing my best."

The food arrived shortly after: a tapas of salads with two bowls of sauces, mini-baguettes with spreads, and two glasses of raspberry smoothie.

"Wow, Seth. This looks amazing. Thank you."

"You're welcome."

"I wouldn't know what to try first."

"Anything. It's all good."

"Certainly. But you're the expert."

"Right. In that case, go for the white sauce with one of the salads."

"Okay." I put a small portion on my plate. I took a bite, shocked by the flavor. "What *is* this?"

"They put magic in the sauce."

"That's not possible."

"I'm sure it's possible." He smiled.

It was time to try something. Test his reaction. "You can't put magic in a sauce. You can create the sauce magically, but not put magic in it." I knew he'd think I'm just kidding.

"So, you're a good cook, too." He laughed.

Not quite the response I'd hoped for—he'd shown no curiosity at my comment.

"How do you know about these places?" I asked, after trying a few more things on the table. "First the Chinese from last night, then this."

"My lab partner writes a freelance food blog. She

keeps getting invitations and brings a group with her."

I felt a pang of jealousy and wondered what she looked like. "Sounds lovely." I composed myself. "I'd happily join next time."

"I've already told her about you."

My chest warmed. "Good things, I hope."

He didn't answer. He looked me in the eye, then down at my lips, then at my eyes again. His hand reached across the table to mine, and I closed my eyes, waiting to feel his lips again. It was a soft, calm kiss this time and surprisingly, it had an even stronger effect.

I heard myself moan and pulled back. "Sorry."

He caressed my cheeks. "Don't ever apologize for that."

"It's...embarrassing."

"To whom?" He looked into my eyes. "It's just us. I'm sure nobody heard it."

I wasn't as certain.

We ended up staying at the cafe for a little over an hour. Seth seemed eager to learn more about my life before Oxford. I told him about Harley and my parents. The usual stuff.

When he asked about the rest of the family, I said I didn't really know them because they lived abroad. It was a partial truth. My mom said that some of the family members liked to move a lot. For all I knew, they could be in England too.

I added the anecdote that I used to like school as a kid and was curious to learn different things, but then my dad sent me to science camp, where I met the really intelligent kids, and got discouraged.

"Yet, you made it to Oxford."

"True." I never saw it that way. "I just liked to read books. So, how about you?"

He had an older sister, Lisa, who was a designer in New York, married with two kids. She was an inspiration during tough times. One of the biggest hardships came just when he started getting interested in fencing.

His dad was an engineer and the firm he was working at went bust. His mom was the main caregiver while his dad had built his career and her job progression had, as a result, been slow. Cash was tight.

"We couldn't afford the gear, or the lessons. We could hardly afford basic necessities."

"I'm so sorry. How old were you?"

"Thirteen."

"Thirteen? That must have been extremely tough." I always felt empathetic when anyone had to struggle that hard. Harley and I never had money issues. Our parents invested well, as they had the advantage of coming from the future and knowing what was going to happen in the markets. Of course, they'd been careful not to overdo it and draw attention, so though we weren't rich, we never wanted for anything either.

"It was. Especially at school. Social life was suddenly limited."

Was that why he was so critical of me at first? "What did you do?"

He smiled. "Actually, my sister proved a good role model to follow. She had to defer on her last year of college in New York. She was devastated at first, but then she decided nothing would stop her from getting what she wanted. Lisa's like that," he said, proudly, admiringly. "She got herself an internship with a small company, and they really liked her. They ended up raising the money for her tuition and board, and she had a guaranteed job when she graduated."

"That's so inspiring." I looked at him, impressed. "So, how did you...I mean, clearly you did get to learn fencing."

"I worked all summer, building websites for small companies, and saved up."

"What? How? You were thirteen."

He chuckled. "Nobody checked. I communicated with everyone through emails."

"You're amazing, Seth. I mean...you did it, all on your own, despite the obstacles."

He paused, and I was met with his grey gaze. "I can't believe I'm telling you all this!"

I reached out for his hand, and he took mine in his, feeling that undeniable electricity between us.

"I...didn't do it all on my own. I had a good mentor, who offered to teach me for free and refused the money even when we got out of the financial situation. Even when my dad did very well."

"Do you still work with him?"

"Of course. I also save tickets for his kids for every competition."

"That's great of you."

After that bonding talk, we got more focused on the food. We ate silently, our hands brushing as we moved the plates around, each time smiling and looking into each other's eyes.

I ate slowly, in no hurry to finish. I knew that the closer we got to the end of the meal, the closer I was getting to raising the inevitable subject of magic.

His opening up to me and telling me about his hard times was a constant reminder of the things I had to say to him.

When we were done and he'd ordered the bill, I could delay no longer.

"Seth, there's something I need to tell you."

"What?" He pulled slightly back and there was a look of worry on his face.

"It's...a very personal thing about me. Something that I couldn't say here."

"Is it...bad?" It was as if a dark shadow was suddenly cast between us after the lightness of our breakfast.

"No. Not at all. It's just...a bit complicated."

He gave me that look of *that sounds worse.* "Okay. You can tell me anything, Kim."

I doubted *that.* "We'd have to go somewhere where I can speak openly."

"We could walk back to the dorms."

I shook my head. "I'd need somewhere a lot more discreet. I'm sorry. I know that sounds weird."

"It's all right," he said, though I knew there was no way he understood. "Where would you feel comfortable?"

"I don't know. I can't think of any place private enough in town."

Before the missing witches, I would have gone for the canal or Christ Church Meadow, but now nowhere in the city felt safe.

Seth looked at me, puzzled. Then, he said, resolute, "It's fine. I could drive us somewhere else. I'm parked right next to the college."

I considered that. "Yes, I think that would work."

The waitress arrived with the bill and a paper package. "Your dessert to go."

"Thank you," I said to Seth. I wanted to compliment him on still being the romantic, but it appeared out of place. He seemed very tense.

The waitress asked for his autograph on a picture in a sports magazine. He was polite and did it. Then, we got up and left.

We walked in silence again, holding hands, but distant. From time to time, he'd glance at me, trying to put on an encouraging smile, but that was it.

We had walked so fast that we reached his car in half the time I'd expected.

"Anywhere, as long as it's remote?" he asked once we were inside.

"Yes."

"Okay." He put the key in the ignition.

We were off, and soon the busy streets with old gothic buildings gave way to open roads and farmlands. After that, it was fields and small country roads.

His silence bothered me. This wasn't how I'd wanted it to be. I had hoped for a happy conversation.

I tried telling him that this was not anything to be alarmed by, but he just smiled and said nothing. I wished I had planned it, and not just asked to speak with him alone.

Or perhaps he was right to feel this tense? After all, I was about to tell him that I was not human.

We stopped near one of the fields, and Seth parked. "We could talk here, or get out. There is a small stream five minutes from us. We could sit there. I've got a blanket."

"That sounds nice." I tried to be encouraging.

We stepped out of the car, and Seth walked to the back to open the boot. When he wasn't looking, I magically changed my shoes, conjuring something I could walk in, and hiding the high heels I was wearing behind the wheel.

He returned with the blanket, ready to lead the way. He noticed the shoes. "Did you bring those with you?"

I nodded. He'd given me an easy out.

A few minutes later, I sat in front of him, under a tree by the stream, a short distance from the path. In different circumstances, this would have been a very romantic place for us.

I had cast a tent spell a few meters in each direction, enclosing Seth's blanket, and ensuring nobody could hear what I was about to say.

"All right, I'm listening." He smiled reassuringly, but his voice was very tense.

"I'm not sure where to start." I felt like I was literally going to swallow my tongue. I'd never thought of this moment. Everyone said it didn't matter, but clearly it did.

Seth put his hand on mine. "Kim, just...tell me. Whatever it is."

"Okay." I took a deep breath. "Remember yesterday's lecture?"

"What of it?"

Yes, what of it? Where was I going to go with that? "Uh...maybe this isn't the right way to explain."

I looked at the water flowing in the stream next to us. I could show him a spell. *No.* That would be too much. Perhaps a direct route was better.

I looked straight into his eyes. "Seth...do you believe in magic?"

That confused him. "I...don't think so. What's that got to do with anything?" Then, there was suddenly a look of understanding and almost relief on his face.

Did he get it? Was it just that simple?

"Wait, is this about faith? Do you belong to the Wicca religion?"

Not that simple.

"No. I am not a Wicca. I'm..." *Here I go.* "I am a witch. As in, I can do real magic."

He tilted his head, for a moment measuring whether I were being funny. Or maybe he thought I might be a little bit insane.

"I can move things with my mind. I can conjure things. Change the weather..."

"Change the weather?"

"In a relatively small area. Say, the valley we're in right now and..."

He shook his head, confused. And then, he looked at me. "Show me."

Definitely not the response I'd expected. He just didn't believe it! He observed me, waiting to see what I'd do.

"Okay." I looked at the clear sky and imagined that through that blue I could see heavy clouds, as though they were behind it. I closed my eyes. *Give me rain. Give me rain.* The image of the drops was clear to me, and when I opened my eyes, clouds started rapidly forming above us. I paused and gave myself a moment's rest from the concentration. I got into the habit of always pausing after a weather spell; they required so much focus.

In less than a minute, there was wind and rustling in the trees and drops of water started to come down from the sky.

"Are you...?" His voice was hesitant.

"Making it rain. Yes."

"How?" he said, but it was rhetorical. I'd just told him how.

The rain got heavier, wetting the path and the ground, creating a strong noise on the water.

Seth looked around, knitting his eyebrows in bewilderment.

"How come we're not getting wet?" he suddenly asked. The ground surrounding the blanket was completely dry, marking the edges of the tent spell.

"I'd cast a protection sphere around us first. Nobody can hear or see us and we're going to stay dry. I can make it warm, too, if you want."

"Or, just stop the rain." Then he smiled. "Sorry. That came out wrong."

"It's okay. It's not a bad idea."

He was still finding it hard to grasp that I was doing this, but at least he was responding. I needed to show him I had control over it. I looked into the sky and this time imagined the sun shining from behind the clouds. *Give me a blue sky. Give me a blue sky.* The image was strong in my mind, and a few minutes later, the rain stopped.

"Incredible," he mumbled once the sky had cleared. "What else can you do?"

I shrugged. "Different things. Like, conjuring. For example, the shoes just now. Or the protection spell."

"Or love spells?"

I did not see that one coming. "Of course not," I reassured him. "You can't control minds."

"So...this...us...it's real?" he asked and then, he suddenly looked down. "I mean..."

He had just said he loved me! Not directly, but he did.

"Yes," I said quickly. *And I love you too*, I wanted to add, but then, he hadn't quite said it. "Actually, that's why I have magic. My powers exist so that I can meet the right person in life, fall for them, and protect them."

"Fall for them." He breathed hard, and then finally smiled. "Kim, you have no idea what was going on in my head on the drive here. Every moment we spend together has been the best I've ever had with anyone, and then you tell me there's something. And I started wondering if you've got another guy, or some illness, or anything else stopping you from being with me."

"No." I shook my head. "Not at all. I'm so sorry. I really didn't know how to tell you."

"It's okay. I don't think there was an easy way."

"I could have prepared this better."

"What? To tell me that you had magical powers? I don't think you could have."

He was coming around. The promise of the guardianship was finally on my side.

I sighed in relief. "Thank you. For saying this."

"You're welcome." He took my hand in his, now smiling. "You really are special, aren't you?"

Chapter 11

Western Scotland, AD 500

Kim sat, leaning on the hard stone wall of the inn room, covered by the warm blanket. Images from the previous evening occupied her mind.

A part of her refused to believe that last night was real. That the things she saw and experienced had happened. That any of it was even possible.

But it was. Magic never lied.

She looked at Seth. His chest rose and fell in his sleep. She closed her eyes and he was still there, as clear as before. As was the couple in the room next to theirs and the innkeeper downstairs who was up early, baking the bread.

She recalled how she woke up from a strange feeling the evening before, when Seth had left her.

She sensed someone, or something. It was trying to hide its presence.

At first, she thought that it was a dream. She turned in bed, but the feeling came again. Someone wanted to not be seen, someone who wasn't human. Her senses focused slowly, as she realized that she was awake.

It was a creature, walking around the village square, at an uneven pace. There was an air of happiness to the way it walked and, yes, it was definitely not human. For starters, it was green and it glowed. It also had a long tail and lizard eyes.

Something about it drew her.

She sat up. A quick glance told her that Seth's bed was empty, which meant that it must still be early in the evening and he'd be speaking with Ealga. She got up, and put her shoes and her coat on.

When she tried the door, it wouldn't open, but then when she tried again, it suddenly did.

The hallway outside led to a long corridor with large open windows. She walked to them. Through them, she could clearly see the village square.

There weren't many people there. A few were dining at tables outside the inn, and she heard a lot of noise coming from the inn downstairs. A family of three were just entering. A couple walked slowly outside, admiring the buildings of Haven, holding hands. And there, right behind them, next to the fountain, she saw it.

Nobody else seemed to notice. Nobody, except an old man sitting on a bench, who glanced at it and then away, pretending to read a book.

The creature was walking, among the people, invisible. It seemed to enjoy not being seen. It was a dragon, like the ones she'd seen in drawings when she lived with the fairies. It walked on four heavy feet, had a round head, and large wings covered its belly on both sides.

It was about three feet high and very different from the brown one she'd seen the night before, towering over the trees, standing on its hind legs with a sharp head, and nostrils ready to blow out fire. That must have been full form, as the knights called it, she realized. Dragons used that in battle.

She was fascinated by what was right in front of her.

The dragon smiled. It walked merrily, as if a tune played in its head. She watched it, marveling at how no one seemed to notice. It stopped and looked at the people who dined at the inn—or, rather, at their plates.

Then, it saw her.

It was too late to hide. It smiled at her and made a gesture with its head. For a moment she hesitated, but then realized it was harmless to respond, so she smiled and waved back. The old man on the bench put his book down and stared at her curiously.

The dragon made a motion for her to come down, and strangely enough, her instincts told her that it was safe. She felt a tingling in her fingers, a sense of awakening, of strength. Like that feeling that was gradually growing in her, changing her awareness. She was not afraid because she felt that she herself was powerful.

She turned from the window and headed down the stairs and out of the inn toward the dragon.

When she reached it, it was walking toward a small street, where the people in the village center couldn't see it. It stopped after the first building and waited for her to walk to where she'd be hidden from sight too. She realized it was so that other people wouldn't see her speaking to thin air.

Still smiling, it spoke in a masculine voice.

"Pardon me for being direct, lass, but you wouldn't mind getting me some warm soup and a piece of the roast?"

His style made her giggle.

"What?" He chuckled.

"Who are you?"

"I'm Leonard. I come from the dragon clan of the

Great Loch."

She'd heard of the dragons of the Great Loch. They had been created long ago and most of them remained there as a tribe. "I'm Kim. I'm...traveling."

"That makes the two of us."

The reality of her situation suddenly dawned on her. "I'm sorry. I...just realized I'm talking to a complete stranger in the middle of the night." *And for some reason this feels safe.*

"I can tell you my life's story, if it makes you feel any better, but then you'd want dinner too. And breakfast."

She laughed.

"Of course, *you* can always conjure food if you're hungry. Makes me envious."

"Conjure food?" The very thought of it was ridiculous. "You must think I'm some sort of mage. I'm afraid you're mistaken."

"'Course you are a mage, lass. And not only are you a mage, you're also a direct descendant of Ivan of Camelot, or one of his pals. The men who created us."

She shook her head. The situation had become comical. There she was, in the middle of the night, in a foreign place, speaking with a dragon and trying to assure him that she was human.

"Ah, but I have a way of knowing," said Leonard.

"You do?" She smiled.

"Well, for starters, you can see me."

"There was another person who saw you walking down the street."

"What?" He seemed concerned. "Where?"

"He was on one of the benches." A quick look behind the building informed her that there was no one there anymore. "It's empty now, but there was an old man sitting there, reading a book. He looked straight at you."

"Thanks for the warning. I'll keep an eye out."

What warning? It was strange, that a dragon would need to be careful.

Afterward, Leonard managed to convince her to get him supper.

She walked into the pub, passing right next to a small room where Seth was speaking to an older woman. A few minutes later, when she was at the bar waiting for the order, it dawned on her that she had no way of knowing that he was in there. The door was closed and the inn's restaurant was noisy. Nobody could tell whether the room was even occupied.

But just like at her father's ball the night before, she was able to focus on Seth's voice, separating it from the rest, even through the closed door. Now, she could also hear the princess, and she could amplify the conversation at will.

Then, she noticed that it wasn't just Seth's voice she could focus on anymore. She glanced around the restaurant. At every table, people were talking, but instead of a generic noise, they were separate conversations to her. She could single any of them out at will.

Quite extraordinary. And she could see Leonard, and sense that dragon last night, and Seraphim.

Was Leonard right?

She got the food and went back to him quickly, bringing bread and butter for herself so they could eat together.

Watching him eat was fascinating. He had no inhibitions, showing how much he enjoyed the food.

"Best vegetable soup in the country," he said after one sip.

"You've tried all of them?" she said, munching on her meal.

"Aye. All of them."

She laughed again.

He licked his spoon. "Puts Fergus Mór's chef to shame."

"You've been to the high court?"

"Twice," he said, moving to the roast. "Mmmm. Done just right!"

"How did you get into the high court?"

"Life's easy when you've got camouflage. Getting in was nothing. It's getting out that was the problem."

"How so?"

"Well, apart from that soup, Fergus Mór's got the best chef around. Kept feeding me until I could hardly get through the kitchen door," he said, between bites from the roast. "This stuff is excellent. I'll tip them heavily tomorrow. Breakfast's on me, by the way."

"Oh. Thank you. But you don't have to do that."

"Don't worry. I'll get them to make you their special oatmeal cake. You've got no idea how great cakes can get."

"Do you know the innkeeper?"

"Aye. Excellent chap when you get a drop of the pure in him. Otherwise, a bit on the rough side." He took another sip from the soup. "So, where are you from?"

"A bit south from here. I'm the daughter of King Áedán."

He put his food down and looked at her, puzzled. "That can't be right. You can't be a princess. You're a mage."

"I think you're mistaken about me." She had to say it. Though she was eager to find out what he knew and why he thought she had magic.

"Lass, only mages born to Ivan or one of the dragon makers can see through the camouflage, and I've got it on the entire time."

"All the time?" She had a feeling that he didn't want to be seen, but that was more emotional. She couldn't tell there was any camouflage. She could see him clear as daylight.

"Aye. All the time. Safety when you travel."

"And you think I'm a mage because I can see through it."

"I know you're a mage. I'm just surprised *you* don't know. So you've never tried any spells?"

"Not that I can recall, but I can sense people coming. I could sense you."

"Aye. You're a mage all right. Maybe your powers are waiting for something."

That was a new way to look at it.

Leonard didn't seem interested in pursuing the subject any further, and they moved to speaking about his presence in Haven.

"Do you always travel alone?" she asked.

"I'm not alone. I'd bore myself. We're a group of five, but the rest wanted to stay another night on our previous stop. How about yourself?"

"I'm here with a...friend."

"*Friend?* Is that what they call it these days? I thought people said 'cousin,' or 'uncle,' or 'long distant ex-brother-in-law twice removed and adopted at birth.'"

She held her stomach, and tried desperately not to laugh too hard. "It's not like that. He kidnapped me. Well. Sort of. I came willingly, knowing it would prevent bloodshed."

"Ah, a pirate! How romantic."

"Actually, he's a knight. His name is Seth. He's a teacher to the head knight, Niall."

Leonard stopped eating. "Seth. As in Fergus Mór's knight Seth?"

"Yes. Why?"

He raised his eyebrows. "Are you sure he kidnapped you?"

"Why is that so hard to believe?"

"The only reason a man like him could ever do such a thing would be to protect the king."

"Well, that was kind of...but wait, what do you mean, a man like him?"

"You don't know him from before?"

She shook her head. "We met for the first time yesterday."

"Hmm... You missed out on a lot. I was there at Fergus Mór's court when he was first knight."

"What? Seth was first knight?" *No!* Suddenly, a lot of things made sense.

"By far the best one there's ever been. Never seen anything like him. Always traveling the kingdom, helping where there was a need, never wasting too much time at court like all those other ones. And you had to see him at the tournaments."

"Sword tournaments?"

"Aye. Before he broke his wrist in battle, Seth was legendary. People who saw him fight started believing in magic. Given a decent sword, that man was a demon. Literally, a walking myth. Had fans too. People would travel far and wide when they heard he was going to compete."

"What happened?"

Leonard sighed, slowly. "We failed him."

"We?"

"The dragons. And we didn't fail just him—we failed all of you. When Harthenon sacrificed our kin, two survived. Became deranged. There was a change in them; they became faster, less predictable. And they had a lust for human blood. We never managed to kill them. Got close a few times, but they kept eluding us. Then, one of them got caught and Seth killed him. Did our job for us. And his hand got injured so badly that he had to resign his post."

So, that was how it happened! She recalled the weakness of his right hand.

"I...think he killed the other one yesterday."

Leonard raised his eyebrows.

"I was there."

"That man's a devil." Leonard shook his head. "Not even the injury could stop him."

"How did he learn to fight like that?"

"Who knows? There are all sorts of rumors around Seth."

"Like what? What are they saying?"

"All sorts of things. That he's a conjured human—not that that's possible. That he was raised by pirates. And the best I've heard was..."

"What?"

"That he's from France."

After the meal, Leonard walked with her to the back door of the inn.

"I want to check if the innkeeper is in the wine cellar and say hi. It'll only take a moment. Do you want to join?"

"No. I think I'll pass. But thanks." She felt ready for bed.

She held the door for him. It opened outward and

a staircase let down from it.

"Are you sure? He's a nice fellow. He'd be on the booze by now."

"Really. Thanks. I'll just head back to my room, if that's all right by you."

"Want me to walk you to the front?"

"It's fine. I can see it clearly from here." The street was well lit and the first outdoor table was just a few feet away.

"Okay. See you in the morning." He went downstairs.

She closed the door behind him.

And then froze. Her heart missed a beat.

Behind the door stood the old man from the bench. He had a small crossbow pointed straight at her chest, and his face was somber.

"Scream, and I shoot."

She felt a numbness in her feet, and her hands began to shake. "Who are you? What do you want?"

"Quiet, I said. I *will* shoot and self-healing from my arrow would take such a toll on your powers, that you'd lose consciousness, and you know it."

She didn't understand his words. She hardly heard them. But it didn't take much to understand a crossbow.

"Now, come with me. Quietly."

She followed, trembling. Fear built in her with every step. *Where was Seth when she needed him?*

He led her down the street and into an empty stable. Once there, he locked the door and stood a few feet away, examining her.

She breathed hard.

"You don't know how much you're saving me. I thought I was going to die before fulfilling my destiny, but you're here."

She couldn't speak. Thoughts of what he might want with her raced through her mind. For a moment, she thought—or even hoped—that she was going to faint on the spot.

"You're silent. Very wise. There's no point denying anything, of course. You and I both saw the dragon." He stood close to her now. "Look at you. Ivan's own kin. Just like myself. The only ones who could carry the message."

Again with that? She had to say something. Maybe there was a chance he'd let her go. "I...have no idea what you're talking about," she managed.

"Nice try." He laughed. Something about that laugh reminded her of Seraphim.

"No, really. Please. I think you've made a mistake. Please, just let me go. I'm not the one you want."

"Oh...but you are. You're probably one of the

stronger mages out there."

"No. No. I'm a mortal."

"Pah. Mortal. Of course you are!"

"Really. Let me go," she begged.

"You're not going anywhere."

He smiled and pulled one of her hands firmly, holding it in his. In a sudden flash, the crossbow turned into a knife. He twisted her wrist and then made a small cut.

The pain was intense. "What are you doing?"

But then, that feeling of warmth spread through her, just as it had the night before, rising to the surface and closing the wound, healing it completely.

"Mortal indeed! My long wait is finally over," he said with excitement. "A young one, too—you're not using any age spells. Seraphim would love this."

What did he want with her and what did Seraphim have to do with it? "I—"

"Stop talking." He smiled, for a moment observing her. A look of gratification covered his face.

Then, he made a movement with his hand. A ball of fire appeared there.

"Defend yourself, witch!" And he shot the fireball right at her.

She screamed, in sharp, piercing horror. And then instinct took over. Not knowing what she was doing, she held out her hand in self-defense. The ball of fire stopped between them, and then shot back at the man.

He let out a cry of agony as his chest burned from the impact. Yet then he smiled, content. "I was right." And those were his last words. He fell, catching her hand.

All of a sudden, she was somewhere else, in another realm, another world. His world. There, he was still speaking with her, but without words, without a voice.

This was the illusion-realm, he told her. To take someone's magic, you must kill them magically and physically at the same time. She had just done that. He'd made her kill him. In his last moments, she, his killer, would be able to see and absorb his spells, knowledge, and experience. When she would wake up, they would be hers, her magical talent tapping into them whenever she wanted.

He had been dying already. And it was now, in his final days, that the greatest of all things had happened to him. The night prior, he suddenly received the visions of the prophecy of Camelot.

It was something that the entire world of magic was waiting for. There was no mistaking it. It had the fires of battle, the child-king's mother, the protecting wizard and, of course, the child himself. Arthur was his name—the king who would reshape the rules of society. And he would make the small, half-ruined village of Camelot into a glorious city with a massive influence on the world of men, just as Ivan had foreseen long ago. It would be the final step in mages losing their earthly dominion.

The visions came to two people at once. One would know who the king's mother was. That was him. The other would know who the king's father was. That second one, Merlin was his name, couldn't be trusted. He had other motivations than the rest of the mages, because he would rule along with the king, become his first mage.

But that didn't matter. Killing the king's mother was enough to stop the prophecy from coming true. Igraine was her name. *Just a commoner, but what a commoner!* Her very life threatened all mages.

He himself couldn't do it, of course. His days were over. So were Seraphim's, though no one knew yet. But now *she* could. A young and powerful mage to carry the knowledge and prevent the prophecy.

Seraphim would pave the way for her, send her to the Order of the First Shrine, the strongest order of mages in the world. It was Ivan who made them into what they were today. When he and the mages of the

Order created the Blue Diamonds – one hundred magic rings through which they shared their powers. Every mage who wore one could sense the others' magic, no matter where they were, and could draw upon their power to enhance spells. Ivan used it to defeat Harthenon.

And what powers the Order had now! Whoever brought the details of the prophecy to them would become one of the Leading Five once the king was dead. After that, they could reignite the fire of Avalon and rebuild it to its former glory, undoing the Curse.

Seraphim was once part of the Order – they even let him keep his ring! He would be her way to them now.

The old mage showed her the images from the visions again and he also showed her his magic, for her to use.

After that, the old man's words started to disappear, becoming more quiet and faint. His life had reached its final grains of sand. The illusion-realm was dissolving, breaking the connection with him.

Kim felt her own powers now. They had been there long ago, and now they moved through her every cell.

She'd had had magic before, but it was in another world. Another time. The details of that world were not clear, but the magic was.

Then, there was Seth. A different Seth. Yet, both had much in common. The word that she had managed to lock in her mind when he had touched her now came to her consciousness. *Seduction.*

She remembered waking up in his bed, next to him, and feeling an incredible surge of magic rumble through her as her powers ascended from the intimacy they'd shared, from sealing the bond with her Charge. She was not just a mage. She was terribly powerful.

She recalled what it felt like to have magic, seeing the spells she had cast in the past. It was like remembering old songs that you once learned by heart, and realizing that you still knew all the words.

It was clear now why meeting Seth again had started the renewed awakening of her powers, and why she began to feel the way she did about him. They'd been together before, in that other world, but somehow they got separated here.

Did Morgan know about Seth? Was that why she had opposed the marriage to Domangart? Maybe she even tried to contact Seth?

"It doesn't matter." The old man's voice was faint.

He was almost gone now. "Forget guardian love. You don't really have a choice. You must prevent the prophecy from coming true."

And then he gave her an image. It was of a young woman mage, just like her, being burned at the stake. Her clothes were torn and there was blood between her legs.

The old man's final rays of magic ended and she awoke. She lay on the cold ground of a dark, empty space, next to his dead body.

She tried getting up, but it took effort. She was so tired. It took a few more attempts and she eventually managed.

She walked back to the inn, half asleep. Seth was there. He was speaking with her, but it was too hard to concentrate on what he was saying.

Soon, she was in bed, where she cast the dream-realm. It was a spell she had used in her other life. That old man liked to use it too. He would cast it on himself and practice magic unnoticed inside it. To the rest of the world, he was only asleep. All the magic he did there was untraceable.

Seeing it in his memories reminded her of it now, and she spent the night practicing her magic. Old and new. Sometimes, she would stop and consider her changed position in life.

She was no longer a king's daughter, and she might never be a king's wife. Not in this world. Not where it was forbidden for mages to rule.

Here, she was just a woman, even though she was a witch. The things she had seen or heard of in the villages around her father's court came into mind.

A peasant girl once knocked on the doors of her father's palace. Yes, King Áedán was still her father, even if he wasn't the one to give her life. The girl had a black eye, a deep cut on her cheek, and other blue and purple bruises all over her body.

She had come to the palace hoping the king would overrule her family's decision to marry her to the old town butcher. It was her own brother who had hurt her. To punish her for going to the butcher and asking him to break the engagement.

Áedán granted her wish, and she became one of Kim's servants. But a month later, when she was sent to collect a package from the village, she disappeared and was never seen again.

A woman's heart did not belong to her.

And neither did her body.

But somehow she knew that in that distant world, where she and Seth had come from, things were different. Her memories of that world felt safe—the kind of safety she never felt here as a woman. Not even now that she had magic.

She now recalled that image that the old mage gave her. The woman who had burnt at the stake.

It was a known story. She had first heard it from a mage who came to her father's court. He was leaving the Order of the First Shrine because of it.

That woman was one of the mages of the Order. But a mistake she made put her at odds with the leaders of one of the villages. The Order decided that this was too big a stain to their institution. She was alone against ten of them on the day that the village leaders decided her sentence.

It was a man's world. Not a mage's one. Even the Order knew that.

No woman was safe. Not even a witch.

But she could change that now, Kim realized. If she could get the details of the prophecy to the Order of the First Shrine with Seraphim's help, there would be hope. She was still young. She had years in front of her to use her magic, and that of the other mages. They could undo the Curse of Avalon.

Though deep in concentration, she could still feel Seth, breathing in the room next to her sleeping body. He was the only thing that could stop her plan from working. If she could think past guardian love, there would be nothing she couldn't do.

Chapter 12

Oxford, Present Day

Mindy texted me after the morning with Seth. I was at the library, trying to concentrate on readings for the upcoming lessons, but ending up just staring at my computer screen. Fragments of the conversation near the stream kept running through my head.

Seth texted me shortly after I'd entered the building and got set up at a desk. "Thank you for telling me. I think you're great. Xoxo."

The next text was Mindy's. She had a last-minute trip to Bicester Village and wanted to meet up. She was hoping Jane could join. I added Jane to the SMS chain, and we all agreed to meet for a late lunch.

Jane and Mindy had a good click. Unfortunately, It didn't work that way with Scarlett. In Jane's mind, Mindy "did all the donkey work" while she was partying, and she felt that Scarlett was using her. I had tried to explain that Scarlett had networking skills. That it was thanks to her that the more high-end clients came to the salon.

But Jane could be really stubborn when she felt there was an unfairness. Especially if uneven financial backgrounds were involved. "Not all of us can *afford* to party our way through life like her," she once said, and I wondered what she'd think of me, if she found out my dad was Mark Ralston.

When I was done with the reading, I found myself looking him up. Ralston was now in Edinburgh. On the first page of the search was a large image of him cutting the red rope to a new exhibition he had funded at the National Gallery. The young version of my mother was in the picture too. She'd be pregnant with me at this point, though it wasn't showing. The article spoke about his company's latest acquisitions and praised the young self-made billionaire.

"What are you reading?" Jane stood right in front of me.

I immediately closed the laptop lid. "Ahh...just something about a picture in a museum in Edinburgh. It was an accidental click." Luckily, I was on a part of the page that had only text and no images.

She tilted her head and then smiled.

"What?"

"I don't know. You're different. Ever since you met *him*."

Phew. She thought *that* was the reason I was on edge. "Yes. Seth's really great."

"Is he now…" She looked at her watch. "How about we talk about him on the way to lunch?"

What? What time was it? I glanced at the wall. The library clock showed quarter to one. We were meeting Mindy at two.

"I'm sorry. I totally lost track of time." I got up quickly and put my computer and notebook in my bag. "Thanks for coming to meet me."

"Uh-huh." She shook her head.

"What?"

"You are in so much trouble." Then she took out her phone. "So, are we taking a bus or a train? There's no traffic."

"Train." Buses were not really my thing, but I loved train rides. Stable and comfortable.

We ended up talking about Seth the entire journey.

I told Jane what I could share, leaving out the whole part about magic and making it sound like normal dating.

"At least this one doesn't play games." The fact that we already met more than once impressed her.

"Maybe he's just not afraid to show he's interested."

"Can you blame him?"

I laughed.

She said he was mature for his age, which was the highest compliment she'd give a guy. Oliver, of course, was *extremely* mature for his age. The conversation shifted to him. He was gone for a weekend teachers' seminar. This year, he was cutting down his workload to have time to interview for post-graduate jobs. She was trying to help out, but her own job-hunt burden was high.

When we reached Bicester, Mindy had already saved us a table at the cafe. Her trip there had been a success, and she was eager to tell us all about it.

The London salon was expanding and she was getting tired of the fast pace of the city. It was becoming too much and she wanted somewhere more quiet. Scarlett loved London, so they agreed that Mindy would start searching for a different location, where she could open a new branch.

One of Bicester's larger designer outlets was looking to sublet some of their space. Her branch would have two entrances—one from the street and another from the shop, to help both businesses gain customers.

Mindy said she'd also been feeling lately like it was time to break the partnership, and she and Scarlett were looking at how they could keep the name and still collaborate after they split the business. Scarlett's father knew a lawyer who could help them with the paperwork.

She asked Jane about the job hunt.

"It's a bullet in my brain. This year is so competitive."

"But she's got four research professors she's in close contact with," I said, "and two conferences she's arranging this term."

"Three," Jane corrected, "and one of the guest professors has a reputation of being a handful."

"Can't you share the load?" Mindy asked.

"I am sharing, but managing a group of students is sometimes worse than doing it all yourself."

"Hmm... Look, I know this sounds funny coming from me, but you need a break."

"I wish! I can only rest once I've got a placement for next year."

"You're more likely to get one if you took some time off. Quality over quantity."

"So far, quality hasn't been a problem."

"Yes, yes. We've heard all about it. The world of academia can't be lucky enough to have you arrange its conferences."

"Hey! I'm just doing my job, and I'll be dammed if I don't do it well."

"You're exhausting yourself, Jane."

There was no winning that one.

The food arrived and we decided to share the mains. When the bill came, Mindy pulled out vouchers that the outlet had given her. Jane and I were impressed.

On the train back, Mindy wanted to hear about Seth, and I filled her in. She typed his name on her phone and looked at a photo. Then, she gave me an impressed look.

"Yeah, I know..." I blushed.

"He sounds nice. What do you think?" She turned to Jane.

"Hey, why are you asking her?"

"Because," Mindy started, her voice light, "you are not known to be a good judge of character when it comes to guys."

"Seth's as good as they get," Jane said.

"Thank you!" I said.

"A real goody-good, geeky, got a bit of an attitude —but nothing a decent spanking won't cure," she added with a naughty smile.

"Stop it!" I elbowed her.

Mindy laughed. "My worries are set to rest, and I can now sleep soundly."

When we started approaching Oxford, Jane invited us for a girls' night in at her place during the weekend. I said that my parents were coming over to say goodbye before their sabbatical, so we arranged for the next Saturday.

It would be nice, to be just the three of us. Especially because this might be the last year when we'd all comfortably be in the same area.

Soon, we reached the station, and Mindy continued onward to London. Just as Jane and I were coming out, my phone rang. Most of the time I could magically feel who it was, but this time it didn't work. I picked it up, hesitantly.

"Hi, is this Kim Taylor?"

"Yes. Who is this?"

"Hi, Kim. This is Police Officer John Anderson. I understand you are head of the Junior Common Room at Christ Church College?"

"Yes," I replied.

"Kim, I'm afraid I have some bad news."

I looked at Jane, and felt that the world was suddenly dark, and I needed to sit down or throw up or... I didn't even know what. With his brief words, he'd taken the happy events of the afternoon away, and reality came banging on my door. I knew exactly what he was about to tell me.

Two of the missing students had been found. Dead.

Bradley was still missing.

Jane held my hand as we walked out of the train station and crossed the road, until we found a place outside in the fresh air, where I could sit, my head between my legs.

"Do you want an aspirin?"

I shook my head. I just wanted space to breathe. Somewhere where I could quiet myself. Jane's warm hand was on my shoulder, soothing. My mind was blank. I had no idea what to think.

"Idiot!" I heard her say, angrily, and I knew she was talking about the police officer. "With the head of a smashed nut! If it were me on the phone with him, I would give him a piece of my mind. You don't just spit out news like that."

"Yes," I mumbled. For a moment, I wished she knew the rest of it: that the missing students were witches; that so was I, and that I was now in danger too.

Then, I realized that there was someone who did

know. Someone who had tried to warn me. I took out my phone and texted Fiona Morganstein.

Jane walked with me to the Old Bank Hotel, where Fiona was staying. As we made our way there, I had some time to think. I resolved to tell Jane the truth about who I was, but not now. I'd wait until this crisis was over. It would make sense to have her confidence, if anything like this were to happen again. Plus, she was my closest friend. I wanted to share stuff like that with her.

"I didn't know you two were in contact," Jane said when we reached the hotel.

"It's about the Junior Common Room students. The professor knew one of them personally," I lied.

"Oh. I'm so sorry."

We called from the lobby, and Fiona told them to let us up. One of the staff escorted us to the room, where she was waiting with the door open.

"Please, come on in."

We both walked in, but Jane stopped at the entrance. She and Fiona had a quick chat and then she tactfully left us, telling me to call if I needed her for anything.

"You've got a good friend," said Fiona, once Jane was gone.

"I know." I looked around the room. Or rather sensed it. Magic had been cast here.

Fiona saw my gaze. "I put up the tent spell, so we could speak freely."

A tent spell. So, she was a witch after all?

She walked into the middle of the room, to where the sofa chairs were and as she crossed the edge of the carpet, she disappeared.

There was no point hiding my magic anymore, if she were being *that* honest about hers.

I followed her, and we both took a seat on opposite sofa chairs. I took out my phone, put it on silent, and left it on the table.

"Thanks for the warning last night." I figured I should start with something. So far, she'd been fair, letting herself get exposed without asking anything in return.

"You're welcome. How have you been?"

"All right. A bit shaken. I just found out what happened to two of the missing students."

"Hmm." She looked down. She did not seem surprised.

"You knew?"

She shook her head. "It was a guess. Like I said,

similar things have already started happening in Edinburgh."

"But why? I mean, you said that someone is accumulating power. What for? Why is all this happening?"

She sighed, and then said two words. "Avalon's Curse."

The Curse. The one that Zhi Ruo had referred to in the lecture.

I remembered that story well. Before the Curse, it was mages and not humans who ruled most of the earth. Until the great mage and king of Avalon, Harthenon, was driven to madness and created a curse that in the event of his death would make mages bound to serve as protectors of mortals, ending our earthly dominion. It also created guardians and immortal love.

"What of it?" I asked.

She smiled. "I'm glad you immediately knew what I meant. Not all mages are aware of it."

"Yes. I know."

"It would seem that there are people in this world who would rather...reverse things."

"Reverse things?"

"There have been previous attempts in history to reverse the Curse, and it seems that now it's happening again."

I vaguely recalled my mom mentioning it too, when she first told me the story of the Curse. She warned me about it. She called it a "forbidden road."

"But wouldn't that require tremendous powers?"

"Exactly. And there's been one known way throughout history to...become stronger."

Killing witches. I gulped. "I see..."

"I'm sorry."

"No...it's best that I understand what is going on." I thought back to her lecture. "And clearly, you are against this."

"Yes. The world has been better since the Curse."

"How so?"

"You already answered that one in my class. Humans nowadays must behave with respect to each other, because no one can *magically* fix their deeds. You've learned history. Think about the social advances of the past two thousand years."

History. Her words sounded as though she knew for certain and not just read it somewhere. But that was impossible. No mage lived that long. Unless...she wasn't a mage at all.

The images from my dream of her flashed in my mind. They reminded me that there was a type of people who had immortality. Fairies. There was only a handful of them in the world, and most lived in Ireland.

They normally chose to seclude themselves, though some, like her, were active in the world of humans. Sometimes, they would end up having families with humans and their children would be witches, like me. Some of us believed that that was how the first witches were born and why we could live for a few centuries even though we were mortal.

I breathed out. "Can I ask you a question?"

"Please," she said.

"Sorry for being direct, but are you speaking from experience, and not just from knowledge?"

Fiona smiled. "You're very clever. Yes, I am speaking from experience."

"You are a fairy, then." I decided to take my chances, while we were being honest and revealing who we are.

"Yes."

I couldn't believe I was meeting a fairy! I tried to keep my composure. "So, all this has happened before?" I managed.

"It was once common. Especially right after the Curse got activated. Mages trying to reverse it and other mages stopping them. It's been rare in recent centuries. Like I said, the world is far better where magic is not commonly used."

"Do you think it's even possible to do it?"

She shook her head. "I don't know. It would require reigniting the fire of Avalon that was extinguished to create the Curse. Some say it can be done with enough power. Others believe that there is a natural equilibrium in the world now and that we can't go back to what was before, no matter what we do."

"Thank you. For sharing all this with me."

"You're welcome. I wanted to help you since it's clear you don't have witch friends. Not many witches are sole practitioners these days. You must be careful, Kim. You would be at higher risk. Maybe you could go away for a while? Stay with your family and do remote study?"

"Unfortunately, they're all traveling soon."

"Can you join them?"

"Not really." Not yet. We were still not certain as to what dangers would lie ahead for my parents when they returned to their lives.

She thought for a moment. "You can come with me to Edinburgh. There's a...community there."

"Thank you, but, I wouldn't know who I can trust there." I didn't mean for my tone of voice to come out the way it did. It hinted heavily that I still did not really trust her either.

She didn't seem offended. Perhaps it was only reasonable to assume that I would react that way. "You're smart. Let me know if you change your mind. The offer stands and always will. Whatever you do, be careful."

"I will."

There was nothing more for us to say. Not now, anyhow, though I had a ton of questions for someone who had lived for thousands of years. I knew I'd want to meet her again.

She got up and I rose, too.

"By the way, how did you know that I'm a witch?"

"That's a whole other conversation. Let's just say I'm very perceptive."

Did fairies have a way of sensing a mage even if they were not using spells? I didn't know that much about them, and her cryptic answer bothered me. It would definitely be something to take into account if I chose to take her on her offer.

"Call me if you ever need help," she said. "You have my number. Don't hesitate about the hour. Fairies don't sleep."

That, too, was news to me. "Thank you."

I was just about to take my phone and put it in my bag, when it started ringing, silently. The picture of my mother flashed on the screen with the word "Mom" on it.

"Sorry." I reached for it.

Morganstein saw it and her relaxed mood changed immediately. For a moment, she stared at my phone and then mumbled something to herself. Her whole frame of mind was suddenly different, stressed.

She showed me out of the room, hurriedly.

Though it made no sense, I had the strange feeling that seeing my mom's image on my phone had caused this change in behavior. But why?

When I got back to my room, I shut the door, put on my favorite music and tried to relax. I decided not to tell my family about the things going on in college until they got here tomorrow. I didn't want to have to deal with anything else tonight.

The past few days had been a complete drain and I needed to let my mind rest.

When I lay on my bed, trying to relax, my thoughts wandered back to a poem that was my comfort through tough times.

It was in an old, used book, handwritten opposite a beautiful illustration of a fairy princess, added after the book had been printed.

The drawing itself was exquisite. From the illustrator's angle, you couldn't see the fairy's face.

There was a lot of detail on the woods around her and the full moon shined on her long black hair. My subconscious mind must have used these elements to create the dream about Morganstein.

Mistress of time and enchantress of old
Ivan's kin awaits your spell to unfold
She alone knows who will bear the king's son
She will give birth to his knight number one
Born to both earthly power and magic
Bring us the prophet whose fate is so tragic

When I'd first read it, all those years ago, it was cryptic to me. To this day, I didn't understand all of it. I assumed the poet spoke of the birth of King Arthur, because it referred to Ivan, who was the first person to foresee the coming of Arthur. Lancelot must have been that "knight number one."

The last line resonated with me, with the isolation I'd experienced all those years, away from other people who were like me. Other witches, who knew what it was like to have spell power. To me, growing up like that was harsh.

I felt this way again now. Isolated, and in danger.

I never told anyone about that poem. I had torn the page out of the book and kept it somewhere safe, reading it, with tears, in hard times. I did this now.

The crying helped. It released the pressure, and I remembered the day when I'd first discovered the poem. It was the day that my mother had told me the truth about who we were. It came as a shock, and I made up my mind that if I couldn't have a normal life for a witch or be part of a witch family, I would make my friends my new family. That I would pave my own road to independence. I'd try to live the teen dream, be that desired girl, the one who was active at school social events, the one who was irresistible to the guys.

But it was during college that I slowly learned that all of these things were just distractions. Running away from the things I truly wanted and couldn't have.

I'd always kept the poem close. Sometimes I'd read it at night, before going to sleep.

On some occasions, it gave me the courage to deal with the truth about my family. I'd even look up my parents and watch Ralston grow from a small startup to a multi-billion dollar company, with more and more articles about my dad appearing in newspapers.

Once the tears were dry, I felt better, ready to be optimistic. On Monday, my parents would be back to their old lives and I would have a large family that could support me. I only had to survive the weekend.

I'd had enough of that low mood and decided to take a nice long shower and try one of the body lotion samples that Mindy had brought us on her visit.

This proved to be a great idea. Once under the warm water, I felt as though my mind was slowly shutting down, and switching to a low gear. A nice, fuzzy feeling spread all over me.

Back in the room, I massaged the lotion into my skin, spreading the scent of lavender in the room.

I was just done, when there was a knock on the door.

"Who is it?" I asked. I didn't feel like using any magic.

"It's me."

Seth?

I put my bathrobe on and rushed to open it.

"Your intercom wasn't working and...wow!" He stared at me.

"I've just had a shower."

He paused, smiled, and bent down to give me a quick kiss. "You smell amazing," he whispered, and a soft tingling ran all over me.

He was here, so close, and I was wearing nothing but a bathrobe. "Come on in," I said, and he did, looking at the room.

"It's very pink!"

I laughed.

"I'm glad you're okay." There was worry in his voice.

"Why? What happened?"

"I suppose you've heard about the students?"

I nodded.

"There's...been rumors that...they were *pagan* in some way."

Witches. "I know," I said. "Someone warned me. But...you came to check on me?"

"I...didn't know how magi...the thing works, so I didn't know if it was safe to text you. If somehow someone can see it."

They wouldn't need any special abilities for that, of course; they could just hack my phone. But he didn't think about it.

"It means so much to me that you're here, Seth." I kissed him.

When the kiss broke, he looked at me hesitantly. "Do you...maybe want to come over? It might be safer if no one knew where you were tonight. That is, unless you have plans."

Come over? We'd be spending the night together in his apartment.

I took a deep breath, and then said, "Yes."

Chapter 13

Western Scotland, AD 500

Breakfast at the inn was unusually good for what Seth had remembered of the place. The innkeeper was entertaining a special guest who liked to travel a lot and had to make an impression.

He ordered seconds and thirds. Kim, on the other hand, didn't seem to have much of an appetite. He asked her whether she remembered anything from the previous night, but she didn't want to speak about it. She sat quietly, watching him eat.

She looked at him differently too. Observing, and deep in thought.

She surprised him when he said he needed to check if anything had come from Niall. "I won't be long. Will you be all right on your own?"

"I'll come with you," she replied. "I need to send something."

Huh? "Send something? To your father?"

She smiled, but it was that irritated type of smile. The kind that spoke of impatience. "No, but maybe I should write *him* too."

If not her father, than who was she writing to? And should she be writing her father at this point? He'd had a chance to speak with Ealga shortly before breakfast. Fergus Mór had written back, thanking him and Kim and informing them that he had arrested both his son and sent his knights to summon Áedán to court.

When he told her that about her father, a silent tear made its way down her cheek, but she said nothing.

In different circumstances, he would have thought that this was what was bothering her, but she was distant and distracted before he had told her.

Still, he didn't want her to be hurt.

"It might be too early to write your father."

"I will do it if I think it's the right thing. I'm no longer your prisoner," she said, coldly. "You delivered your message to Fergus Mór. My part is done."

Prisoner? They had an agreement that fit both sides, didn't they?

The final course arrived and she left her plate half full, leaning backward and staring blankly at the food. The curiosity she had had the day before was gone.

When he ordered the bill, a note came instead, along with two large slices of oatmeal cake. The note was from Leonard, a dragon he'd met at Fergus Mór's court. Leonard apologized to Kim that he couldn't join them and said that the meal was on him.

What? When did she meet Leonard? She didn't want to speak about that either.

What had happened to her last night?

"Maybe you'd want to go for a walk?" he suggested.

She looked up. "What?"

"The bird hut opens in half an hour. We could get some fresh air, and then go there together."

She hesitated, looking blankly at the table. Then back at him. "Okay."

It almost felt like an insult. As though it were *him* she was not interested in. Surprisingly, that bothered him.

He asked the serving girl to pack the leftovers and send them to the room. Kim waited, seated at the table, staring out the window.

"Shall we?"

She took a deep breath and got up.

When they got to the entrance, he opened the inn

door for her. For a moment, she smiled, gratitude in her eyes.

It had a warm effect he didn't expect. He tried to ignore it. Tried to lock away what being around her felt like.

When they reached one of the many forest paths that stretched around the village, he offered her his hand. He wanted to see how she'd react—it wasn't rough ground like before, and she didn't need help walking.

She took it. "Thanks." She wasn't looking at him, but her voice had a softness to it. A softness that felt familiar.

It made him think of something Niall once said. Something he would catch himself rolling over and over in his head when he lay injured, wondering why his betrothed never came during evening hours. A thought about his past: in those years of his life that he couldn't remember, did he have someone?

A letter was once sent to him from one of the fairy tribes, after he had become known as first knight. They said they wanted to speak with him, in discretion. The thought had crossed his mind then, that it may relate to his previous life, but he had just gotten engaged and he knew he had to choose her over anything he had before.

Just to be safe, he paid one of the king's secret agents to try to dig information. He wanted to make sure he didn't have a family somewhere. The agent couldn't find anything.

And then, he got injured and everything changed. He promised himself to visit the tribe in person once he healed. But then Fergus Mór started negotiations over Domangart's marriage and wanted him in court until it was complete.

Now he wondered about it again. Niall had said that Kim reminded him of that woman he was going to marry, but could it be that both of them were like another? A third woman. A woman he had left behind.

Kim's hand was warm, delicate in his rough fighter hand. It was hard to think for long when he felt her touch.

"You seem different today."

"I've got a lot on my mind." She was looking at the trees around them, and it felt as if she were miles away.

"Is it...the things that happened in the past few days?"

"You could say so."

He let her have her silence.

At a clearing, near a small pond, they walked by a

bench. He asked whether she'd like to sit down and she nodded.

He offered her a sweet roll from the inn that he had brought with them. She thanked him and then looked at it for a moment, as though considering whether it was really what she wanted, before taking it and nibbling on it slowly. He waited, eating with her quietly, until she was done.

"Kim, what happened last night?"

"I...just did some thinking, that's all." She didn't look at him. She didn't seem to look at anything in particular.

"I'm sorry about everything you had to go through with your dad, and...that you can't marry the prince like you wanted to." It might be slightly direct to bring it up, but it could help her to speak about it. Though Fergus Mór had thanked her, there was no knowing what would happen to her father, or to her, now that she was a traitor's daughter. He would do everything he could for her.

"What? Why do you say that I can't marry him?" She spoke fast, looking straight at him, her eyes now focused, alert. She didn't seem sad—she seemed stressed.

"Because he's in prison."

"Oh. Yes. That." She relaxed again.

An unexpected response to his words.

"What did you think I was saying?"

"Nothing. Sorry. I'm finding it difficult to concentrate."

She was lying. There were signs.

"I know what it's like. I, too, lost my hopes once."

"Yes, I know. Someone yesterday told me that you were first knight. And then there was that battle and you got wounded."

"True. But that wasn't the only thing I lost."

"What then?"

He swallowed hard. "My love." It hurt to say it, but after the words were out, there was a sudden relief. "I was going to get married."

"Seth... I'm so sorry." She was back with him now, empathy in her voice.

"It's all right. It was a while ago."

"What happened...if you don't mind me asking? You don't have to say anything." She looked at him with her large, clear blue eyes, somber.

"Domangart happened." These painful words sounded cold when they came out.

She was shocked. "Seth...how horrid! When was this?"

"While I was laying injured."

She closed her eyes and shook her head. "Oh no.

That's just... I...I don't know what to say."

"You don't have to say anything."

But the fact that she truly cared was like a ray of sunshine to the ice he'd been carrying with him all this time. She took his hand in both of hers and caressed it. For a moment, he closed his eyes and the sun came out, amplifying the warmth.

When he looked back at her, he was met with her sky-blue gaze. "I can't believe he did that to you, or her."

That almost made him chuckle. "What he did to you is far worse."

"No, it's not." She looked down. "Maybe...we wouldn't have gotten married anyhow."

"Don't say that. I sometimes said that, but it didn't make it hurt any less. Loss is loss. It's okay to be in pain."

"I didn't love him, Seth. I didn't even know him. So, it's not the same at all."

They were silent for a moment. He needed to tell her that he'd be there for her when she'd need it soon. "You know, Fergus Mór appreciates what you've done. I will speak for you. And he would welcome you to his court. I know it's not the same as getting to the high throne, but..."

"Seth, I'm not going back to be a court lady." She

stated it as though it were a matter of fact.

"Why?"

She shrugged. "It can't happen. That's all. I'd rather not talk about it." Back in town, a bell started ringing, informing them that the bird hut would open soon. She got up. "Thanks for the chat."

"Anytime."

"And Seth...she won't be your last love. I'm sure."

It was hard being around Seth now that she knew he was her Charge. Guardian love was known to be irresistible.

She'd have to be a lot more careful around him. She had said to him that he'd find another love. What was she thinking?

Every moment with him brought out the warmest side of her and everything about him drew her to him. Only thoughts about her visions kept her clarity of mind. Once the Order of the First Shrine managed to reverse Avalon's Curse, there would be no more guardians and Charges.

She walked by herself now, trying to distract herself with the beautiful streets of Haven, but the conversation with Seth kept weighing on her mind.

Back at the bird hut, he was surprised that she wrote Seraphim. He looked at her, confused, but didn't say anything.

Her message was brief: *"I met your friend in Haven. I have a private message for your eyes alone. It is urgent."*

The mailing attendant said that they'd let her know immediately when there was a reply by leaving word at the inn.

Seth asked whether she wanted to write to her father too, but she said it was too early. After that, he left. There was no message from Niall, and he went back to speak with Ealga.

These thoughts brought her back to her internal conflict. She was being unfair to Seth, leading him on when she was going to deliver the knowledge of that prophecy and end their destined bond.

They could still be together, couldn't they? Like a regular couple, without the guardianship—if they met again and chose to; no destiny involved? Ivan himself was in love with his Charge before the Curse. She was the reason he wasn't afraid to kill Harthenon, even if it meant activating the Curse, because he had foreseen guardian love with her.

But she and Seth were different than other couples. Those images in her mind from that other place in which they had already been together were definitely from another time—a future one. Like the dreams she had on the night they'd danced together, with the strange buildings and the people who spoke in a strange language.

Would reversing the Curse of Avalon prevent them from ever meeting?

A child's voice disturbed her thoughts.

"But Snow White was beautiful!"

What?

She had just turned a corner, to see a group of kids laughing in an alley. A large mirror was speaking with them. It was resting on a stone-stepped pedestal.

"No, she wasn't," said the mirror, in a grumpy voice full of certainty. "That's why the queen was so angry. Because I kept telling her that she wasn't any prettier than the ugly Snow White."

The kids laughed.

"Morning, lass. Enjoying the show?" Someone pinched her leg.

She turned to see Leonard.

It was a pleasant surprise. He was not someone you could be emotionally down around, and she immediately felt like a load was off her mind.

"How've you been?"

"Okay. Thanks so much for breakfast," she whispered, in case his camouflage was on and only she could see him.

"No worries, lass."

She looked around quickly. "Can the others see you, or am I sort of speaking with myself right now?"

"Ah, not to worry. I never hide myself from kids. They like the entertainment."

She laughed. "They seem to be getting enough now."

"Who? Shraga?" He looked at the mirror. "Aye, he's a hit. Convinced he's from a world of fairy tales, from the future. My doing."

"Your doing?"

"I took him to a mage who could see the future, who's now a great wizard down south. He went to magic school near my loch when he was young. Meeting him got Shraga's head slightly confused."

"Wait, did you say there is a mage who can see the future?" *How was that even possible? Did it mean that there were other answers to the questions on her mind?*

"Aye. And now, Shraga is convinced that he's from there. From about a thousand years from now. Though, he does seem to mix times a bit."

"And you're to blame for the poor fellow's confusion."

"Blame? He's been having the time of his life since. You should have seen him before. All alone, head filled with stories. Now he's got the right setting for them. He's famous, at least in these parts. The magic mirror of Haven. Parents travel with their kids to see him."

The kids were thrilled, sitting around the talking mirror.

"So...about that mage who could see the future. Do you still know him?"

"Aye. His name's Merlin."

No. It couldn't be. It was the same name of the mage who had the other part of the prophecy's visions. If that were indeed him, it was best to avoid talking about it. She couldn't know which side of things Leonard stood on.

"So, what have you been up to today?" He changed the subject, to her relief.

"Not much."

"Come on!"

"Really."

"Okay, have it your way."

She laughed. "Have your friends arrived yet?"

"They're coming for lunch. I've got the kitchen on their feet!"

She shook her head. "I don't know how you do it."

"The art of being liked." Just then, behind him, Seth was coming toward them with a note in his hand. Leonard turned. “Hey, mate!”

“Leonard!” said Seth. “Great to see you here. Thanks for breakfast, by the way.”

“My pleasure. Sorry for not being there. Had some important business in the morning.”

“Important business?”

“I had to sleep in.”

Seth laughed.

“Nice lass you got there. You two an item?”

Seth winked. “Not yet.”

Not yet? And then, suddenly, his words sent an image flashing through her mind. They were together, alone in an unfamiliar bed.

She quickly thought of something else.

“I’ve got a note for you.” Seth handed her a piece of paper.

It was a short line from Seraphim, asking her to come as soon as she could, and inviting her to his castle.

“Well?” asked Seth.

“He wishes to see me, but I don’t know how to get there.”

“I can take you. It’s on the way to Fergus Mór’s court. I have to go there since there’s still been no word from Niall.”

“Thanks,” she said, though it would mean

spending some more time with him. It was hard to know whether that would be confusing or give her some clarity.

"We should get going then. It's at least half a day's ride to Fergus Mór's court."

That felt too long. She was confused, and she was eager to meet Seraphim and get some answers. Was there no faster way?

"You guys need a ride?" said Leonard.

"Really?"

"Sure. Where do you need to go?"

"Fergus Mór's court."

"Seraphim's castle."

She and Seth had spoken at the same time.

Leonard had a funny look on his face. "Seraphim?"

"What?" she asked.

"He's a bit too old for you, lass."

Seth snickered.

"Seraphim used to belong to the Order of the First Shrine." Leonard was serious now. From his tone, it was clear he didn't like him. "He still has his Blue Diamond—he's affiliated with the Order. That institution is not what it used to be. They're full of political chaos and their leadership is split. That's not a friend you want to make right now."

He seemed concerned. But, of course he didn't know she had the visions of the prophecy. "I just want to talk with him."

"Okay, lass. I'll take you to him, if that's what you want," said Leonard.

"I really appreciate that," she said.

"Follow me, then."

Seth gave her a funny look. She tried to ignore it. She wasn't going to explain to him what she was about to do.

Leonard led them down the street toward the woods. When he put his camouflage back up, he informed her so that she could pretend not to see him, just like everyone else.

She caught another curious glance from Seth when Leonard did that. He was trying to figure her out. Had been for a while.

For a moment, her chest tightened and the genuine wish to tell him everything washed over her. In that flash of emotion, she wanted to forget all about the prophecy, leave it behind and never speak with Seraphim. Just be with him and tell him that they were both from another time and place and that they were destined to be together. That she had magic and could see dragons.

But she kept walking, looking away. There were

many things involved in the complexity of her choice, not just the guardianship.

Once in the forest, Leonard led them to a space between the trees.

"Hope you're not scared of a dragon in full form, after the other night."

"We're good," said Seth.

Leonard motioned them to step away. His green glow began to change. There was a blast of magic around him and his feet started to stretch out, sharp nails growing from the claws. His figure straightened. He got taller fast, and stood on his hind legs, expanding. His small wings opened into gigantic ones, larger than sails.

Soon, he looked fierce, standing higher than the trees, and his skin had turned light brown and hard as a rock. His back was covered with spikes. His nose had sharpened, and for a moment, it seemed as though he might want to breathe fire all over the forest.

He smiled at them. "Ready for a ride?" His voice was deeper now, resonating in a massive body. Then, he bent down and took each of them in one of his claws.

"In the case of emergency, the exits are right under your feet. That is, if you can fly."

Chapter 14

Oxford, Present Day

Seth's apartment was a five-minute walk from my dorm. It must have been six degrees out, but I felt such heat at every step that I didn't even put my gloves on.

Under my coat, I wore a tight buttoned white shirt and warm skirt, with lacy underwear. Seth had turned when I dressed, back in my dorm, but I could tell by how tense his back was that the images in his mind were probably stronger than if he had looked straight at me.

His hand was tight around mine, his walk tense. A couple of times, he looked at me and his eyes lit up.

When we reached his building, we went straight up to his floor. It was quiet, and I concentrated to see whether I could sense anyone else was there, but the rooms seemed still. A large sign on the message board advertised a dorm party downstairs.

Seth stopped by one of the doors and took a key from his pocket. Then, he turned and looked at me, a hunter's gaze in his eyes.

"Come here." He pulled me to him.

I stood between him and the door.

"Wrong move," he whispered in my ear, and a second later, I felt the weight of his body against mine pushing my back against the closed door, his muscles tight.

I let my hand slide down his back. He pulled it gently and then pinned it to the door.

"We're still in a public area," I said in a cheeky tone.

"What are you going to do about it?" His lips almost touched mine.

There was no one around. I put my free hand on the doorknob and magically felt the inside of the keyhole. Rapidly, I used spell power to turn the lock.

The door flew open and we nearly fell.

In a swift move, Seth caught me and helped me stand straight.

"Hmm...nice one." He locked the door behind us.

"Thank you," I said.

He turned on a soft light and took my coat, his eyes stopping at my tight buttoned shirt.

Slowly, he put both our coats on a table at the entrance, still looking at me.

I took a step back, and then turned and looked around.

There was a wide couch and a small kitchen with a large, sturdy table. A door led to another room.

"Would you like a tour?" he whispered.

I turned back to him. "The tour can wait."

He grinned and walked toward me.

I walked backward, toward the kitchen.

"Damn it, Kim." He shook his head and followed me like a lion stalking his prey.

I stopped when I reached the kitchen table. I put both hands on it and pulled myself up to sit, crossing my legs.

He reached me. "Uncross your legs," he commanded.

"And if I refuse?" I giggled.

He laughed. "You'd be playing with fire, lady."

"I like it that way." With a telekinetic wave of my hand, I undid all his shirt buttons.

"Wow." He looked at me. Then, he took it off and threw it behind him.

"Mmm..." I looked at his athletic chest. Then, I let my index fingers move slowly from his neck downward.

He closed his eyes, but stopped me when I reached his belt, took my hands in his and put them behind my back. "Keep them there." He looked at me now, as he bent down and then placed his own hands on the table, on either side of me.

His face was above mine and he stopped, his lips just about to kiss me. But he didn't move. His chest rose and fell, his breathing hard.

"Teaser," I said.

"Teaser, yourself."

"I don't think so." I freed one of my hands and, with another quick move, I undid my own shirt buttons and let the fabric fall to the sides. I was wearing a lace-only bra. White. The one that never failed me. And by Seth's stare, I could tell it didn't fail me this time either.

"I can't go on like this." His hands reached out to my back in search of the strap opening.

"It opens at the front."

"God, Kim!"

He pushed against me, and his strong hands led me to the table.

It was then that I first saw them. Blue lights. Shimmering.

They happened when he touched me. His hand was softly caressing my skin, and there was a strange glow where his fingers went, the light moving like an ocean wave. I looked up. His eyes seemed to shine, and I could almost hear the lapping sound of the waters on a faraway shore.

When I undid his belt, the metal sparkled. His hands moved down to my skirt, and I was suddenly aware of the fabric, rough, too tight around me. Goose bumps ran up my legs when Seth pulled the garment off and again when he reached for my thong. I heard myself sigh, but that sound was far from me, an almost distant echo.

The shimmering waves grew stronger.

Soon, they were everywhere, surrounding us. I could still see him through them. I was in both places: with him, but also out at sea, about to welcome a glorious storm. I ached for him. His hands caressed my bare skin, from the tips of my toes, going upward, and I wanted to scream from impatience.

"I can't stop thinking about you, Seth," I heard myself whisper.

"Me too," he said.

There was a loud, thundering sound, pounding fast, and I realized it was my own heart.

I pushed myself upward, kissing him with the force of the hurricane building inside me, and put my hands on his back, pulling him to me.

He moved his lips away and bent to whisper in my ear. "Close your eyes and count to ten. Slowly."

The waves got higher.

And then, we were one. I watched his perfect eyes through the dancing waves. I was intoxicated, melting more and more into an endless ocean, feeling every touch as though it resonated within it.

The waves started mingling, moving faster, dancing around each other, spiraling into a giant whirlpool and then...

For a second, all was silent. It was as though I were nowhere and everywhere at the same time. All physical feelings were at their most intense but also at their dimmest.

Suddenly, there was a stillness.

From a distance, two identical balls of light flew toward me. They hit me at the same time with tremendous power—a power that felt like my own magic, only magnified in force. Words whispered, *"Born to both earthly power and magic."*

Someone was panting hard. Someone who had my voice.

The images disappeared and Seth's hands were caressing my hair. The table was warm under me. The soft light of the lamp was glowing behind us. I was back in the room.

"Still breathing?" he whispered, his chest moving fast.

I nodded and smiled. "You?"

He shook his head, a look of bewilderment and daze in his eyes. "I never thought it could be this..."

"Neither did I," I said, though I knew he didn't experience it the way I did.

It was at that moment that I recalled that guardian love was different in the way it worked physically.

But there was something else, something that was slipping my mind.

I remembered later, after we'd gone to sleep and I woke up with a start from a dream of the two balls of light hitting me. In them were the waves, rising inside me, charging me with force. The sensation was still there when I lay beside Seth, my eyes open and my body shaking. The powers were moving in me like a storm, and then I remembered: the first time I'd be intimate with my Charge would release my powers to their fullest.

I slid out of bed and stood. Under my feet, I could feel the floor, spreading toward the walls, and the rooms on either side, then all the way to the ground and basement, and every room in between.

I took a step, and when I moved, the edge of the linen touched my leg. I could sense its texture, its components, the threads that made it, the tiny electrons moving around the nuclei.

I kept walking. The feeling dimmed, like a scent you got used to. It was about concentration, I intuitively realized.

The door to the room was half open, and through it, I could see the small kitchen window above the sink, with the moon shining down on the dark roofs of the town. Beyond them, millions of miles away, between the dust surrounding Saturn, two small asteroids crashed.

I closed my eyes.

I never had such powers before. Not even close! I could feel them, bubbling inside me, aching to shoot out of my hands. Images of what they could do raced through my mind. Large tsunami waves crashed on the shore, a comet was pulled from orbit, wind blew strongly enough to blast a skyscraper, fireballs the size of elephants.

Those two balls of light. *What were they?*

"You can never tell her *that*."

I suddenly heard my father's voice, somewhere from the past. My parents were talking in hushed tones, the night before the trip to Glastonbury. I never heard the part that came before.

Then, I recalled my mom's words, when she was

training me: "Be careful with magic. If you use a massive power to its fullest, it can destroy you."

How strong was she?

I was beginning to feel dizzy. *It's all about concentration*, I thought. *Just block out the stimuli.* The alertness started to dim. I was tired. I retraced my steps and went back to bed.

Seth felt the movement of the sheets and his warm hands reached out to caress me.

When I woke up in the morning, the images from the night were still vivid in my mind. I was hungry. I got up carefully, to not wake Seth, and headed to the kitchen. His fridge was surprisingly well packed. For a guy, at least.

Making breakfast without magic was suddenly a lot more difficult. Those new powers of mine wanted to be used.

A printed calendar page, stuck on the fridge with a magnet caught my attention. My sleepy mind wandered. *What day was it?* Ever since I'd met Seth, I was losing track of time. Things with him were always so intense. It felt as though we'd known each other much longer than we really did.

I checked my phone. Saturday.

Saturday... Hmmm...

Oh no! My parents were coming to Oxford tonight.

I had completely forgotten about that.

Noises from the bedroom informed me that Seth was awake. I put my phone back in my bag and turned to see him by the door.

"What are you doing?"

"Making breakfast."

"No, you're not! You are my guest. You sit down. I'll do the breakfasting."

I giggled and turned away, picking up a wooden spoon.

"Now, you put that thing down."

"And if I refuse?"

He laughed and moved until he stood right beside me, his face above mine. He bent to kiss my neck, and I closed my eyes. An instant later, the spoon was out of my hands.

"No fair," I protested, and he smiled, winningly.

"Now, please, sit down and enjoy the ride."

"Are you a good cook?"

He was an excellent cook. No wonder he was such a foodie. In fact, he was so good that it was a surprise that he bothered to eat out at all.

We ate, smiling, looking at each other between bites. I told him about my parents' visit. To my relief, he seemed excited to join and meet them. We talked about having dinner together. I asked him which restaurant he'd recommend.

After breakfast, Seth went to practice. He invited me to stay at his apartment until he returned, saying it was best that no one knew where I was just for a few hours longer. He also wanted to spend some time with Bradley's sister, to see whether there was anything he could do. There was no more news about him yet. I had made some calls myself, but there was no new information.

I texted my parents to say that Seth would be joining us, and then used the rest of the morning to do some reading for my upcoming tutorials and look at a few online papers. Around noon, I got a message from a number I didn't know.

"I have to tell you something. Could we meet at the meadows?"

"Who is this?" I texted. Every idiot in college had my number.

"Zhi Ruo."

I hadn't saved her number before. I did that now.

"I'm sorry, but I can't today. Could we speak on the phone?" The meadows didn't feel like the safest place for me to be alone with anyone.

The thought crossed my mind that she might be under threat. She was definitely not keeping a low profile, and that Adam guy who had attacked us knew her. She could have somehow figured out that I was a witch, like Morganstein did.

She might need my help, but I had to be extra careful.

There were only two days left to protect the family secret. I recalled the image I had seen with the Ralstons. My mom was pregnant with me. Any move that risked exposure could mean that they couldn't go back in time and I wouldn't be born.

Another text came.

"Please, Kim, I need to speak with you. Face-to-face. It's important." She was persistent.

I texted back. "My weekend's packed. I can do a quick five-minute call. Or, we can meet Monday. Late afternoon." By then, my parents would have replaced their younger selves.

"Okay. I'll call you," she replied after a few minutes.

I waited, but no call came.

Seth returned, and I decided to go back to my dorm and do some more reading before dinner. He insisted on walking me there.

He seemed stressed out, after the failed attempts to find out any more about what had happened to Bradley.

Before we left, I told him about Zhi Ruo.

"How come she's not hiding her magic like you?"

"Not all witches do. It's a long story, and it has to do with my family. I promise you'll hear about it tonight."

We walked back to my building, holding hands, and parted outside.

"Do you have a busy afternoon ahead of you?" I asked.

"Yeah. I've got an application for an internship to finish."

"An internship?! When will you have time for that?"

He laughed. "It's just a remote one. Next summer. I wouldn't want sword fighting to be the only thing on my resume after I graduate."

I giggled. "So, where is it?"

"The office is in Edinburgh, but it's work-from-home. They've got a great reputation."

"Let me guess: Microsoft, or...Google?"

"They're probably working with both of them. They're called Ralston."

Crap!

I texted my parents immediately when I got to my room. My dad texted back not to worry, that they'd take care of it.

Then, my parents called half an hour later. They'd changed the dinner plans: my mom upgraded the hotel room to a larger place and ordered takeaway to be delivered from the restaurant. Everything was moved to a private setting.

"Don't worry, Kim. Remember, it's guardian love. Seth will accept you," my dad reassured.

"Easy for you to say. You didn't have to deal with dating the daughter of time travelers as well as magic when you met Mom."

"Yes. But that doesn't mean that Seth won't. And when he accepts it, you'll see the humor in this."

"Humor?"

He was silent, but I could imagine him raising his eyebrows.

"It's not funny!"

"Well, we'll do everything to ease this."

Seth showed up at my dorm showered and shaved, wearing a blue collar shirt. The guy was making an effort.

I smiled nervously. I couldn't get anything done since the call with my parents. There was no point trying to concentrate. I was reading the same lines multiple times.

"Sorry about the change in dinner plans," I said on the way. "Something came up and they had to stay in."

"It's cool, Kim." He was tense.

When we walked into the hotel room, I immediately sensed the traces of my mom's magic. She had cast the tent spell around the dining table and the entire living room.

"Hi." She seemed excited, smiling, as Seth and I walked in. "You must be Seth. Kim has told us so much about you."

"It's nice to meet you too, Mrs. Taylor," he said, shaking her hand.

"Please. Call me Julie."

Not Julia.

I looked around. My dad was nowhere to be seen.

"My husband had to take a call. He'll be with us shortly. Please, feel free to take a seat and help yourselves to the starters." She motioned to the couches, where there were a few plates set up on a small table. "The meal will arrive in half an hour."

We all took a seat. Seth held my hand, while picking up a toothpick with vegetables from one of the dishes and telling my mother how great it was.

My mom smiled at us. "Kim said you were very supportive of her being a witch."

"Of course. It's part of who she is."

I was impressed. Clearly, he was still trying to take

it all in, and under the stress of meeting her, it was not obvious he would answer so well.

"Yes." She smiled.

My heart began to pound loudly.

She heard it and looked at me. "Well...there is one more important aspect to our family story."

To my surprise, he was curious. "Kim did mention you hide your powers and not all witches do that."

"Yes." She took a deep breath. "We could discuss it now, if you like."

He looked at me, then back at her. "I'm all ears."

"Well... My husband and I...we had to do something radical to save Kim's life."

"What?" There was a look of concern on his face.

She gave me a meaningful glance. She wanted him to hear it from me. It made sense.

I put my hand on his. "They had to travel back in time. They did it so that I could be born in a safe time."

For a moment, he was puzzled, just as he was on our talk before, when I told him I had magic, trying to comprehend what I had just said. "Wait. You're from the future?"

"No, no. Just them. I'm a millennial, like you. And they are just from the recent future." The *very* recent future.

He paused. Then, after thinking about it, he asked, "So, there's another pair of your parents somewhere?"

I nodded. "But nobody knows. They have a different family name. They have no idea that we exist."

He looked at me, a question in his eyes. "Is this... something you...I mean, witches do?"

"No. I've never heard of it happening before. It was done by..." My mom shook her head. *Too much information.*

"It's a long story," I concluded.

"Kim, this is...a lot." He looked at my mom, then at me.

My mom got up. "I'll be right back." She wanted to give us space.

Seth closed his eyes and shook his head. After that, he was silent for a long time.

I pulled my hand away, to give him space. The thought even crossed my mind that he would never want to see me again, guardian love or not.

But, to my surprise, he eventually looked up and said, "It doesn't matter."

What?

"You're still the same girl, right? You just have a different family name."

"Seth, you're amazing!" I can't believe he'd just said that. Tears rolled down my cheek and he leaned gently toward me to wipe them. "And...I'm actually keeping the name Taylor. Only close family will ever know the truth."

We could never reveal that Harley and I were their kids—my mom would be in her late twenties and I was twenty-one.

"When are they going back to their old lives?" he asked after the emotional surge ceased.

"Do you really want all the details now?"

He smiled, caressing my face. "Probably not. Maybe, just...tell me their last name. So I can meet your dad."

My mom walked into the room. She'd heard us. "Kim's father needs me. This is the key." She placed a plastic card on the table and left, giving us full privacy.

"Okay, so what is it?" he asked after she left.

I shook my head. I didn't want to tell him.

"Come on, Kim. I'd rather take it head-on."

"No." It was too much. The tears started coming again.

"Is it someone I might recognize?"

I nodded. *How did he do that?*

"Then, it's best if you told me, right?"

I shook my head.

"Come on, Kim."

I swallowed hard and then mumbled, "Ralston."

Chapter 15

Western Scotland, AD 500

She'd never flown before. Few had. In fact, not many people had seen a dragon in full form and lived to tell the tale. Dragons only used it in battle, which hardly ever happened. Being peaceful was part of their ways.

At first, it was so scary, she had to close her eyes. The very thought of looking down at her feet, and seeing the world move under them, was terrifying. But Leonard's hands were strong, and a quick glance at Seth to see the look of thrill and excitement on his face was convincing enough that it was safe.

It wasn't a long flight. Soon, it was over and the landing was soft, in a valley with tall trees towering over a stream. A short path led from there to Seraphim's castle.

"You might want to sit for a couple of minutes,"

Leonard said to her, as he morphed back to his regular form. "You look flushed."

"I'm fine. That was amazing! Thank you so much," she managed between fast breaths.

"No worries, lass."

"You know, you talk kind of plain for a loch dragon."

He chuckled. "Hmm... I should probably work on that."

She smiled at him. "By the way, did you use camouflage during the flight, or did people think we were in the air by ourselves?" The words had come out of her mouth too fast, without thinking. She immediately regretted them. Once again, her secrets were revealed to Seth.

Seth stared at her. "How come you can't tell?"

Leonard looked at them, and then cleared his throat. "I'll give you guys some privacy." He turned and started to walk down along the stream.

She could have tried to stop him, but he wouldn't have listened. The sound of his footsteps grew softer and fainter, as he put a distance between himself and them.

They were alone now, and Seth observed her with anticipation.

She looked around. "Can we sit?"

"Sure."

They took a seat on a couple of small rocks, near the stream. Her heart beat fast. She was about to tell him who she really was.

He waited.

There was something so undeniably impressive about him. Even sitting, he was far taller than her. Strength radiated from him, and his whole face glowed when he looked at her.

"I've...recently discovered I can see dragons." It was as good a start as any.

"I know. You saw the one that attacked us." He spoke with anticipation, expecting a confession now.

"I...have magic."

"Yes," he said after a short pause. "And you've been very good at hiding it."

"What?" *Was that what he was thinking?* "No. I've only just found out."

He breathed out loudly. "That was my second guess. I was wondering how come you randomly told me you sensed Seraphim, if you were trying to conceal the fact that you have magic."

"I was surprised myself. Things started happening to me and then I...met someone who helped me remember I had powers. Leonard realized it when I could see him camouflaged."

"How are you doing *that*? Mages can't see dragons."

"There is an exception to that rule." There was no harm enlightening him about that. "Those who are descendants to the mages who had created dragons are able to see them."

"You're saying you're a descendant to one of the dragon makers?"

"Yes." She took a deep breath. "Ivan."

Why was this so hard?

She didn't have to tell him the truth. She owed him nothing. But it felt as though she did. And she was more worried about what it would make him think of her than about any of the complications that awaited her now that she was a mage.

Fight it! she thought. But, suddenly, all the rest didn't seem to matter, not even the prophecy or anything she'd gain by telling Seraphim about it.

He was here now. Here with her. For what could be the last time. Before Seraphim would send her to the Order and she might not be able to return.

Even if she did come back, things between them would be completely different once the Curse was reversed. He'd be human, mortal. She would always be a mage. And there would be no guardianship to bridge that gap.

"So, you couldn't marry the prince anyhow."

What?

His words brought her back to the moment. "No. I'm a mage." *Marry the prince? That was the least of her worries.*

"Yes," he said. "And this means that you have a Charge somewhere." There was an unmistakable sadness in his tone.

He loved her. Even if he didn't quite realize it yet, like she did because she knew he was her Charge.

"Somewhere."

"Well," he suddenly got up, resolute and ready to walk away, "we should get you to Seraphim now." He was disappointed.

"Wait, Seth." There was one thing she could still do for him.

He turned.

"Before we go...there's something I'd like to try." She pointed at his injured wrist. "May I...feel that?"

Long ago, in that other world where they'd been together, she could perform healing spells. And the old mage who had shown her his powers used them too.

"You want to feel my wrist?"

"Your wound. I'd like to see it, if it's all right by you, see if I can sense it magically."

To her surprise, he just put his hand in hers. Without resistance or questions. He took a seat on the stone next to her.

She closed her eyes.

It was badly damaged, that much was certain. She could feel the impaired structure of the bones, the blood vessels wrapped around in a twisted way.

There were traces of different magic there. Most of it was done by witches. Medicinal spells. But there was also dragon magic. It was not exactly the same as what she and Leonard had in common, but it was similar enough.

"Can I try to heal it?" She opened her eyes.

"What?"

"This was a dragon wound. I feel..." She didn't know exactly how to explain it. "Like I should try."

He observed her, hesitating, strong doubt in his eyes.

Many must have tried before, greater mages than her. But she did have a magic that they didn't. Ivan's powers flowed through her...the source of dragon powers. And she was also his guardian. In theory, she should be able to heal him from anything.

"I guess it could do no harm," he said in the end.

She smiled. "Thank you. For trusting me."

Then, holding his wrist with both hands, she

closed her eyes again.

The first thing she felt was that magic of the others, the mages who had attempted to cure the wrist.

They had tried to treat it. Like healers would. That was their mistake. They should have instead eliminated the cause. But they couldn't.

She could. She knew it when she felt her powers slowly reaching all the way to the core wound. There was poison there. It felt almost identical to the kind of magic that came from the beast who had attacked them in the night. She could make it flow out of him, draw it out, release it in a similar way to how she healed herself, leading the toxins out. All she had to do was open the pathways that had been blocked by scarring and by the spells of others.

She concentrated, feeling the warmth in her heart grow and transferring it to him through her fingers, bypassing the magic of others and reaching all the way to the core of the wound.

From there, she started to pull. All of it: the medicines, spells, the poison itself, the tension that the injury had placed on Seth's hand, and any traces of unnatural interferences that had lingered there.

The wrist shook as the bones moved back into place.

Seth twitched, releasing a sharp cry of pain, and then, almost immediately afterward, a sigh of relief.

There was strength in the wrist now, growing, rebuilding the damaged tissue and making the blood flow as it naturally would.

His body shook and he turned his hand in hers. "Kim!"

She kept her eyes closed. Focused. There was still healing to do. An injury like that would have its effects on the rest of his body. His posture would have changed, the way he moved his arms. She kept pulling all of that out of him and spreading warmth to where the organs needed rebuilding.

Rejuvenation and lightness flowed through his body, as her powers moved through every cell, restoring it to what it used to be.

It took a lot of concentration and it exhausted her. Her breathing became shallow. *Hold on!* she whispered to herself. *Just a bit longer*. And she kept her attention on the healing until the last of it was complete. Then, she breathed out, weak from the effort.

She gave herself a few moments of rest before she slowly opened her eyes.

Seth shook his head, looking at both his hands.

"How is this possible?" There was a tear in his eye.

"Kim! You're...you're incredible. You did what no one else could!"

And then, suddenly, he bent down and kissed her.

She stopped, for a moment holding her breath. Seth's lips were full of warmth. And heat. That seductive heat she had known before. A flow of images from that other world, where they had been together, rushed through her mind.

A passion like that! How could she even think to resist him? She gave in, absorbing that heat. Wanting more. Her hand moved to his neck, pulling him toward her. A sigh escaped her, and she could feel him. All of him. Only in memory, but the connection was there, an imprint he'd made on her body long ago that she couldn't, nor would she ever want to, remove.

What power could have possibly broken the bond that they'd previously had, making them not remember each other?

The past images merged with his kiss now, and she let the intoxication take over, melting into it, forgetting the world. Nothing else mattered.

Their lips parted and he looked at her, dazzled. "Have we...done this before?" Then he shook his head. "Sorry. I didn't mean to say that. I...don't want to confuse you."

But it was she who was confusing the both of

them. She managed a smile.

"You look faint." He had noticed her fatigue.

"That was some wound, Seth. I'm drained."

He looked at her, concerned now. "I'm so sorry. Is there anything I can do? Do you want to stay here for a while?"

Stay forever. Never go to Seraphim. Never deliver the prophetic visions that could threaten such a love. Never lose each other again, the way they had already done once before.

A sound of heavy footsteps coming closer informed her that Leonard was about to join them.

Seth let go of her hand, still watching her with worry.

"Why is the lass all worn out? What did you guys do?" Leonard winked.

Seth laughed.

"Do you want another ride? I could fly you right up to the castle. Though it might give some of the people and livestock a fright."

"It's okay. I'll walk with her when she's ready," said Seth.

No. Please, no. She heard a soft voice in her heart. She closed her eyes, wanting to go back to that kiss. To stay there. But when she closed them this time, the images of the prophecy came again, a reminder.

The conflict inside her was strong.

When she was ready to walk, Seth helped her up and they walked together in silence, holding hands again, his now strong arm helping her.

But every movement was painful in her heart.

They reached the castle and went to a side gate. A guard recognized Seth.

She almost turned there. Almost told him everything. Almost.

"I'm sorry about...before." He meant that kiss.

"I'm not sorry, Seth."

She let her hands move to his chest and up to his cheeks.

With a look of excitement and disbelief, he bent down and kissed her again.

Fergus Mór's palace seemed smaller than when he'd left it, Seth thought. His mind was with Kim, who was safe in Seraphim's castle.

He walked more confidently now that his wrist was what it used to be when he was first knight here. He caught the looks from a couple of the court ladies, as he went up the stairs. He ignored them.

Those lips of hers were impressed on his mind. It

had felt so right. And when she touched him the way she did, something in it awakened a longing he had forgotten. A longing that was there with him right after he had awoken two years ago.

She was a witch. She had a Charge. Somewhere, there was someone she was meant for.

Was it at all possible that it might be him? Was it really against all odds? Niall would say it was just wishful thinking. But both he and Kim didn't remember their lives up until two years ago. *Could they have shared the same life?*

If he were her Charge, would she already know? Is that why she kissed him? But then, wouldn't she have told him?

"Fergus Mór is waiting for you in the war room," said the servant who had led him.

The war room? "Is Niall with him?"

The servant stopped. He looked as though he were about to say something, but then changed his mind. "No."

They turned a corner and went up a side stairway.

In a large sunlit room with a hard wooden table in the center, Fergus Mór stood, surrounded by five of his ministers. About fifteen knights and ten advisers were there with them. Servants came in and out, bringing food.

But no Niall. His absence was strikingly

noticeable.

"Seth." Fergus Mór raised his head and smiled. His eyes were bloodshot, surrounded by dark circles.

"Your Majesty." He bowed.

Fergus Mór made a motion with his hand. "Come." The others made way.

"What's going on, sire?" He approached.

The table had a large map of the country with pieces on it, just as it would when a battle was expected.

"Here, read this." He handed him a letter in Niall's handwriting, dated the night before.

Sire,

I regret to inform you that I have been captured on my way to you, by agents from the kingdom of Alt Clut. The man carrying this letter is one of them.

They asked me to write to you, on behalf of your imprisoned son, who had an alliance with their king. They demand his release and marriage to their princess, and that you abdicate, passing the throne to him.

Should you refuse, or if their agent is harmed, they will take arms against you. Their armies will march tomorrow, accompanied by the head of the Order of the First Shrine. And in such a case, I am informed that I will not live to see this fight.

Anticipating the only response a true king can give, I would like you to know that the time I had served as your first knight was the height of my life, regardless of how it ends. Please send Seth my sincere regrets that our friendship, that was so dear to me, must conclude this way.

Your humble servant always,

Niall

Seth stared at the note.

"His body was hung in the village of Aerras," Fergus Mór said.

A sharp pain spread through Seth's chest and anger bubbled in his veins. Niall was dead. His best friend. The closest thing he knew to a brother.

"Damn it!" He pounded his fist on the table, shaking everything on it.

Everyone in the room stopped talking and looked at him in silence.

"How...did you just do that?" said one of the ministers. The other knights, who had known him all this time, looked at his fist.

"Son," said Fergus Mór, his voice filled with concern. "That was your injured wrist."

He paused. It was not something he wanted to expose yet, but there was no ignoring the king when he spoke. "She fixed it," he heard himself whisper.

"Who?"

"Kim. Áedán's daughter. She's a mage."

There were gasps and murmurs in the room.

Fergus Mór looked at his men. "Leave us. Take a break."

Once they were alone in the room, the king started to pace, treading the stone floors in anger.

"Sire?"

"So, Áedán was going to trick us after all." He spoke in a low voice. "I had let him go in return for money for hiring mercenaries. But he had his witch daughter helping his plot against me all along."

"What? No. Áedán didn't know. Even she didn't. Her powers just awoke."

"Just awoke? She did something my best mages couldn't do. With such strength, I'd be very surprised if she's not already working with the Order."

"I don't think that's what's going on, sire. She really didn't know about any of this. Not about her own magic and not about her father's betrayal."

There was another option, of course. He could also be her Charge. And then she could heal him from anything. But Fergus Mór's mind was as far as could be from even considering that. He was looking at him straight in the eye and raising an eyebrow.

"You seem to have taken her side."

"She doesn't have a side."

The king paused, then smiled wearily and shook his head. "Seth…come on. It's the oldest trick in the book. Surely you wouldn't fall for it."

"What?"

"She's a beautiful woman. She's got your mind twisted."

"No. It's not like that."

The king just shook his head. "Where is she now?"

"With Seraphim."

"Of course she is! I've been suspecting *his* loyalty these last few months. Always on the road, that mage. Never in court when I needed him."

The king paced again, his feet getting faster.

From experience, Seth knew that there was no point interrupting this semi-trance.

Fergus Mór continued speaking, half to himself. "Seraphim still has his Blue Diamond. He and Kim are both working for the Order. And we are left with no strong mage to fight the head of the Order. First, when I read this letter, I thought she was a ruse, to hide my son's plan to marry the Alt Clut princess, but this is far worse. However…" He turned to Seth. "Since she healed you, you can be my first knight again. The men look up to you and this," he pointed to the table, "will now be your responsibility. Perhaps my spies can find out for certainty where Seraphim stands. If I were you," he patted Seth's shoulder, "I wouldn't speak about Kim again."

Seraphim's castle was a small one. There were hardly any guards. Of course, with his powers, that would have been an unnecessary hassle.

He had taken her request for discretion seriously. She was led to a small, heavily furnished room, with a large, dark rug. The walls had heavy tapestry, to block sound.

"So, how can I help you?" Seraphim said, once they were sitting, facing each other.

She would have to play tough. A man like him would despise any show of weakness and use it against her. "I met your friend in Haven."

"My friend?"

"The old mage. He never mentioned his name."

"His name is Rokus. What of him?"

"He's dead." *The power of a direct approach.*

Seraphim moved back in his chair.

It worked.

"But he gave me a message for you."

"I'm listening." There was no more of that

condescending tone. He observed her intently, eye to eye.

Silence was a powerful thing. She let him look at her for a few moments, now immune to his penetrating gaze, before she responded. "It is not a message to deliver lightly."

The door opened and a servant walked in, carrying plates for them. She thanked him and then waited for him to leave.

"Before I say anything else, I should tell you that I healed Seth's hand this morning." She had bested him.

It was his turn to be silent. He observed her long before saying, "You are kin to dragon makers?"

"Kin to Ivan. Just like your friend."

"I see."

"My message concerns the Order of the First Shrine."

"And he wanted you to deliver it to me."

"Through you," she corrected him. "I will meet with the Order. Once they give me a position as one of the Leading Five."

"The Leading Five."

He was catching on. Slowly, as she'd intended him to.

"I think we both know of what I speak."

His fingers tapped on the armrest of his seat. “Rokus passed a vision on to you.”

“Rokus passed a vision on to me. One that the Order is sure to reward you handsomely for helping me deliver.”

He didn’t like these last words. “The head of the order, Khonsu, will be here tomorrow,” he said, stressing his strong position with the Order.

“Khonsu?”

“Originally from Egypt. You can stay in this castle and speak with him then.”

“Thank you very much for the offer. But I’d rather stay at Fergus Mór’s court. I will return to meet Khonsu in the morning.”

“I’m afraid that won’t be possible. Fergus Mór and Khonsu are now on opposite ends of a war.”

A war? What war?

What was he talking about? Fergus Mór was about to fight and Seraphim was hosting the mage who supported the enemy?

“You’re not going to fight?” *Who was going to protect Fergus Mór?*

Seraphim picked up his plate and sat back, leaning into his chair. “Politics is a tricky game and magic often gets caught in between, but none of this is our concern. It will all be over tomorrow.”

He was just going to sit there.

And Seth would be back at Fergus Mór's court by now. *Seth could die!*

Chapter 16

Oxford, Present Day

Seth stayed for the dinner, but it was as if he wasn't there. He hardly touched the food, and he kept staring at my dad. He ended up leaving early.

"I'll call you," he said dryly.

I was depressed. I thought I'd feel relieved once Seth knew the truth about me, but this wasn't the same as telling him that I was a witch. This was more than any Charge had had to take. I regretted not finding a way to somehow wait longer.

During the meal, he'd asked when my parents met. I could sense by the nature of the question that he was keen to know that it was only after my dad's company had become a success, and that this wasn't achieved using magic.

"He needs time," my mom said when he was gone, leaving me with them.

To my great relief, he called early in the morning. My heart leaped when I saw his name on the phone. He wanted to meet up, which I thought was good, but he didn't sound excited or happy, like before. He asked whether I could be ready around ten, and whether I had some sports clothing I could wear.

At least it didn't sound like he wanted to meet in order to have a heavy talk, or that he needed a break.

I had chosen to stay with my parents that night. The place had an extra bedroom, and I was too tired and too despondent to go back to my dorm and be there alone.

During breakfast, I filled them in on what was going on in college with the witches. I decided to leave out the part with Morganstein. Telling them that witches were being targeted was bad enough.

My dad was very concerned. He and my mom exchanged a meaningful look. And she whispered, "Same pattern?"

"I don't know," he said, and then immediately checked the news. There were five new cases of missing students since Friday morning.

"What do you mean, same pattern?" I asked.

They looked at each other and then at me.

My mom sighed. "We've seen this before."

In Edinburgh? The thought crossed my mind that

their younger selves might have the same knowledge that Morganstein had. I almost told them about her then, but I decided against it. Tomorrow would be a better time. Right before they headed to the airport, so that they could process it when they weren't busy getting the last bits of their plans finalized.

My mom said that I should get away, that one of my aunts, Angela, lived in London, and had a large family with three grown-up sons who all had strong powers. Tomorrow, once she and Dad were back to their old lives, she would call her and arrange for me to stay in the city, near them, for a few days.

I'd have to somehow convince Seth to join me. As my Charge, he was under threat too, but I had no idea how he'd feel about any of this so early in a relationship. Yesterday's dinner was no help.

I checked my voicemail. Things in college had escalated too. There were messages from the undergraduate student union about police visits. Word got out that two of the missing people were dead and students were going to be interviewed. There was still no sign of Bradley, to my relief. The Junior Common Room inbox had exploded with emails from parents and freshers. One of the other union members had been answering them. He also wrote me, concerned, to ask where I was.

The dean requested that we set up auto-responders to direct calls and emails to a helpline that was set up by the university, for all the colleges.

There was one email from Jane, that Professor Morganstein had traveled back to Edinburgh. That surprised me. Especially after she'd offered to help me. The email said it was a personal matter, and that Morganstein hadn't yet canceled any of her lectures for later next week. I couldn't help but suspect that it had to do with the missing witches.

Seth showed up at the hotel lobby at exactly ten, two sports bags of different sizes on his shoulder. His eyes were heavy. He said he'd taken a sleeping pill. I said I did something similar. I had cast the dream-realm, but not for practice; it was just a way to guarantee I'd get sleep.

His expression was distant. "I'm sorry. I just really don't feel like speaking today."

"Neither do I," I confessed.

He smiled. "I still wanted to see you."

And I was thankful for guardian love, keeping us together after last night.

We walked out, silent again. He took my hand, but his touch felt cold.

I assumed we were headed to the sports center, which proved correct. When we got there, he led me to a private training room, where he pulled out a key and lay his bag on a bench. Then, he closed the door behind us.

"I'm assuming this will be your size." Out of the bags came out a few smaller supermarket plastic bags, one of which he handed to me. And then, a pair of fencing swords.

"Here. Feel it." He gave me one of them. "What do you think?"

Was he going to try fencing with me? "It's...lighter than I'd imagined," I said, holding it.

He chuckled.

"What?"

"It's just...that's what I said the first time I'd held one. I'm hoping we'd try this and see if it's fun for you." There was something apologetic in his tone. He hadn't asked me first. Under the current circumstances, though, this was a step forward. He was welcoming me into his world.

"I'd love to give it a go."

"Good," he said, with relief.

Getting ready took some time, and I needed help dressing. Once done, he placed a sword in my hand again.

"Try to think of it as an extension of you."

He started by demonstrating how to hold it, and

then explained that there were different types of swords.

When he showed me the right posture and his large hands correcting my body, I felt that undeniable spark between us again. It was as if slowly, through this, the top layer of the ice between us was starting to melt.

The lesson was very different than what I had imagined. It was almost as though, at any given moment, Seth was connected to the very core of what fencing was. I'd had a few karate teachers in my life and learned other forms of sports at times, but his approach was nothing like my other instructors.

He said that all arts are about your raw talent. It's tapping into that unique gift that was in every one of us. Sometimes, it was hidden so well that you'd think you lacked it at first. I could tell he was speaking from experience. There were other hints during the lesson that his road had not been a straight or swift one, and that that was his advantage. He'd been through the ins and outs of it, trying and failing until he found what worked.

His strong hands guided mine when he showed me how to connect to the sword. He spoke about getting a feel for the opponent, their movements, the focus of their actions, their intent, even their spirit, before they even made an attack.

Once you were tuned into the essence of the art, there was no more opponent. There was only you and the moves, and those had to be done instantly, without thinking. "Never stall. You get the best points for winning."

This was a different Seth. He was in a zone, at his tournaments, where there was nothing more important or more real than fencing. So much so, that it almost seemed as though there were no tournament at all. That this was his way to breathe. Like my magic.

"It's sometimes hard to switch off," he said, helping me out of my equipment after what had felt like no more than twenty minutes, but the clock told me we'd been there for over an hour. "Some of it stays with you."

"Seth, that was..." I shook my head from side to side, so moved from the experience that I couldn't find the words.

He smiled in satisfaction. "Glad to hear it." There was a sparkle in his eyes. We'd connected again.

He finished helping me out of the equipment, and then stopped and stood in front of me. His hand moved slowly to caress my cheek. "Thank you. For doing this with me." And then he bent and pulled me toward him.

There was something in that kiss that was out of this world. Simple, but powerful. It was almost as if it resonated, sending waves around us.

After a quick shower, I switched to a dress, and towel-dried my hair. Seth was waiting for me at the entrance to the complex, his short hair damp and slightly messy. It was cute.

We walked back to college together, holding hands. There was a different type of silence between us now. A silence of intimacy.

I felt the muscles in his arm tense when we got in through Canterbury Gate. I looked up. He looked away, but smiled to himself.

"Are you busy right now?" he asked when we reached my building.

"What do you have in mind?" I teased.

"If you have to ask..." He had that neon look in his eyes again, and I blushed.

"Would you...like to come up?"

He stopped. "You sounded hesitant just then."

"It's just... I wasn't sure."

"Kim. I want you. Never doubt that!"

He did? After last night? I pulled out my key and almost dropped it again. My hand trembled as I twisted it through the hole in the main door. Then, we walked briskly up the stairs and into the room.

Seth locked the door behind us.

"Get on the bed," he commanded.

There was so much enticement in that sentence, that I sighed before I obeyed.

"Lay back." He took off his shirt and threw it on the floor behind him.

I started to take my dress off.

"Leave it on." He unbuckled his belt and stepped out of his pants. "Just take your bra and underwear off from underneath."

My heart began to pound fast.

I watched him undress, his eyes on my every move, and then the shimmering waves took over.

Lunch was an array of sandwiches that my mom made for us to take outside for a picnic. She was glad that Seth and I had met so soon after last night.

I still had no idea how I was going to bring up the trip to London, but the problem got solved on its own shortly afterward. One of Seth's coaches wanted to schedule a training week in the city. I quickly texted him that I was planning to go down too. He said I should stay with him.

"He loves you," my mom said.

"Or, he's just afraid I'd party too hard if left to my own vices."

She laughed. We spent the afternoon working on my magical training, now that my powers had ascended. She would give me advice and then I'd take a dream-realm nap and practice.

She knew my powers, or a variation of them. The core was similar to hers, but there were differences.

Conjuring was her forte. It seemed I had a lot of power there, but overall my magic was more intuitive. I'd always found telekinesis to be my strength.

My powers were in tune with natural elements. Fireballs and wind seemed to come at a strength and magnitude that amazed her when I described them. My range was larger, too, though I lacked her spread. Her weather spells could cover an area the size of a large city. Mine were more limited in space, but I could affect a farther place.

The passive awareness of the world around us was also different. Hers had more detail than mine, but I could feel things far away.

"You're much like your grandfather. That's how his powers work." She couldn't wait for us to meet. She said he was also an excellent trainer.

Her instructions were with me in every practice,

but she wasn't the only one there. With many spells, I would find myself back in the sports center, with Seth. His words on fencing now applied to my magic. Blending my new powers into the old was like connecting to the sword he had put in my hand. He was teaching me, part of me now, in every spell.

"Have you thought about telling your friends about magic?" my mom asked when practice was done and we were waiting for my dad to finish off some business, so that we could go together for an early dinner.

He was working hard at closing last things before the trip, going over an old file he and Mom had prepared right before traveling back in time, of all the things they'd need to know upon their return.

I said I wanted to tell Jane, maybe Mindy at some point, but not Scarlett. "I don't think she'd get it, no matter what I'd say. I can't help but feel bad about that."

"Honey, we all have different types of friendships. Scarlett is more your fun buddy. That's wonderful too. You have a deep connection with Jane and Mindy."

Though she didn't speak much about the life they'd left behind, I knew she had a friend who was in on the big secret. Someone named Kendra.

"Mom, I have a question."

"Sure."

I looked at her. The question I was about to ask had been on my mind for many years. "How powerful are you?"

She took a breath. "Does it matter?"

"I can't talk about magic with other witches. All I know is you and Harley, so I'm thinking that if you're very strong, then I could be too."

She smiled. "It doesn't really work that way. It's more like...musical talent. You can find a family of musicians where some of the siblings are tone-deaf. Your magic would feel similar to that of other family members, but its strength depends on your own ability to connect with its depth."

Again, her words reminded me of Seth's fencing.

"Also, I don't want you to think that the amount of power is what counts."

"*It's not the size of the dog in the fight, it's the size of the fight in the dog.*"

She grinned. "Yes. You'd find that your smarts serve you far more than your magic ever will."

"Right. So...what is the answer to my question?"

She laughed. "Persistent. Just like your father." She paused. "I never really knew, but based on what our family had seen in other witches, we assumed..."

"That you were one of the top mages of your time."

She didn't answer.

"Is that what happened? Is that why you and Daddy needed to run away? Were you persecuted for your magic like the witches in my college?"

"No. It wasn't like that. It's...best you don't know certain things. Not yet, at least. There will be time. Lots of time, after things settle."

Yes. She and Dad didn't really know what they would be going back to and how they would deal with the dangers they had escaped. Their only certainty was that Harley and I were now adults, and in control of our powers.

"Kim, I'm so glad your powers ascended before we had to go back."

My dad joined us shortly after that conversation. He had just gotten off the phone, explaining to the tenants who had rented our house the complex workings of a boiler.

During dinner, an email arrived from Harley and Amber, addressed to all of us, and Mom read it out loud. They were somewhere in Canada. Hiking. There was a college there that Amber wanted to have a look at, and they'd be staying for the rest of the week.

It was a relief to my parents. Harley and I would be their largest secret, and the fact that they were mobile during this critical time made them safer.

After dinner, they went over the flight details again. They had arranged for a safe time barrier, to allow them to arrive at the time they had planned.

Looking at their itinerary made it all suddenly real.

"I'll miss you," I heard myself saying.

"Really?" said my dad. "I recall how eager you were to leave home. Get your independence."

"Yes. I know."

"We'll see each other very soon," said my mom. "It's just that we don't know exactly when."

My dad suggested an evening walk to look at the town. He loved Oxford. When he'd first come up with me, he had me walking around for hours, getting in and out of colleges and visiting touristy areas, or places where famous films had been made.

Before going out, I had a quick check of my phone and the Junior Common Room inbox. Some people had ignored our request to use the helpline, and left messages for us. I quickly replied that they should contact it. Then, I searched online for any news. One more student, from Magdalene College, was missing.

"Try not to think about it," my mom said. "Get some sleep tonight. Tomorrow you're going to

London with Seth."

I got a message from him, right before going to bed back at the hotel, asking whether I could be packed and ready for the four p.m. train to London. I replied that I would, and he said he could pick me up and we'd walk to the station together.

He ended with, "My concentration has been completely off today. Can't stop thinking about this afternoon."

His words made me feel a nice warm sensation in my chest, and relaxed some of my worries about the missing students and our safety. I also felt more confident about the tension that had built between us. We would get through it. Even though he needed his distance. Maybe slowing down the pace was good for us, after all.

As I drifted into a deep non-magical sleep, I started dreaming of that trip long ago, when my mom took me to Glastonbury.

✧

I was at a charity shop, holding an old book, that I could tell had been well cared for. It had beautiful pictures of knights and castles. My mother was looking out the shop window at the rain-covered street. The drive up had been long, and we'd spent it singing along to our favorite songs. Loudly.

Many witches lived in Glastonbury, and it was also a pagan center. People spoke about magic freely. It was the safest place to have *the talk.*

I knew it was important for her to do it right, and I was eager to finally find out why we were living under such restrictions.

We had a quick tour of the town and got lunch. The shop was just across the road from our hotel, and Mom seemed to want to take our time before we got there. I could tell she was stressed under the happy-tourist facade.

She went to pay, and I put the book in my bag.

"Anything else you want to see?" she asked when we were outside the shop.

"Not really. I think we should check in."

Waiting would have just made it more stressful. I was like my dad, preferring to be hit with all the information at once and sort it out in my own way. I didn't like to delay dealing with things.

We went upstairs. Once in our room, my mom locked the door and closed her eyes. I knew that she could feel the building, the other rooms, and the people inside. She was checking whether we were alone.

Then, she cast the tent spell around the small table. We both took a seat and she pulled out her laptop and turned it on. That last action had seemed strange to me.

"I know you have a lot of questions about magic," she said after a short silent pause.

"No, Mom. Not *a lot* of questions. Just one." My dad often said I was an easy teen. Most of the time. "Why do we keep our magic a secret?"

She smiled. A sad smile. What she was about to tell me was clearly difficult for her. "I want to show you something."

She punched two words into a search engine, then turned it to me. The words were "Mark Ralston." A few results came up, including an address of a startup in New York, near the Hudson River. She clicked it and a website loaded. Then, she hit the About section. On the screen was an image of a young man who looked like my dad. He was much younger, with different hair and minus the beard, but there was a definite resemblance.

Then, she opened another window and typed the name "George Evans." The search results showed a middle-aged doctor, also in New York. She opened an image of him with a beautiful woman and beside them was a young woman who looked like my mother. There were differences, but they were in many ways still very similar.

"I...don't get it."

She waited, giving me time.

"Why are you showing me people who look like you and Dad?"

The power of denial could not be underestimated. It took what seemed like forever for me to notice that they also had the same first names. Well, sort of.

"Something happened to your father and me," she started again. "We got threatened. By very strong mages. And I was pregnant at the time. Nobody knew. In order to protect you, we chose to do something radical."

I looked at the images on the screen. It was as though the things that she was saying were trying to come together in my mind, but it was impossible.

"What exactly are you saying to me?"

"Your dad and I...we chose to go back in time."

"What?!" *Was she serious?*

And then, I started laughing. I didn't know why. It just all seemed ridiculous. *It couldn't be real, of course, could it?*

"Kim." She laid a warm hand on my shoulder.

"You're joking, right? This is funny, right?" I took the computer from her and looked at the images.

Then at more images.

"I can cast an age spell to show you what I used to look like."

I heard her voice, almost as though it were underwater. It made no sense. *Time travel was impossible.* And yet, here were two people who could be her and Dad when they were younger, alive in our time.

"No witch could travel in time," I said in the end.

"It wasn't a witch who cast the spell."

Suddenly, I was angry.

If she *was* telling me the truth, why did she wait this long? Surely, she could have trusted me enough to keep this secret, or at least parts of it. And I had a family! A family who never knew me.

I got up and held tight to the computer, tears in my eyes. "I'm going to tell them. I'm going to write these people and..."

A force of power sent the computer flying out of my hands and into hers, reminding me that my mother only avoided heavy spells, not that she didn't have the ability to cast them. I had often wondered how strong she really was.

"You can't do that!" There was alarm in her voice.

"Why not? I might even prove you're lying."

She closed the lid. "For you to be born, an exact

combination of sperm and egg has to happen. You cannot contact these people. You can't have any interference with their lives. Anything you do..."

"Can mean I won't be here," I completed her sentence, my voice weak, breaking. In that moment, I finally believed her.

I sat down and looked at my knees. *How did this happen? What did this mean about who I was?*

I had a thousand questions. I wanted to know why they did it, what had happened that caused them to be persecuted. She said she couldn't tell me that, because it wasn't safe.

I kept asking questions: *Why didn't they go forward in time?* They'd thought it was safer to go to a time that they knew from experience.

And then, I asked, *Why didn't they ask the Guild for help?* The Guild was the top authority of mages in the world, dating back to Avalon days when they had been called the Order of the First Shrine. Her answer there was evasive, and the way she reacted to the very mention of the Guild made me suspect that they were somehow supportive of the people who threatened her and Dad.

In our long conversation, one thing was certain: They didn't have a choice. Nobody could help them. No place was safe enough for them to hide, so they chose to time travel. To save me.

I walked out of the hotel room that evening, confused, and wandered the streets of Glastonbury alone. For the first time, I didn't hear her say the family warning: *Remember, no magic unless you absolutely have to.* In fact, there was never a need for her to tell me since.

I wandered aimlessly, ending up somewhere in Glastonbury Abbey, where I sat between the ruins and cried. I was angry at her, angry at the world. At myself, too, for not pushing them, for not making them tell me who I really was.

That gap between my parents and me that formed back in Glastonbury took a long time to bridge. It happened gradually, during my college years.

I had waited so long for the time to arrive when they'd be going back to their lives and I would have a family. Witches I could speak with and relate to.

Finally, this was going to happen.

I woke up in the middle of the night, back at Oxford, in the hotel with my parents, thinking about the fact that I had an aunt in London! And I was going to meet her tomorrow.

Something was making flashing lights in the room. It was my phone. I looked at the time. Two a.m.

The number was Zhi Ruo's. I cursed her and rejected the call. A text followed.

"I need to know what side you're on."

Chapter 17

Western Scotland, AD 500

The armies started arriving shortly after dawn. They marched slowly, rhythmically, a small but growing dark cloud in the distance.

Kim stood at the top of the northern tower of Seraphim's castle.

She had awoken to the sounds of footsteps going up and down the halls outside the guest room, where she'd spent the night. She lay awake, listening. The servants were speaking, recounting stories of the damages that the marching troops had already caused on the way. Horror and violence spread where they treaded. It made her heart sad to hear it.

Why did war extend beyond battles? Why was there kidnapping, theft, slavery, rape and murder?

Somewhere in the back of her mind, she knew that there was a world, far away in another time, where things were, to an extent, better.

Was that world ruled by mages?

If not, was it the choice that she herself would make about the prophecy that could cause things to change? But which choice was the right one? How could she have memories of a better world in the future, where she and Seth were also together, if she reversed the Curse now?

Maybe she was not his guardian then? Or was it that she didn't reverse the Curse, and it was Arthur, when he became king, who changed the way that people behaved and set an example that created this better world?

Now, from the tower, she looked at the waiting troops of Fergus Mór's forces. Mercenaries were arriving all the time, joining the army lines. Seth was there, dressed in the first knight's armor.

That was her doing—her healing him that enabled it. He was first knight again. But where was Niall?

They desperately needed a mage. They may have found a few who could help, but the power needed to offset a ruthless army like Alt Clut, with the head of the Order on their side—it would take someone like Seraphim, and he had betrayed them.

"You've impressed me, Kim." She heard his voice, climbing up the tower from below. A second later, he appeared and joined her. "Two days ago, you were the daughter of a traitor. Now, you're about to join the Order and become queen of the world."

It wasn't for those reasons that she was going to the Order. And though it hurt that he called her father a traitor, it was ironic coming from him. "I'm doing what's right."

"You're doing far more. Without the child-king, Camelot won't become the kingdom Ivan spoke of and you and the other mages will align and reignite the fire of Avalon and reverse the Curse."

She turned to look at him, the dying mage. How powerful he still was at the end of his days. If it weren't for the fact that Rokus had told her, she wouldn't have guessed that his life was nearing its end.

"What was the world like before the Curse?"

He shook his head. "My dear, you have no idea. The type of power we mages had... There was magic in Avalon that your generation can't even dream of. You'd know something about that, of course, being Ivan's kin. No one now can create dragons. Avalon was the center of the world. People came from all over to marvel at it. We could heal anything. You think Seth's wound would have been a challenge? It's why Harthenon created the Curse in the first place.

He never believed anyone would take the chance of starting a course of events that would lead to this power being lost."

"Yet, Ivan did."

"Ivan was a romantic. He did it for guardianship, to save the woman he loved."

Was that not reason enough to do something, even something that changed the world? She looked at the battlefield.

Seth sat proudly on his horse, giving away nothing of the fears he must have of the inevitable defeat, keeping morale up for the sake of his men.

"Maybe Ivan was right. We've seen the guardianship now. There's much to lose."

Seraphim laughed, his low voice rolling. "Don't take after your forefather, Kim. There was no guardianship when I was born. No shackles."

Shackles? "Guardianship means everlasting love."

"It's overrated, Kim. Those born before the Curse will tell you. Khonsu will tell you, after the battle. He was alive then too." He leaned on the balcony edge, looking at the armies on both sides. "The Curse let humans rule. Just look at them! Feeble. Helpless. That's why they are such greedy beings. They're afraid. It's all about power for them, because power means self-preservation. But they destroy themselves with it. And us."

Once again, she remembered the woman who was burned at the stake.

"So many of them will die today," he continued.

That last sentence sent a shiver down her spine. "You despise them."

"No. I just don't sympathize with them."

"They're just like us. We kill each other for power too."

"That's rare. We are normally peaceful to one another. And to the world around us. We don't seek to exploit it. Ever since *they* have had our powers at their disposal, it's been nothing but accumulation of things, buildings. Destruction of the natural world and plundering of resources is everywhere."

"But perhaps it is because they rely on our powers to fix it all. Maybe we are still too powerful." Again, she was thinking of that woman. It was mages who had helped humans kill her.

"You sound like Ivan. He was very convincing. He thought the world would be better after the Curse, but he was just blinded by love. I was part of the Order then, when he joined us. We told him not to go against Harthenon. If we'd known that he'd ignore us, that he'd still use our shared powers through his Blue Diamond, we would have stopped him. And now the world is in the hands of mortals instead of mages. In the past five hundred years, all mages combined haven't done the damage that humans do in one day."

She looked at him. So sure of his ways. "But you could have stopped Ivan. You could have taken the Blue Diamond rings off."

"It happened too quickly. He killed Harthenon in a very short battle. Most of us didn't understand what was going on."

"Perhaps it was destiny, then. For things to happen the way they did. Like guardian love."

He laughed. "Destiny? You think guardian love is destiny? It's nothing but an illusion. All love is. You know what happened to Ivan's?"

"He twinned his powers and gave to her a magic identical to his. She died from the insanity it caused." She recalled the fairies didn't like to mention this part of the story.

A look of immense sadness crossed Seraphim's eyes. "She didn't just die, Kim. She killed many people, ruthlessly, and we had no choice but to kill her. Ivan, too—to get to her. She was worse than any horror Harthenon had caused. Ivan died for the myth of guardian love."

"What about your Charge?" The words came out

without thinking. It was an impulse, caused by the surprise of how much he'd spoken against guardian love.

Seraphim wasn't caught by surprise. "She was a wonderful woman," he said.

Something must have happened to her.

Everyone knew that mages could bring a Charge back to life, but only within a certain window. A few days. *Did she die and he couldn't find her?*

Was that why Seraphim was dying? Did he want his life to end, rather than live without her?

It was that very thought that finally solved her conflict. No world was worth living in without Seth.

Suddenly, her mind was completely clear. Guardian love made being with a human possible. Without it, Seth would one day die, and she would go on living. Their time together would be nothing but a memory. One that would haunt her every day for the centuries that she would walk the earth. Alone. Longing.

She knew exactly what she had to do. She had to leave Seraphim and get to Seth. He was leading Fergus Mór's army into a battle that couldn't be won. They needed a mage and if no one else would stand beside him, then she would.

She needed an excuse. A way to get out of the

castle and to the battlefield, without Seraphim standing in her way. She looked at him. "I can't watch. I'm going downstairs."

"Kim... How do you expect me to send you to the Order, if you can't even watch a simple battle? Once in the Order, you'd be part of wars."

"But it wouldn't be in a place I'm attached to. This was going to be my home." Those words seemed a smart argument, but he took them in a different way than intended.

"So you're saying I betrayed Fergus Mór?"

"I'm just saying I don't want to be here right now."

"Yes. I know." He had that haughty tone again. Like the one he used when they'd first met. "You want to go down there. To Seth. That's what's confusing you so much."

She froze. There was no way he could know that. No way, except...that kiss. His guards must have spoken to him about it. And, knowing she had healed Seth, he must have come to the conclusion that he was her Charge.

"But I'm afraid I can't let you do that," he continued. "You see, I am here to get you to make the right choice."

"Then it's not a choice."

He smiled.

"You can't force me. What would you do? Keep me prisoner until Khonsu arrives?"

"If I must." His voice was enigmatic.

"That would give you nothing," she said with resolution. "I've said all I could to you. My message is for Khonsu's ears alone, and I will choose under which terms I deliver it. You can't get the visions of the prophecy out of me without my consent. Now, excuse me, I must go."

"You're not going anywhere."

He had a strange look on his face. Something that was a combination of malice and satisfaction. He *wanted* to fight her.

"And you are wrong if you think I need your consent." He stepped toward her.

It was a death threat!

She took a deep breath. He was between her and Khonsu, between her and Seth's battle.

She swallowed hard. She was strong. Her memories had told her that. But he was Seraphim. And even if she won, she'd be weakened when facing Khonsu afterward.

Deep in her mind, she heard Seth's voice. It was a voice from another world. Their world, where they had been together. He was wearing a strange white helmet, trying to teach her something. Something about battles. He was saying to her that she should end a fight in as few moves as possible.

She turned to Seraphim and looked him straight in the eye. Behind her, in the battlefield, she sensed strong magic, telling her that Khonsu had started his attack.

Seraphim smiled. Then, he made his first move.

A gush of air pushed her backward. She resisted it. He tried again.

He was strong, that was evident. He also had the experience of many years, but it was also clear that his magic was fading, his life leaving him.

At first, he was just testing her. A couple of times with the wind spell, then switching to using telekinesis to throw tower blocks at her. He was trying to see what she was made of.

In the battlefield, the men shouted in pain. She glanced behind her. That mere moment was enough for her sharp eyes to inform her the men had been infected with lice. How Egyptian of Khonsu!

Remove the lice from the men, remove the lice from the men, she thought.

When she turned back, there was a fireball in Seraphim's hand. "Fighting for Fergus Mór?" He laughed. "You're nothing. A low princess. What do you have?"

Spell power, she thought, *and experience.* His weakness was that he assumed she was new to this. That all she knew was what she'd gotten from Rokus.

She remembered Seth's teachings. *A fast battle.* She looked at the sky. *Give me lightning.* At the same time, she also focused on her hands, and thought of fire.

The spells were rapid. A large fireball appeared in her hand and she threw it at Seraphim. Her lightning hit him from behind, while he was focused on shooting his own fireball against hers.

She managed to hurt him and extinguish both flames at the same time. For a moment, he seemed surprised. But he was a fast healer.

In the battlefield, large balls of hail started to fall from the sky. She heard cries, and she could easily feel Khonsu's strong power.

Before she could do anything to help Seth's men, the floor moved under her. She tripped and fell. A second later, Seraphim came and stood on top of her.

She thought fast. *Set fire to his clothes, set fire to his clothes.* His heavy robes caught fire. She looked at the sky. *Another lightning,* she thought rapidly, and another appeared, hitting him hard, pushing him backward. *Again.* He was hit and she rolled, back to her feet. *Again.* Before he could respond.

Speed was on her side against Seraphim. But time was running out for the men in the battlefield. They needed her. In a moment of complete focus and concentration, she brought down one final lightning strike, ten times stronger than any of the previous. The light itself was blinding and she had to look away.

When she looked back, Seraphim lay beside her, unconscious but still breathing. His clothes were burnt and his skin was red. She turned and stood beside him.

She'd never killed anyone before. Her hands trembled. She didn't want to do it. Didn't want what it would make of her. It was strange how quickly one could cross red lines, become a beast.

She could just leave him there and it would take him hours, maybe even a few days to heal. But then, he would come after her. He might even fully align with the Order and they'd hunt her down together.

They would find her, kill her, and extract the knowledge when she was dying.

"I'm so sorry." A tear ran down her cheek. "I don't want to do this. Please believe me." Then, she looked up to the sky one last time and brought down a final bolt of lightning.

It hit Seraphim's chest, shaking his entire body,

and then he lay motionless. Defeated. She listened for a moment. He had no heartbeat.

She felt an inner pain grow inside her. She'd done it. She killed a man. It felt strong, but awful. She walked carefully around him and put her hands over his eyes to close them.

She didn't take his powers when she could. She let him die in dignity, but it didn't lessen the shame she felt. She knelt beside his dead body, saying a prayer for him in her heart.

Then, she got up quickly. She couldn't linger. She rushed down the steps of the tower.

She needed a horse. Somewhere in the building, there would have to be a stable. She focused. The noises of the castle came to her mind, first as a blur and then, with more clarity. Inside the variety of sounds, she found the beasts. Five horses. She followed their sounds.

The stables were near a side gate. She mounted one of the saddled horses and then she was out, riding toward the battle.

The closer she got, the stronger she could feel Khonsu's magic. She passed through a small wood and though she couldn't see the soldiers, she saw fireballs in the sky above them.

Give me heavy rain, she thought. *Give me heavy rain.*

Rain started to fall, countering Khonsu's magic. The fireballs stopped and she stopped her own spell.

As she neared the fighting men, she could see Khonsu himself. He was on a horse; a tall man in armor stood next to him, instructing him.

According to conventions, Fergus Mór's mage should be at his side to serve his plans. That's where the men of Alt Clut would expect her to go. But she could do better. A dramatic entrance would send the message that she was here to challenge Khonsu directly.

She entered the battlefield and put her hands on the horse's mane. Through it, she could feel the beast's body, all the way to its strong legs, and its connection to the bare ground. There, she imagined heat and flames.

Where her horse stepped, on either side, she arose a wall of fire, marking her path and creating a barrier between Fergus Mór's men and the forces of Alt Clut.

Behind her, Khonsu's spells diminished the flames. She kept going straight toward him.

"You dare challenge me?!" He roared and a ball of ice shot from the sky, toward her.

She waved her hand and the ice ball changed directions and headed straight for the Alt Clut king.

Khonsu waved his hand and pushed it away. "Leave at once, girl. My mages sense your spells through my ring. Win, and they will hunt you down. No one will protect you."

She was about to answer, to take part in this battle of wits, but deep in her mind, Seth's voice was guiding her again, an image of him in a white mask. "Never stall." The first clear words from that other time, in another language—and she understood them!

She looked up, through the skies, all the way to the place where the blue ended, and the darkness of the night that surrounded the world in its never-ending peace started. There, she could see the stars, gas balls burning bright. Small and large bodies of rock were there too. Some near and small enough that she could move them out of their course. And one was very close.

She pulled it. It took a lot of concentration, a lot of strength, but it responded, coming down to Earth, down to the battlefield. At great speed. When it neared, the men started shouting and running, as its shadow covered them from above.

She directed it straight at Khonsu.

He waved his hands and she saw the glow of his Blue Diamond, calling on the powers of the Order.

The massive rock stopped in the air. Khonsu concentrated on it and it started to move away. But he was distracted by it.

Just then, an arrow flew toward her. She slowed it down and caught it. As Khonsu was moving the hot mass of rock so that it hovered behind him, she used her powers to hit him with the arrow.

She heard the cry of the king and the shrieks of the men as the mass of earth suddenly fell to the ground and Khonsu tumbled off his horse.

"Surrender your armies. Call off this battle," she yelled and let the wind carry her words to the king. "Or I will destroy you." There was a pause. "I *will* do it."

The king turned and signaled to one of his men. A white flag was raised.

Kim was just about to let out a breath of relief and give herself some time to regain strength from the toll of the spells, when something happened. There was a faint whisper in the air, coming from the battlefield.

It was Seth, calling her. But without words. In complete silence. That cry resonated within her, and she felt a sharp pain in her chest.

She turned and looked. There, on the rough ground, Seth's body lay motionless.

Chapter 18

Oxford, Present Day

From the lobby, I could see my mom's face in the cab. There were tears in her eyes. For months, we had spoken about this day with so much excitement. Now, it was all happening.

"We'll see each other very soon," she said at the end of breakfast.

Then the cab arrived, and we had a short but emotional goodbye. My dad seemed anxious. They texted three times from the airport before boarding the plane, and we agreed they'd call as soon as it was safe.

They'd waited twenty-two years for this to finally arrive. I once asked them why they had gone back specifically that far. They explained it was part of how time travel worked, from what they'd been told. That only certain options were available to them on the day of travel.

They couldn't choose a date that was too close either. I needed to be old enough for it to be safe for them to return, so that I could protect myself when needed. The same went for Harley.

That was all about to be tested. As I was packing for the London trip, trying not to dwell on my mixed emotions about my parents' departure, my thoughts wandered to the message from Zhi Ruo. *Did she want help, or was she trying to challenge me?*

The interactions with her went through my mind, along with everything that had happened in college since I'd first realized that witches were in danger.

Less than a week had passed since Veronica went missing.

I didn't have time to check my voicemail, the Junior Common Room inbox, or the news. I had promised myself that I'd do it first thing once Seth and I were on the train to London.

Morganstein's words now went through my mind, and I realized that I had completely forgotten to tell my parents about her. A quick check of the airport website confirmed that their plane had already departed. I would have to text them later.

Packing took a lot less time than I'd thought. The small mundane tasks were a welcome distraction from my worries.

I had just zipped up my bag when the phone rang. It was Seth.

"Hi, baby."

He'd never called me any nicknames before. And of all the ones to choose from... I felt a surge of heat rush through my body.

But the tone of his voice betrayed worry. I didn't need magic to know that something was up.

"Hey, Seth... I'm just done packing for our trip."

There was a pause. "There's been a development."

Development? "What do you mean?"

"I've been asked to attend police interviews about Bradley. They just called me. But...it's on campus. Right next to your dorm. Hopefully it won't cause us too much delay."

My phone made a buzz. I looked at it. An incoming call from an unknown number. "One second," I mumbled to Seth and focused.

The number had no emotional sense. Something that felt like a form you'd fill. Something institutional. But protective.

Something that had a uniform... The police.

"I think they might be calling me too."

"Answer and phone me back."

Twenty minutes later, we were both sitting on

wooden chairs that had been arranged in a row in front of a closed door, waiting to be called in. The hallway had three other such doors, with people waiting in front of them.

On the right, I saw some faces that I recognized from the JCR party, waiting too. On our left, I saw Zhi Ruo.

I smiled at her. She looked away. *How was she involved in all of this?*

"It shouldn't take long." Seth held my hand. But his touch was tense.

I caressed him. "We're helping Bradley."

"Yes."

The door opened and a tall, stout man, who I guessed was in his early thirties, came out. "Kimberley Taylor and Seth Damian Rivers?"

We rose.

"Follow me."

"Both of us?" The words escaped my mouth instinctively. I bit my lip. Probably not a good idea to question police methods.

"Yes." He gave me a sharp look.

Seth held the door for me and we walked in, just as Zhi Ruo's name was called too.

The room had a large desk and a few chairs. All the other furniture had been pushed to the side. The desk was bare, except for the interrogator's laptop, notebook, and pen.

"Take a seat." He closed the door behind us.

His coldness made me feel uneasy.

The only light in the room came from a window behind him and outside, it was starting to rain. We were on the ground floor, and I could sense the earth absorbing the drops as the skies got darker.

A woman with a red coat stopped under a tree and looked at us through the window.

"I'm Lieutenant Abraham Watson." He introduced himself. It was an unusually old name for someone this young. "We understand that the two of you were harassed on Thursday evening and the police helped you."

I looked at Seth, thinking what to say.

Lieutenant Watson didn't wait for an answer. "We also know you were acquainted with this man." He picked up his notebook, took out a clip that held an inserted page at the front, and turned it to us. It was a picture of Bradley.

He closed the notebook fast, but slow enough for me to notice that it was new. The pages flipped, empty, as they shut. There were no other notebooks on the table.

Surely we were not the first people he had seen today?

"I am," said Seth. "She met him once."

Watson looked at me, but said nothing.

Outside, a young man wearing a long black coat joined the woman under the tree, who was still staring at us.

It was then that I also noticed a door on the left, that connected our room to the next one, where Zhi Ruo would be. I focused, to see whether I could hear her voice, but my magical sensing could hardly reach past the door. And yet, I had no trouble hearing people speak in the quad.

I started to feel on edge and tried to calm myself with the thought that it was just my response to being in a police interview. But my father's words came to my mind: "Always trust your instincts, Kim."

"Are you still with us?" Watson looked at me, his head tilted.

"Sorry. I got distracted there." I sat up straight in my chair. "Could you repeat the question?"

"I didn't ask you any questions."

"Right. I do apologize. I'm all attention now. It's... just a bit stressful to be here. But, I'm very interested in helping find Bradley. What would you like to know?"

Two other people joined the ones under the tree. They stood there together in silence, all looking at us.

Except for the one in the long black coat, who had his back turned.

Watson put his pen down and pointed at me, then at Seth. "How long have you two known each other?"

"A few days," Seth answered quickly.

Why did that matter?

"Where did you meet?"

"Here, on campus."

"Do you have a lot of friends in common?"

"No. Why?" I said, challenging him. I wanted to know how he'd reply.

"Let me ask the questions." He suddenly glanced toward the door that connected the rooms. "I'm assuming you're a couple?"

I felt on edge again. Alert. This was none of his business! "I'm sorry, but how exactly is this helping you get information about Bradley?"

Watson ignored me. "Have you been intimate?"

"What!" Seth rose.

Watson smiled.

And then, two things happened at the same time.

The man with the black coat turned and for the first time, his face was visible. I had seen him before. He was Adam, the student who'd threatened us!

A chill passed through me, and I grabbed Seth's hand. And then the door to the next room opened and Zhi Ruo stepped in.

I got up and turned toward the main door, but in the corner of my eye, I saw her move her hand and the chair I'd been sitting on moved to block my way.

"Please, do take a seat." Her voice had a combination of sneer and sweetness.

"What do you want, Zhi Ruo?" I remained standing. My heart beat fast.

"You know what we want."

"I couldn't possibly imagine!"

But I knew. She wanted my powers, or my allegiance.

It was just like Morganstein had said. And it was clear why she'd only entered the room after Watson asked whether Seth and I had been intimate. It meant I'd have more powers and she knew it.

And Watson was either a mage or working with these people. How many others like him did they have?

Outside the window, there were seven people now and they started to walk toward us.

My hand shook.

Nobody knew we were here. And even if they had, the only people who could help were my mom and Harley, and both of them were out of reach. We had no one. We... Wait! There was *one* person I could still call. Morganstein. Even if she herself wasn't here, maybe she knew someone else who was.

In a flash, I closed my eyes and used my powers to text her my location and the word, *Help!*

But the magic got interrupted. My pocket was suddenly torn open and the phone flew toward Zhi Ruo's hand.

Did it send? Did my message get through?

"Trying to text Mommy?" Zhi Ruo raised her eyebrows. "Too bad she's on a plane."

How did she know that? I suddenly recalled her using magic on my computer. *What else did she find out about my parents? Was our secret still safe?*

"You must be strong, Kim. Is that why you hide? No coven. No friends with magic."

So she didn't know. At least I could rest assured that she couldn't expose my family.

"Leave her alone," Seth snapped.

She laughed.

"My magic is my own concern." I took a step forward. I had to buy time. If my message had somehow managed to get through, Morganstein might be able to send someone to help us. That is, if she knew anyone here who could still be trusted. A thought came to mind on how I could delay things. "You will fail, Zhi Ruo. You couldn't possibly have enough power to reignite the fire of Avalon."

"Oh, so you figured it out. Congratulations, Kim. And, why would we fail?"

"Because it can't be done. It's been tried in the past. Surely you don't think you're the first?"

"Oh, we've done our research. We know how and why others failed. So...we're back to whether or not you'd join us *willingly*."

"Because you'd kill me if I don't? Like you killed Veronica and Bradley?"

"Oh, don't worry. Nobody killed Bradley. He made the right choice."

Bradley was with them?

And then I saw him. Outside the window, joining Adam and the others.

"What?" Seth's voice was half a whisper.

Cold sweat ran down my spine and my breath went shallow.

"So," Zhi Ruo started again, with artificial warmth in her tone. God, I hated her. "You know you can't win, dear. And you're probably guessing that we wouldn't want to leave any witnesses."

Seth! She was threatening him now.

Could I fight her? There were a few of them and one of me. *But how strong was I in comparison? How much power had they accumulated? Did I stand a chance or would I just go down trying?*

But then, what choice did I have? We still had no one.

"We could start with him." Zhi Ruo looked at Seth.

"Don't listen to her." Seth took my hand in his.

My heart pounded hard. My mind raced. *Was there a way out of this?*

"We won't make it quick." Zhi Ruo sneered at Seth. "And we'll make sure Kim won't know where you are. And yes, the kiss of the guardian can bring you back to life later. But some things can't be cured. The kind of things we do when we torture people... you'll live with it for the rest of your life."

"No!" My cry echoed in the room, as if spoken in a hollow space. Like in a dream.

Everything else was silent.

Nobody moved. No, wait. It was more than that. They were frozen.

Even the people outside. I couldn't sense them breathing. The raindrops had stopped touching the ground; the trees were motionless. Everything stood still.

There was no sound. I could feel Seth's hand in mine, but he, too, was still.

What?

"Kim."

I heard a warm, familiar voice.

Morganstein?

Suddenly, just like that, she was there, standing in front of me. Between me and the table; between me and the mages.

She looked at me, her face glowing. There was mist surrounding her, enclosing us and Seth.

She put her hand on mine, and it felt like the touch of the summer sun rays, warm and soothing.

Was I awake? "How are you here?"

"Fairies live between the physical and the spiritual worlds. We walk in the In-Between, the space between the material reality and eternity, and between life and death."

I didn't understand her.

"You can't see it, so we pass unnoticed by you." She smiled, bathed in a shimmering golden light. "Now, we must hurry. I can't hold this for long."

"But there is nothing we can do."

"There is *time*."

There was something significant about the way she said that word.

I closed my eyes. I felt suddenly sleepy.

"Stay with me, Kim." Her voice brought me back. "The In-Between is distracting for mortals. You have to concentrate."

"You can freeze time?" I opened my eyes again and looked at the people around me.

"Not freeze. Slow to an almost stop."

A humming sound started in my head. "Umm..." I mumbled with it.

"Kim!"

"What?" I was back with her again.

"I can help you. I can send the two of you to a place and time where no one can hurt you."

"Time travel?"

She nodded.

And then it clicked, somewhere inside my blurry head, that she'd just been to Edinburgh. "Wait...did you send my parents back in time?"

"Yes. I'm the only one who could."

"How?"

"There was once a mage who could control the speed of time and, combined with my powers... Kim... stay with me..."

"Seth and I...we don't want to live in the past."

"Your case will be different. It won't be like your parents."

"How could you know?"

"Because all of this has already happened."

Of course.

When she first saw me, back at the lecture hall, she looked at me with recognition.

"Why didn't you tell me?" I didn't know whether I finished the sentence. She was saying something, but I didn't hear it.

"What if we end up right back here again?" I mumbled.

"You won't. You'll come back to a different place."

A thousand questions raced through my mind, but they were numbed by this strange floating sensation. The golden light was clouding my senses. And right behind it were witches waiting to kill me and Seth.

Deep down, I knew that it didn't matter what she said. We had no choice. "Seth must agree."

"Of course."

His grip on my hand suddenly felt stronger, as the speed of his time aligned with mine.

In a few short words, Morganstein explained the situation.

"There's too much you're not telling us," he said. "But..." Seth looked around.

He saw it too. We just had to take that risk.

"I love you, Kim." His grip of my hand went tight.

"I love you, too, Seth." A tear dropped from my eye. I looked down. It stopped mid-air.

Morganstein was whispering something, her voice

soft and growing fainter. It was in a language I didn't understand. The light around us became blinding.

My eyes felt too heavy now. And then everything went dark.

"Kim?" Morganstein's voice was now distant.

Seth's hand was still in mine. He was here. But it felt as though I wasn't. Not really.

The flow of time changed. In what seemed like only a few moments, the floor under our feet dissolved and we were on the bare earth, though it felt as if we weren't standing on it. Or on anything at all. Buildings around us were replaced by trees.

Slowly, I was aware of a swirling motion. We were in the center of it. All around, everything was moving. Backward.

Somewhere, far away, was my life in Oxford. My parents, whom I'd just said goodbye to. The extended family I so longed to meet. My friends. Harley. It was all becoming increasingly distant.

Where in time was she sending us?

This wasn't a couple of decades like my parents were sent back in time. This was centuries. *Had we been tricked?*

Morganstein! I wanted to call out. But I could no longer feel her presence. I could only feel her spell, as its effects were becoming more noticeable to me. And more rapid.

My senses that were in tune with nature told me that change was happening around us. Forests were growing denser, oceans were receding. The Earth was turning clockwise, against its natural movement, with great speed.

Time flowed differently for us. It seemed as though we were frozen in it, but everywhere else, there was constant rapid motion. It was as though we were in a safe bubble, while outside it a whirlwind was spinning everything.

I couldn't tell how long it lasted. When it finally slowed down, I felt Seth's hand slide away. Exhaustion finally took over, and I drifted into dreamless sleep.

I woke up to the sound of a familiar voice.

I moaned and tried to open my eyes. *How long was I out?* I blinked once. I was lying on a bed. It was broad daylight and birds sang above me in a tree.

A bed in the middle of the woods. *What? Where was I?*

I must be dreaming. But when I blinked again, the view was still the same. I tried to open my eyes wider, but only managed to see things between half-closed eyelids. The light of the sun was too strong.

Next to me was a woman, wearing a white, lacy

dress. Her long black hair was loose, a silver tiara in her hair. She reminded me of the fairy picture in my old book.

She had large, almost translucent blue eyes. She looked a lot like Professor Morganstein. But it wasn't her. Not exactly.

She held a note in her hand, a page torn from a lined notebook, and discussed it with someone in a strange language.

The other person called her Morgan.

Morgan? Who was Morgan? I didn't recognize the other person's voice. *And what was that note?*

Amongst the strange words she read out, I picked out my own name, and then Seth's.

"Seth?" I stirred, but I was too weak to rise. "Seth?"

He didn't answer.

"Seth!"

The woman who looked like Morganstein lay a warm hand on my arm. She said something soothing, as though trying to tell me that he was all right.

What was that language? It reminded me of a course Jane and I took on old Celtic literature. Morgan said something that sounded like the word for shirt. Yes, Seth was wearing training clothes. His name had been embroidered there.

Then, someone else spoke. In a whisper. They said Seth's name and then the word for "gone" and "crazy."

Seth had wandered off?

I needed to get up fast. Find him. I managed to push myself up, as far as my elbows, but I saw stars and fell right back to a lying position.

I looked behind Morgan. There was a gazebo with silver decorations. I had seen a similar one in a picture from Ireland, where the fairies lived.

Clearly this was somehow in the midst of the woods, with one of their Irish tribes. *Maybe they were trying to speak Gaelic with me?*

"Am I in...*Ireland?*" I pronounced the word as clearly as I could.

They didn't understand. They answered with a question.

"Am I in Ireland?" I repeated.

"Ireland?" Morgan asked, puzzled.

They didn't know about Ireland?

"Ireland. Ireland, the large island near England."

"Shhh..." Morgan's hand on my arm moved softly, trying to soothe me.

They really didn't know about Ireland. *How was this possible? Where could Morganstein have sent us that people didn't know about it? Or...when?*

I lay back. There was no point trying further until I had regained my strength. At least Seth was here. He'd return to me, and we'd figure this out together.

The fairies went back to discussing the note. Morganstein must have slipped it into one of my pockets right before she'd sent us here.

I was tired. Tired from whatever journey I'd just been sent on. All I could think about was Seth.

If I could think at all.

There was a buzzing noise in my head and I started to feel blurry.

Slowly, the memories of what had happened right before and my life until now began to dim and the voices around me seemed warmer, safer. And that strange noise in my head became stronger.

Every time I blinked, the colors around me were more vivid and the fairies' voices louder and clearer. But other parts of me were shutting down, closing my mind to any thoughts and memories that didn't belong here.

Edinburgh Royal Infirmary, a few days later

There was a loud, irritating noise. Something was beeping. Like a pulse: constant, but high-pitched and unnatural.

"She's coming to," someone said.

Coming to? To what?

I tried to speak, but I couldn't. My head felt hard. It was lying on something soft, but the surface itself was rough. The rest of my body was motionless, heavy, flat on a fabric surface.

I tried to move.

Somewhere deep inside me, a powerful warmth was spreading through my veins, giving me strength. *Magic.*

The beeping noise became faster.

I managed a murmur.

"She's about to wake up." It was a man's voice. The same one I'd just heard.

The warmth spreading through me was charging every cell and the weight I was feeling disappeared as the sensation of my limbs became lighter. Strength was coming back to me.

"Will she be all right?" A familiar voice. Filled with concern. Warmth. Love.

Seth!

"Don't worry, son. You have no idea what she's made of."

Who was speaking? The voice was deep and belonged to an older man. Where did I hear it before?

And then I remembered: a spell brought Seth and I back to our own time, safe but wounded. There was a doctor with us when we emerged. He had healing powers similar to mine – he guided me as I drifted off, from exhaustion and from my wounds. And I also knew who I was: the memories of the present and past had suddenly come together.

A large hand caressed my cheek now. *Seth.*

I breathed in. It was a strong breath. The beeping was now much faster. *What was making that noise?* From behind closed eyelids, I could tell that there was a lot of light in the room.

Seth's warm hand was a comfort in this strange place, whatever it was.

"Seth." I only managed a whisper.

"It's okay. Take your time," he said. "I'm here."

The warmth now vibrated in me, charging my bones, my muscles, my cool breath. I opened my eyes, but there was too much light. I closed them again.

"Your family is here too," said Seth. "Your parents are in the other room."

"My parents?" My voice was faint, but definitely more than a whisper now.

"Should I go call them?"

"Not yet," replied the older man. "Let her magic heal her first."

He knew I had magic? Who was this person? I tried to get up.

"Easy, now," said the man. "No rushing it."

I opened my eyes again, slower this time. The light seemed less severe. Two figures stood next to me. Slowly, the image cleared. Seth was there, smiling.

"Seth."

"We're okay, Kim. We made it."

As my mind was becoming clearer, an image came. That one thing that I wanted to hold on to the most, but couldn't bear to remember. *No. Not that thought!* It was too hard to deal with right now. Too painful. Impossible.

I turned my attention back to my body, blocking my mind.

Something was annoying me on my hand. It was stuck to my finger. I tried to take it off.

"Leave it, sweetheart. It's the heart monitor."

"It's all right," said the other man. "We can take it off now." He bent and removed the device. His hands were strong, but their touch gentle. He smiled at me. I could see him clearly now. There was something strangely familiar about him. Something about his face. *What was it?*

Right. His eyes looked a bit like Harley's.

"Harley?"

"Your brother is not here," said Seth. "Still traveling."

There was a sudden boost of magic inside me, as if that healing warmth had turned into a wave. It swept through me, ridding me of any remaining weakness and fatigue. The heaviness in my neck lightened completely, and then the warmth went through my head and removed any fog I felt there, pushing me to full consciousness. The rest of my muscles felt flexible. Strong.

I stretched my arms and pushed myself up so I could sit.

The room was small. Everything was white. There were machines of all kinds around.

"Hey... I'm not in a hospital, am I?"

The older man laughed. He wore a statoscope. "She's back." He patted Seth's shoulder.

Seth smiled at me. I took his hand in mine and held it strong. Then, I looked at the doctor who had helped bring me back. "Thank you," I said. "You're a really good doctor."

"He's not just a doctor," said Seth.

"What do you mean?" I asked.

The old man smiled. "I'm George Evans. Your grandfather."

Chapter 19

Western Scotland, AD 500

The castle was quiet.

Near the gates, people stood in line, waiting for their turn to ask the two clerks about the names of their loved ones who hadn't returned from battle. In scattered tents, mages who could perform low-level healing spells were helping with the injured.

The main court stood empty and the great hall was open only for meals. Portraits of Niall and Seth stood on elevated canvases at the entrance to the gallery.

Kim noticed them when she passed through, led by one of Fergus Mór's servants.

The evident emptiness of the castle was daunting. It spoke of mourning more than any of the grim faces and tearful people she saw. It was as though death itself had settled there, and the portraits were its children.

A woman stood next to Seth's, in tears. Her fingers were closed around an object. For a moment, she paused and looked down at her hand, opening it. The object was a small ring.

The former fiancée.

Kim paused. "I'm sorry for your loss."

"Thank you," the woman replied in a soft tone, not looking away from the portrait. "I lost him long ago," she said, half to herself.

The servant had noticed Kim stop and beckoned her to follow. "Your Highness, we must continue."

Hearing the words *Your Highness,* the woman turned to look at her. "You," she muttered. "You're the mage who saved us."

"Yes." She glanced at the woman and then at Seth's portrait. *I am the one who didn't betray him.*

The servant led her through a side passage that bypassed the great hall, and then down a flight of stairs that ended in a small corridor with arched doorways. They walked past empty rooms, where workers would have been on a different day. The silence was heavy and her footsteps that echoed in the dark passages made her feel a chill.

At the end of the corridor, the servant opened a heavy door.

Three steps led down into a low-lit room. There

were a few torches on the walls and a man sitting on a wooden chair rose when she entered. It was King Fergus Mór.

On either side of him was a table. His two first knights lay there, dead.

She thanked the servant who left, closing the door behind him, and approached the king, bowing when she reached him.

There was gratitude in his eyes, a thanks for her coming to their rescue, but when he looked back toward the tables, his expression was hollow.

She approached Seth.

A quick glance at the other table told her that Niall had not had an easy death. Signs of torture covered his body.

Seth had been hit hard too. His wounds were severe, almost surprising in their magnitude. Each one of them alone might have caused another man to cease fighting, or even perish. A sword wound to the throat was what had caused the final, fatal blow. Blood stains covered his body in different points. His left leg was twisted and he was missing two fingers.

She touched his cold hand, remembering what it was like to feel it holding hers.

"You shouldn't be here." She heard the low, broken voice of the king. His words were uttered slowly. "The Order will be on their way to challenge you. You've killed their head, and Seraphim, one of their greatest allies."

"We don't know if I killed Khonsu. He might still be alive. He could have healed himself."

"Then you will have him to fight too."

"I know. But don't worry. I won't be here long. I wouldn't want my presence to endanger your kingdom."

Fergus Mór sniffed. "Worried? I would offer you the place of first mage, if it weren't for the fact that it would put your life in danger."

"Thank you."

Her hands moved to caress Seth's bloodstained hair.

"He was right about you." The king smiled with kindness and fatigue, the smile of a grieving man. "I told him you'd tricked him."

"You were both right. I had a choice to make." A choice that might now cost her life.

"And we are all grateful for it, but you must leave, Kim."

"I have one more thing that I have to do. When it's complete, ask Seth to take me away somewhere safe. I need to go south."

"What do you mean, ask Seth?"

"I'm his guardian."

"Guardian!" His grieving expression turned immediately into surprise, with a ray of hope in his eyes. "Seth can live?"

"Yes. I can reverse all of this. Start his heart. Rebuild his whole body, every tissue."

"But you will faint. He's badly injured."

"Yes. I know."

"Risking your life for him again."

"He would have done the same for me."

There was no point talking about it. It was the most fundamental thing related to having a Charge: saving their life so you could continue being together —the kiss of the guardian.

"You will tell him? Go south."

He nodded.

She turned to Seth and bent down until her lips touched his.

Immediately, she felt the pull. Deep inside her, her heart, her pillar of life, started to slow down. A soft white light came from it, and through her lips, it reached Seth.

The light was the magical bond inside her that connected them. Through it, she could feel his love and his life-force. In her mind's eye, she could see him, covered in the light, protected and warm.

In the depth of her heart, she heard a noisy ring. The timeless clock of a human spirit stood parallel to her own. Its immense power was dazzling, bright and brilliant.

She felt Seth's fierceness and liveliness.

That force of life moved out through her, back into Seth's body, closing wounds, regrowing organs, starting his heart, filling him with strength. And depleting her of it. Her eyes, which were already closed in concentration, now shut in weakness. Her own flame was dimming.

Slowly, softness spread through her limbs and the feeling of her own body became numbed, faint.

She was in an ocean now, deep under the water, with her leg caught under a large stone. As unable to move as she was back at the clearing when fear took over and Seth was fighting the dragon for her. Only this time there was no one else there. No Seth to save her.

The waves were wild above her, but she was so far below that the water around her was calm.

She was running out of air slowly, but she was not angry, fearful, or sad. She lay there in peace. All around her was a warm silence, like a never-ending afternoon siesta.

The last of Seth's life-force flowed from her

fingertips. She let go of her own.

The sun was setting, casting long shadows on the rocks below the cliffs near the water.

The west coast was the safest way south. There were caves along it that could serve as shelter. With Kim's magic, the best trackers could be escaped on that road.

Seth rode hard, Kim's warm body on the horse beside him, slowly coming back to consciousness.

He was her Charge! That was all that mattered. She had come for him. Again. Risking her life.

And that kiss of the guardian. It had awoken something in him. Memories. They were not clear ones, just fragments. He knew that they came from another world, another time, where they had been together. All the images were of her, and everything around them was a blur.

There had indeed been a third woman in his life. This other Kim from his past.

Something had happened to separate them. Making them both forget who they were and forget each other. Whether or not that had been intended, it was all in the past now. She was here. Here in his arms.

She mumbled something, trying to move.

"It's all right," he said. "You're safe."

He kept riding until his horse was too tired to continue and she was beginning to wake up. Slowly, he directed them down a path that led to the coast.

The light of the moon revealed a dark space between the rocks. A cave. When they reached the sand, he aimed for that and stopped by it.

He looked at Kim. Her eyes were open. At first they seemed to stare, but then they became focused.

"Seth."

"I'm here. We're on the coast. South."

"Uh..." She turned. She was still feeble, but when she moved her fingers, he saw the strength return fast.

"Can you stand?"

She mumbled, but then her voice became clear. Strong. "I don't think that I can get down."

"Don't worry. Just sit still." He dismounted gently and then held out his hands. "I'll catch you. Just come down any way that works."

She took a deep breath and then tilted her body, carefully, and landed in his arms.

"Where are we?"

He smiled. "Far from the palace. On the coast."

"How...long was I out?"

"A few hours. Well...maybe all day." The waning moon showed mountain peaks from small islands in front of them.

"Thank you." She caressed his hand.

"Don't, Kim. We're in this together." He repeated her words and took her hand and kissed it.

Then, he helped her to her feet and they walked to the cave. She stopped to concentrate and told him there was no one there, and she held the horse's reins as they gently walked into the darkness.

After finding a place to tie the beast, they sat on the sand and she cast the tent spell, conjuring a comfortable bed for them inside it.

They both slept heavily that night, for the first time feeling safe together.

When he opened his eyes in the morning, his arms were around her. He let himself enjoy having her there. She was fast asleep, a look of peace on her face. She mumbled his name.

The sun was shining brightly. There were no sounds except the waves outside, crashing on the rocks near the shore.

After a while, she started turning and he carefully got up without waking her.

Fergus Mór had made sure they'd been given a

good pack of food for the first few days, so that she wouldn't have to use magic if they weren't in a safe place.

The only instructions were to head south. It was something she had said to the king. He was curious to know why.

She was escaping the Order, which was obvious after the battle with Khonsu. But she was anything but feeble. She'd brought a comet down to Earth. It'd been centuries since any mage had attempted that!

With such powers, she could find allies and stand against the Order. He just had to get her somewhere safe.

The sounds of the waves were the first thing Kim could hear. Then, there was the smell of the food. And the sensation of Seth beside her.

Images from a recurring dream were still vivid. The prophetic visions played in her mind.

She would have them every time she slept. A child, born in the south, who was destined to become king. His mother, Igraine, with her long, curly, red hair, a sign of northern ancestry. She couldn't see his father, but she could see a mage, Merlin. He was always looking straight at her. Waiting. Anticipating her arrival.

She took a moment to enjoy the sound of the waves, the small crabs she could sense, the seals in the water, and the rays of the sun warming up the sand outside the cave.

Less than a week ago, she was trapped in a palace. A contrast to the forests, where she had lived with the fairy tribe. The new luxurious lifestyle was appealing at first, and the gilded cage built itself around her so gradually that she didn't see its bars.

But the longing was always in her for something far away that she couldn't define.

Her mind wandered back to the court's dinners and the perpetual smiles on the faces of the lords and ladies around her. They *all* smiled. It had never occurred to her to ask what was there to smile about the whole time.

Seth had been right. Not just about the expectations she had to answer to as a court lady. That society seemed like a strange show, where all the actors looked alike. Each one of them had an exclusive tailor to sew their outfits at outrageous prices, ending up with exactly the same results.

Their conversations weren't any different. Most of the time, they spoke about nothing. In serious tones, and big words, always trying to sound intelligent to anyone who outranked them.

And then, there was that endless gossip. A way for people who had no life of their own to get some entertainment.

There was no substance there. It was just a competition of who put on the best show.

How monotonous it had all been. And to think that the Order was offering more of the same. Another court, only that of mages. And one that couldn't protect her from mortal laws.

This was not her world.

It would have been like sleepwalking through life: never fully awake, never alive, always in fear. Even if they found her and destroyed her in the end, it didn't matter. She had to deliver the knowledge of the prophecy to Merlin, because that was *her* way.

The sound of the waves and the smell of the food got stronger as she became more and more awake.

As was the presence of Seth. The sound of his movements, his smell, the feeling of being around him.

What lay before them was the unknown, shadowed by many dangers. Only the road itself would be certain: the path to Camelot, where she saw Merlin in her visions. The rest was up to them. Their quest.

She got up and out of the tent.

"Hey there, sleepyhead." Seth was smiling. There was a bundle of food open in front of him.

"Hi." She ran her fingers through her hair. "How do I look?"

"Awful."

She laughed. He'd always make her laugh, that was certain.

"We've got Fergus Mór's finest. A gourmet selection."

"How are you?" She moved to a sitting position in front of him.

"Never been better." He handed her a bread roll, his fingers touching hers. There was an unmistakable spark there.

"Any pains?"

"Nothing."

She took a large bite, suddenly aware of how hungry she was.

He observed her, satisfied.

After they'd eaten, they sat together, holding hands and looking at the sea.

"So, how come you suddenly got your powers back? You never told me."

"It happened at Haven. Someone died and passed

his powers to me, awakening what I'd had before."

"But you did use them the night previous, with the dragon. I knew magic guided my weapons. You were self-healing too."

"Yes. I guess I was, though I didn't do it intentionally. I think it only started happening since I met you."

He turned and gave her a soft kiss. She closed her eyes and let herself be absorbed in the moment.

"Why didn't you tell me I was your Charge?"

"I...had to sort something out first."

"With Seraphim."

"Yes."

"What was it?"

"Well..." It was time to tell him. "Do you know about the prophecy of Camelot? The one that Ivan saw of his destroyed village of Camelot being re-established as a great prosperous city and capital of a kingdom?"

"Ruled by a just king, with one of the greatest mages in history by his side." He completed her words. Then, he paused, his expression changing to surprise. "You're Ivan's kin... No! You have seen the visions of the Camelot prophecy?"

"Yes," she smiled, "but only half. I know who the child's mother would be. Her name is Igraine. I see her clearly. And the mage is called Merlin. He knows the other half—who the father is. He will protect the child, who's called Arthur. I think Leonard might know him."

"Of course he does!"

She laughed.

He thought for a moment. "But wait. This means you can go to the Order. You won't have to run away. They'd take you in with open arms, just to prevent this child from being born. You could restore the power of mages and possibly even reignite the fire of Avalon to reverse the Curse."

She put her hand softly on his. "But I would be reversing us. There would be no more guardians."

He smiled, half to himself. "So, you chose me."

And then he grabbed her, kissing her fiercely. It brought back memories of that other Seth, lighting the heat inside her, the irresistible passion they'd had that was now coming back. She let her hands pull him to her and he carried her back to the tent spell, laying her down as dazzling, shimmering waves started to cloud her vision.

Later, when they were getting ready to leave, she decided to approach the subject of what they used to be.

"Seth, I must ask..."

"Anything."

"Do you remember another *time* when we were together?"

"I'm so glad you said that." He smiled, relieved. "Since you brought me back, there's been fragments, memories where you and I are together, but we were different. We also speak another language. I can't see much else. Do you see it too?"

"Yes. It's just like you've described it. I also see myself use magic. I know it was in a different world, but I can't really see much of it. I keep asking myself: how could we lose that?"

"Maybe you and I are here for a reason."

"Like what?"

"Like you delivering the prophetic knowledge. The very fact that you want to do it makes you different than the other mages here. You're full of surprises."

"Am I?"

He chuckled. "A spoiled princess turns all-powerful mage but is ready to give up all the perks to do what she thinks is right."

She gave him a soft kiss. "Do you like me this way?"

"I like you every way."

"Even arrogant, spoiled, and madly in love with

myself?" She quoted his words to Niall when he'd first met her.

He raised his eyebrows, clearly surprised at being found out. "Well..." he teased. "Maybe we can work on that one."

She laughed.

Then he took her hand, and they walked to where he'd hid the horse.

As they stepped out of the cave, Kim smelled the saltiness of the water, the fresh air of the new day, and the intoxicating and impossible to resist scent of adventure.

A Preview of Merlin's Creed: Prologue

Scotland, Present Day

Jane sat on the chair opposite mine with a half-empty glass of wine in her hand. Her second. I hoped that it would be enough.

How do you tell your best friend that you're not who they thought you were – not even close?

"Kim, I don't think you can surprise me. It's not like you're about to tell me that there are fairies, witches, and magical creatures in this world and that Morganstein's research of Camelot literature is historically accurate."

I froze, my eyes wide open. *No way!* Did she already suspect it?

She stopped, seeing my reaction. Then, slowly, she put her glass down and leaned forward.

We sat there, watching each other in silence.

She took a deep breath. "How much of it?"

"All of it."

Chapter 1

England, AD 500

The dream came every night. So vivid, it almost felt real. But Kim knew she was asleep and these were the visions of her prophecy.

It always started with a woman called Igraine. She had long, curly, red hair, a sign of northern ancestry. She was the most important lady in the land because she would be the mother of King Arthur.

Then, she saw Merlin in his tower at Camelot. He had the other half of the prophecy: he knew who Arthur's father was.

It was crucial to help Arthur's parents meet and protect them, and then do everything possible to keep Arthur's birth a secret. Because the magical world wanted him dead. An older prophecy said that his rule would diminish their influence—slowly, magic would disappear from the world. Their very existence would become myth.

But something went wrong. That part always came next: The fires of battle. She'd see them spread as their heat rose above a town, and mages on both sides cast weather and battle spells to desperately try to affect the outcome. Loud cries from the soldiers would mix with the trebuchets as their rocks hit the castle that lay under siege.

Then, the prophetic visions would be replaced with hazy images of a world far in the future, where men put down their weapons and gave up their rough ways. There were buildings taller than any castle and windows framed in metal. People fought for sport with swords that bent and didn't draw blood, wearing white attires and strange basket-looking masks—you could watch them without being there in person, on small rectangular screens.

She liked to look at one of these *sportsmen* in particular. He was the exception—the one thing she saw clearly. He was tall, with bright-brown hair and eyes as grey as a cloud-covered ocean. His presence brought warm feelings, and a perpetual longing to be with him, always. His strong, masculine voice would whisper in the night, in a strange language that she understood perfectly. And he'd call to her, "Kim... Kim."

Kim opened her eyes. For a moment, the images of her dream were still there. Then, they vanished and the world around came into focus.

She was out in the woods, where she'd chosen to cast a protective sphere called the tent spell. It prevented anyone from seeing or hearing her. Or sensing her magic. The starry night shone between the treetops.

"Kim."

She turned. "Seth."

He was the same man from that future world. Here with her now. She reached for him under her conjured blanket, but his side of the bed was empty. He sat on the edge. In the light of the stars, she saw that he was already fully dressed and armed—ready to protect her if there was a need.

Sweet. But she was the one who was supposed to protect him.

"Here." He leaned and handed her her clothes, placing a delicate kiss on her lips.

She closed her eyes to savor the sensation. "Mmm. What time is it?"

"By the moon, about five or six in the morning. I let you sleep in."

She laughed and picked up the long, warm socks. They were rough on the skin, but their sturdy fabric was essential during the journey.

"Did you have the dream?"

"Every night. The only part that changes is the bit from us in the future. I see different things each time. Tonight, I saw you fencing, but I wasn't there. I watched you inside something that looked like a frame."

He knit his eyebrows. "I fenced in a frame?"

"Yes. Sort of. Or maybe it was some shiny screen." That was the closest way she could describe it. Sometimes it was hard to tell whether the things in those visions were real or part of dreams. And now some things happened inside these strange screens, just to add to the confusion.

"How far in the future do you think this is?"

"I don't know." She rose to put on the warm travel dress. It closed at the front, and Seth came to help her tighten the top.

His fingers trembled on the knots, sending heat through her body and tingles on her skin.

"You could have woken me up earlier..."

"Yes. I could have. But I'd rather save something for tonight."

"Seth!"

"Don't complain. I can tell you like it."

She laughed. He always made her laugh. In that

future of theirs, most of the memories were light. Sometimes she giggled in her sleep.

"Come, saucy lady. Let's get food, before I give in to temptation and we'll start the day too late."

She bit her lip, and fastened the peplos under her shoulders. Then, she conjured food. It was a transmutation spell: the ground under the mattress transformed itself, as it did to sustain the plants and life of this earth. It was the only form of conjuring that was permanent.

It was a breakfast almost worthy of her father's castle.

She used to be a princess. The fresh scent of the bread reminded her of the court life that she had left behind. She closed her eyes. She could almost imagine the taste of the morning stew that had brewed all night, and the sweet baked goods. It was one of the best kitchens in the land. Even Seth said so. He had visited many courts when he was the first knight of King Fergus Mór; dined with noblemen and kings, including her father. Or rather, her adoptive father. The father she had in *this* world.

Over two years had passed, since...since they went back in time and ended up here, forgetting everything they knew. She recalled how hard it was to deal with such a loss of memory. They also got separated for almost two years. They met again only a few weeks ago, and then the memories came. Before that, she just knew herself as King Áedán's daughter.

She had made a brave and dangerous choice to leave it all behind and try to find Merlin.

She looked at the plates in front of her. At court, they had a prayer of grace before eating. She had a different prayer now: that the Order of the First Shrine wouldn't find her.

Seth watched the way Kim picked up a bread roll. Delicately and slowly. He chuckled, recalling her perfect, almost mechanic manners, when they first met, back at her father's castle. And the intense hostility between them then.

"What?"

"Nothing. Well, you."

She smiled at him. Her eyes shimmered. Soft. Loving. She ate the bread and beamed in satisfaction.

"You should try the salad. There's magic in the sauce."

He expected a laugh, but she stared. "I think...you've said that to me before."

He had! That was right. He remembered now. It was long ago, in another time. She sat beside him, her blonde hair loose and her clothes different in style. The table was thinner than the heavy wooden ones he was used to here. They had a selection of salads in small plates. Everything else was a blur. He was nervous, being so close to her. It must have been shortly after they'd met.

He smiled. "Well, this time it's certain. Magic in the sauce."

Whatever spell brought them to this time had taken her away from him, but he found her again and the intense love between them grew every day.

She looked down at her plate. "I think I'm done." It was still mostly full.

"What? But you've just started. You need to eat. It's the final day of our journey. After that, we'll have time to rest and take things slow."

"All right." She sighed and put her hand on his. "We've been lucky so far."

Lucky was an understatement. It was a miracle they were still alive.

The Order of the First Shrine wanted Kim because of her prophetic visions. And they were the most powerful order of mages in the land: they shared their combined magic through a hundred Blue Diamond rings, so a chance meeting with one of them was fatal.

For over a hundred years, the magical world waited for those visions she had—so they could kill the child king, or better yet, kill one of his parents before he was born. A powerful curse, Avalon's Curse, had caused them to become servants to mankind, and this boy's rule was destined to seal their fate.

Instead, she wanted to go to Merlin and save Arthur—who she saw as the king's protector in the future—because she loved Seth. Avalon's Curse had made witches Guardians to humans. She was his, born to fall for him. Mages lived for hundreds of years—this was the only way that they could spend their long life together.

She did have another option. He'd told her that over a month ago, when they started on this dangerous journey.

"You can go to the Order. You won't have to run away. They'd take you in with open arms, just to prevent this child from being born. You could restore the power of mages and possibly even reignite the fire of Avalon to reverse the Curse." It was the one thing many mages wanted.

"But I would be reversing us. There would be no more Guardians."

"So, you chose me." There was no way to describe how much her words had meant to him.

For the last few weeks, they had to look over their shoulders constantly. They even used new names, Adelis and Caradoc, a lady and her bodyguard—not even a couple—to draw less attention. They slept in the woods and stayed away from towns as far as possible.

So far, they only got attacked twice by bounty hunters and both times she managed to avoid any spells requiring a lot of power—mages could sense those, and if someone recognized her trace of magic...

But it was almost over. One last stretch, and they would reach Camelot, where Kim saw Merlin.

More about Merlin's Creed at:
http://reutbarak.com/merlin

Subscribe to get Black Emerald for FREE!

https://reutbarak.com/mailinglist/

www.evanswitches.com

20230928153855